ENCHANTED GLASS

Titles by Diana Wynne Jones

Chrestomanci Series
Charmed Life*
The Magicians of Caprona*
Witch Week*
The Lives of Christopher Chant*
Mixed Magics*
Conrad's Fate*
The Pinhoe Egg

Howl Series
Howl's Moving Castle*
Castle in the Air*
House of Many Ways

Archer's Goon*
Black Maria*
Dogsbody
Eight Days of Luke
The Homeward Bounders
The Merlin Conspiracy*
The Ogre Downstairs
Power of Three
Stopping for a Spell
A Tale of Time City
Wilkins' Tooth

For older readers
Fire and Hemlock
Hexwood
The Time of the Ghost

For younger readers
Wild Robert

Also available on audio

ENCHANTED GLASS

Diana Wynne Jones

HarperCollins *Children's Books*

First published in hardback in Great Britain
by HarperCollins *Children's Books* 2010
HarperCollins *Children's Books* is a division of
HarperCollins *Publishers* Ltd
77-85 Fulham Palace Road, Hammersmith, London, W6 8JB

www.harpercollins.co.uk

1

ISBN: 978 0 00 732078 3

The author and the illustrator assert the moral right to be identified
as the author and illustrator of the work.

Printed and bound in Great Britain by
Clays Ltd, St Ives plc

Mixed Sources
Product group from well-managed
forests and other controlled sources
www.fsc.org Cert no. SW-COC-1806
FSC © 1996 Forest Stewardship Council

FSC is a non-profit international organisation established to promote the
responsible management of the world's forests. Products carrying the FSC
label are independently certified to assure consumers that they come
from forests that are managed to meet the social, economic and
ecological needs of present and future generations.

Find out more about HarperCollins and the environment at
www.harpercollins.co.uk/green

To Farah, Charlie, Sharyn and all who attended the Diana Wynne Jones conference without me.

Chapter One

When Jocelyn Brandon died – at a great old age, as magicians tend to do – he left his house and his field-of-care to his grandson, Andrew Brandon Hope. Andrew himself was in his thirties. The house, Melstone House, was a simple matter of making a will. But it had been old Jocelyn's intention to pass the field-of-care on in the proper way, personally.

He left it rather too late. He knew Andrew could reach him very quickly. If you climbed to the top of Mel Tump, the hill beyond the house, you could see the University where Andrew taught as a dark blue clot on the edge of the great blue-green plain, only half an hour's drive away. So, when he realised he was on his deathbed, Jocelyn commanded his housekeeper, Mrs Stock, to telephone for his grandson.

Mrs Stock did telephone. But the truth is, she did not try very hard. Partly, she did not take the old man's illness seriously; but mostly, she did not approve of the old man's daughter for marrying a Hope (and then dying of it). She therefore also disapproved of the daughter's son, Andrew Hope. Besides, she was waiting for the doctor and didn't want to be on the phone when she should be answering the door. So when she had worked her way through the intricate University switchboard system and arrived at the History Department, and then to a person who described herself as a Research Assistant, who told her that Dr Hope was in a committee meeting, she simply gave up.

Andrew Hope was driving in the general direction of Melstone that evening, returning from a site connected with his research. His Research Assistant, not having the least idea where he was, had simply told Mrs Stock the lie she told everyone. Andrew had reached the curious dip in the road where, as he always said to himself, things went different. It was blue gloaming and he had just switched his headlights on. Luckily, he was not going fast. A figure was suddenly there, dashing into his headlights' glare, dark and human and seeming to wave.

Andrew trod on his brakes. His car wove about, wheels howling, in a long, snaking skid, showing him horrendous detail of grass and blackthorn on both sides of the road, violently lit by his headlights. It followed this by going up and over and down off something sickeningly squashy. Then it stopped.

Andrew tore open his door and jumped out. Into something squashy. This proved to be the ditch in which his nearside wheel was planted. Horrified, he squelshed out and around the bonnet and peered underneath the other three wheels. Nothing. The squashy lump must have been the wet bank between the road and the ditch. Only when he was sure of this did Andrew look round and see the human figure standing waiting for him in the beam of the headlights. It was tall and thin and very like himself, except that its hair was white, its back a little bent and it did not wear glasses like Andrew did. Jocelyn's eyesight had always been magically good.

Andrew recognised his grandfather. "Well, at least I didn't kill you," he said. "Or did I?"

This last question was because he realised he could see the white line in the middle of the road through his grandfather's body.

His grandfather shook his head, grinned a little and held something out towards him. Andrew could not see it clearly at first. He had to go nearer, remove his glasses and peer. The thing seemed to be a folded paper with some kind of black seal on one corner. The old man shook it impatiently and held it out again. Andrew cautiously reached for it. But his fingers went right through it and grew very cold. It was like putting his hand for an instant into a freezer.

"Sorry," he said. "I'll come to the house and get it, shall I?"

His grandfather gave the paper in his hand a look of keen exasperation, and nodded. Then he stepped back a pace, enough to take him out of the tilted beams of the headlights, and that was all. There was only dark road in the dip.

Andrew stepped outside the light himself to make sure his grandfather was gone. Finding that he was, Andrew put his glasses back on and retrieved his right shoe from the mud in the ditch. After that he stood thinking, watching the right front wheel of his car sinking slowly deeper into the grassy ooze.

He thought movements of sky and earth, time and space. He thought Einstein and skyhooks. He thought that the position of the wheel in the ditch was only a temporary and relative fact, untrue five minutes ago and untrue five minutes from now. He thought of the power and speed of that skid, and the repelling power of the ditch. He thought of gravity reversing itself. Then he knelt down with one hand on the grassy mud and the other on the wheel and pushed the two apart. Obediently, with some reluctant sucking and squelshing, the car moved out of the ditch and over the bank and bumped down in the road. Andrew sat himself in the driving seat to put his shoe back on, thinking ruefully that his grandfather would simply have stood in the road and beckoned to get the same result. He would have to work at the practical side of magic a bit more now. Pity. He sighed.

After that, he drove to his grandfather's house. "He's dead, isn't he?" he said, when Mrs Stock opened the door to him.

Mrs Stock nodded and redeemed what little conscience she had by saying, "But I knew you'd know."

Andrew walked through the front door and into his inheritance.

There was of course a great deal of business involved, not only in Melstone and in Melton, the town nearby, but also in the University, because Andrew decided almost at once to leave the University and live in Melstone House. His parents had left him money and he thought that, with what old Jocelyn had left him, he had enough to give up teaching and write the book he had always wanted to write. He wanted to give the world a completely new view of history. He was glad to leave the University, and particularly glad to leave his Research Assistant. She was such a liar. Amazing that he had wanted to marry her a year ago. But Andrew felt he had to make sure she was safely shunted to another post, and so he did.

One way or another, it was nearly a year before Andrew could move in to Melstone House. Then he had to make sure that the various small legacies in his grandfather's will were paid, and he did that too; but he was vaguely puzzled that this will, when he saw it, was quite a different size and shape from the paper his grandfather's ghost had tried to give him. He shrugged and gave Mrs Stock her five hundred pounds.

"And I do hope you'll continue to work for me just as you did for my grandfather," he said.

To which she retorted, "I don't know what you'd do if I didn't. You live in a world of your own, being a professor."

Andrew took this to mean yes. "I'm not a professor," he pointed out mildly. "Just a mere academic."

Mrs Stock took no notice of this. To her mind this was just splitting hairs. *Everybody* at a university was to her a professor, unless they were students of course, and therefore even worse. So she told everyone in Melstone that old Jocelyn's grandson was a professor. Andrew soon became accustomed to being addressed as "Professor", even by people who wrote to him from elsewhere about details of folklore or asking questions about magic.

He went to give Mr Stock the gardener *his* legacy of five hundred pounds. "And I do hope you'll continue your admirable work for me too," he said.

Mr Stock leaned on his spade. He was no relation to Mrs Stock, not even by marriage. It was simply that a good half of the people in Melstone were called Stock. Both Mr and Mrs Stock were extremely touchy on this matter. They did not like one another. "I suppose that old bossyboots says she's carrying on for you?" Mr Stock asked aggressively.

"I *believe* so," Andrew said.

"Then I'm staying to see fair play," Mr Stock said and went on banking up potatoes.

In this way, Andrew found himself employing two tyrants.

He did not see them this way of course. To him the two Stocks were fixtures, his grandfather's faithful servants, who had worked at Melstone House since Andrew had first visited the house as a child. He simply could not imagine the place without them.

Meanwhile, he was extremely happy, unpacking his books, going for walks and simply *being* in the house where he had spent so many fine times as a boy. There was a smell here – beeswax, mildew, paraffin and a spicy scent he could never pin down – which said *Holidays!* to Andrew. His mother had never got on with old Jocelyn. "He's a superstitious old stick-in-the-mud," she said to Andrew. "Don't let me find you believing in the stuff he tells you." But she sent Andrew to stay there most holidays to show that she had not exactly *quarrelled* with her father.

So Andrew had gone to stay with old Jocelyn and the two of them had walked, over fields, through woods and up Mel Tump, and Andrew had learned many things. He did not remember old Jocelyn teaching him about anything magical particularly; but he did remember companionable nights by the fire in the musty old living room, with the curtains drawn over the big French windows, when his grandfather taught him other things. Old Jocelyn Brandon had a practical turn of mind. He taught his grandson how to make flies for fishing, how to mortice joints, and how to make runestones, origami figures and kites. They had invented riddles together and made up games. It was enough to make the whole place golden to Andrew – though he had to admit that, now he was living here, he missed the old man rather a lot.

But owning the place made up for that somewhat. He could make what changes he pleased. Mrs Stock thought he should buy a television for the living room, but Andrew disliked television so he didn't. Instead, he bought a freezer and a microwave, ignoring the outcry from Mrs Stock, and went over the house to see what repairs were needed.

"A freezer and a microwave!" Mrs Stock told her sister Trixie. "Does he think I'm going to freeze good food solid, just for the pleasure of thawing it again with *rays*?"

Trixie remarked that Mrs Stock had both amenities in her own house.

"Because I'm a working woman," Mrs Stock retorted. "That's not the point. I tell you, that man lives in a world of his own!"

Great was her indignation when she arrived at the house next day to find that Andrew had moved all the furniture around in the living room, so that he could see to play the piano and get the best armchair beside the fire. It took Mrs Stock a whole morning of grunting, heaving and pushing to put it all back where it had been before.

Andrew came in from inspecting the roof and the outhouse in the yard after she had gone, sighed a little and moved everything to where he wanted it again.

Next morning, Mrs Stock stared, exclaimed and rushed to haul the piano back to its hallowed spot in the darkest corner. "World of his own!" she muttered, as she pushed and kicked at the carpet. "These professors!" she said, heaving the armchair, the sofa, the table and the standard lamps back to their traditional places. "*Damn* it!" she added, finding that the carpet had now acquired a long slantwise ruck from corner to corner. "And the *dust*!" she exclaimed, once she had jerked the carpet flat. It took her all morning to clean up the dust.

"So you'll just have to have the same cauliflower cheese for lunch *and* supper," she told Andrew, by way of a strong hint.

Andrew nodded and smiled. That outhouse, he was thinking, was going to fall down as soon as his grandfather's magic drained from it. Likewise the roof of the house. In the attics, you could look up to see cobwebby patches of sky through the slanted ceilings. He wondered whether he could afford all the necessary repairs as well as the central heating he wanted to install. It was a pity he had just spent so much of his grandfather's remaining money on a new computer.

In the evening, after Mrs Stock had gone, he fetched a pizza out of his new freezer, threw away the cauliflower cheese and, while the pizza heated, he moved the living room furniture back the way he wanted it.

Dourly, the next day, Mrs Stock moved it back to where tradition said it should be.

Andrew shrugged and moved it back again. Since he was employing the method he had used on his ditched car, while Mrs Stock was using brute force, he hoped she would shortly get tired of this. Meanwhile, he was getting some excellent magical practice. That evening, the piano actually trundled obediently into the light when he beckoned it.

Then there was Mr Stock.

Mr Stock's mode of tyranny was to arrive at the back door, which opened straight into the kitchen, while Andrew was having breakfast. "Nothing particular you want me to do today, so I'll just get on as usual," he would announce. Then he would depart, leaving the door open to the winds.

Andrew would be forced to leap up and shut the door before the wind slammed it. A slam, as his grandfather had made clear to him, could easily break the delicate coloured glass in the upper half of the door. Andrew loved that coloured glass. As a boy, he had spent fascinated hours looking at the garden through each different-coloured pane. Depending, you got a rose-pink sunset garden, hushed and windless; a stormy orange garden, where it was suddenly autumn; a tropical green garden, where there seemed likely to be parrots and monkeys any second. And so on. As an adult now, Andrew valued that glass even more. Magic apart, it was old, old, old. The glass had all sorts of internal wrinkles and trapped bubbles, and its long-dead maker had somehow managed to make the colours both intense and misty at once, so that in some lights, the violet pane, for instance, was both a rich purple and a faint lilac grey at one and the same time. If a piece of that glass had broken or even cracked, Andrew's heart would have cracked with it.

Mr Stock knew that. It was his way of ensuring, like Mrs Stock, that Andrew did not make any changes.

Unfortunately for Mr Stock, Andrew went over the grounds as carefully as he went over Melstone House itself. The walled vegetable garden was beautiful. Mr Stock's great ambition was to win First Prize in all the vegetable classes at the Melstone Summer Fête, either from his own garden down the road or from Andrew's. So the vegetables were phenomenal. But for the rest, Mr Stock was content merely to mow lawns. Andrew shook his head at the flower garden and winced at the orchard.

After a couple of months, while he waited for Mr Stock to mend his ways and Mr Stock went on as usual, Andrew took to leaping up as soon as Mr Stock appeared. Holding the precious door open ready to shut again after Mr Stock left, he would say things like, "I think today would be a good time to get rid of all those nettles in the main flowerbed," and, "Give me a list of the shrubs we need to replace all the dead ones and I'll order them for you," and, "There'll be no harm in pruning the apple trees today: none of them are bearing fruit." And so on. Mr Stock found himself forced to leave his vegetables, often for days on end.

Mr Stock took his revenge in his traditional manner. The following Monday, he kicked open the back door. Andrew was only just in time to stop it crashing against the inside wall, even though he had cast aside his toast and leaped to the door handle at the sight of Mr Stock's hat silhouetted through the coloured glass.

"You'll need both hands," Mr Stock said. "Here." And he placed a vast cardboard box loaded with vegetables in Andrew's arms. "And you're to eat these all *yourself*, see. Don't you let that old bossyboots go pinching them off you. And she will. I know her greedy ways. Puts them in her bag and scuttles off home with them if you give her the chance. So you *eat* them. And don't try chucking them away. I'll know. I empty the bins. So. Nothing particular you want me to do today. I'll just get on, shall I?"

"Well, actually there *is*," Andrew said. "The roses need tying in and mulching."

Mr Stock glared at him incredulously. This was rebellion.

"Please," Andrew added in his usual polite way.

"I'll be—!" said Mr Stock. And turned and trudged away.

Andrew, very gently, nudged the door closed with his

foot and dumped the cardboard box beside his toast. It was that or drop it, it was so heavy. Unpacked, it proved to contain six enormous onions, a bunch of twelve-inch carrots, a cabbage larger than Andrew's head, ten peppers the size of melons, a swede like a medium-sized boulder and a vegetable marrow like the body of a small crocodile. The spaces were carefully packed with overripe peapods and two foot runner beans. Andrew grinned. This was all the stuff that would not be up to the standard of Melstone Fête. He left a few of the most edible things out on the table and packed the rest back in the box, which he hid in the corner of the pantry.

Mrs Stock found it of course. "He's never palmed his rejects off on us again!" she pronounced. "The *size* of them! All bulk and no taste. And what am I to do for potatoes? Whistle? Really, that man!" Then she took her coat off and went to put the furniture back again. They were still at that.

The next day, Mr Stock kicked the door open on behalf of a box full of fourteen lettuces. On Wednesday, for variety, he accosted Andrew as Andrew went out to check the state of the garden walls and presented a further cardboard box containing ten kilos of tomatoes and a squash like the deformed head of a baby. On Thursday, the box contained sixteen cauliflowers.

Andrew smiled nicely and accepted these things, staggering a bit under their weight. This had happened when his grandfather annoyed Mr Stock too. They had often wondered, Andrew and his grandfather, if Mr Stock collected cardboard boxes and stored them ready to be annoyed with. Andrew presented the tomatoes to Mrs Stock.

"I believe you had better make some chutney," he said.

"And how do you expect me to find time for that, when I'm so busy—" She broke off, mildly embarrassed.

"Moving the furniture in the living room?" suggested Andrew. "Perhaps you could bring yourself to leave it for once."

Mrs Stock found herself making chutney. "World of his own!" she muttered over her seething red, vinegary saucepan, and occasionally, as she spooned the stuff into jars, and it slid out and pooled stickily on the table, "Professors! *Men!*" And, as she got her coat on to leave, "Don't blame me that the table's covered in jars. I can't label them until tomorrow and they're not going anywhere until I have."

Once he was alone, Andrew did as he had done every evening that week. He heaved the latest box out of the pantry and carried it outside to where the lean-to of the woodshed made a flattish slope level with his head. With the help of a kitchen chair, he laid the vegetables out up there. Too high for Mr Stock to see, his grandfather had remarked, or Mrs Stock either.

Tomatoes, squash and cauliflowers, were all gone in the morning, but the marrow remained. Careful looking showed a slightly trampled place in the grass beside the woodshed, but Andrew, remembering his grandfather's advice, enquired no further. He took the marrow back and tried to cut it up to hide in the freezer. But no knife would penetrate the crocodile skin of the thing and he was forced to bury it instead.

Friday brought a gross of radishes from Mr Stock and five bloated aubergines. It also brought Andrew's new computer. Finally. At last. Andrew forgot house, grounds, radishes, everything. He spent an absorbed and beatific day setting up the computer and beginning the database for his book, the book he really wanted to write, the new view of History.

"Would you believe, it's a computall now!" Mrs Stock told her sister. She never could get that word right. "Sitting there all day, patter-patter, like dry bones, fair gives me the creeps. And if I ask him anything, it's, 'Do as you think best, Mrs Stock'. I could have given him the boiled teacloths for lunch and he wouldn't have noticed!"

Well, he *was* a professor, Trixie pointed out, and

professors were well known to be absent-minded. And in her opinion, men were all children at heart anyway.

"Professors! Children!" Mrs Stock exclaimed. "I tell you, it's worse than that. The man needs a *minder* to keep him in order!" Then she went quiet, struck with an idea.

Mr Stock looked proprietorially in through the window of Andrew's ground-floor study. He surveyed the new computer and the explosion of thick books and papers around it, on the desk, draping off it, on the chairs, floor, everywhere, and the chaos of wires and cables around these. He was struck with an idea too. The man needed someone to keep him in order, someone to stop him interfering with those who had real work to do. Hm.

Mr Stock, thinking deeply, dropped round at his brother-in-law's cottage on his way home.

It was a very pretty cottage, thatched roof and all, although Mr Stock never could see why a man in Tarquin's condition should put up with an *old* place just because it looked good. Mr Stock much preferred his own modern bungalow with its metal frame windows. Tarquin's windows were all crooked and didn't keep the draught out. But Mr Stock could not avoid glowering jealously at the garden. Tarquin O'Connor had some kind of touch, even if it was only with flowers. The roses that lined the path to the front door now. Mr Stock could not approve these romantic, old-fashioned sort of roses, but he had to admit they were perfect of their kind, healthy, big clusters of cups, rosettes, whorls, and buds and buds coming on. More prizes at the Fête for Tark, for sure. And the bushes so well controlled that not one thorny branch strayed to catch a visitor coming between them to the door. While beyond them – well – a riot. Scents in the air. Enviously, he knocked on the door.

Tarquin had seen Mr Stock coming. He opened the door almost at once, holding himself up on one crutch. "Come in, Stockie, come in!"

Mr Stock entered, saying, "Good to see you, Tark. How's things?"

To this, Tarquin replied, "I'd just put a pot of tea on the table. Isn't that lucky now?" He turned, swinging himself on both crutches into the main room, all the space downstairs bar the kitchen.

Two cups on the round table by the windows, Mr Stock noticed. "Expecting my niece home, were you?"

"No, no, she's not due yet. Expecting you," Tarquin replied, puffing a bit as he got himself and his crutches arranged in the chair behind the teapot.

Joke? Or did Tarquin really have the Sight? Mr Stock wondered, getting out of his boots. Tarquin had nice carpets. Not to his taste, these dark Oriental things, but expensive. Besides, the poor fellow had a job and a half with a vacuum cleaner. Mr Stock had seen him, balanced on one crutch, with his stump of a leg propped over a chair, scraping and pushing for dear life. It didn't do to tread dirt in. He put his boots near the door and sat facing Tarquin in his socks, wondering as usual why Tarquin had grown a beard. Mr Stock did not approve of beards. He knew it was not because of scars; but there it was, a little tufty dark grey beard on the end of Tark's chin. Nor was it for convenience either. You could see the man had shaved round it carefully. Might as well shave the lot, but he didn't.

Tarquin O'Connor had once been a jockey, a very good one and very well known. Mr Stock had placed many a bet on horses ridden by Tark and never been out of pocket. Tarquin had been rich in those days. Mr Stock's much younger sister had had the best of everything, including expensive private medical care, before she died. Their daughter had had a costly education. But then Tarquin had had a truly terrible fall. Tark, as Mr Stock heard it, had been lucky to live, trampled and broken in all directions as he was. He'd never ride again. Nowadays, Tarquin lived on his savings and what he got from the Injured Jockey Fund, while his daughter, the story went, gave up all the millionaire jobs she might have had and stayed in Melstone to look after her father.

"How's my niece doing?" Mr Stock asked, halfway down his second cup of tea. "These biscuits are good. She make them?"

"No." Tarquin pushed the biscuits nearer to Mr Stock. "I did. As for Stashe, I wish she'd have a bit more faith in how I can manage and consider working further afield. She'd surely get something at the University, just for a start, so she would."

"Where's she working now then?" asked Mr Stock, who knew very well.

Tarquin sighed. "Still down at the Stables. Part time. And I swear Ronnie exploits her. He has her doing pedigrees and racing statistics on the computer, until I think she's never coming home. She's the only one there who understands the bloody machine."

The computer. This was what had given Mr Stock his idea. He gleamed. "Wasting herself," he pronounced. "Now my new fellow's at the computer game too. Stuff all over, wires, papers. I'm not at all sure he knows what he's doing."

Tarquin's tufted, waif-like face lifted towards him. Worried, Mr Stock was pleased to see. "But he *does* know he has the field-of-care to look after?" Tarquin asked anxiously.

Mr Stock turned the corners of his mouth down. And I

wish he'd get on and *do* it, and leave me alone! he thought. "As to that, I couldn't say. He's walked up and down a bit, for what that's worth. I think he thinks he's here to write a book. Now, to get back to my niece—"

"But if he doesn't know, someone ought to put him straight," Tarquin interrupted.

"That's right. Show him he has responsibilities," Mr Stock agreed. "It's not my place to. You could do it though."

"Ah. No." Tarquin slumped down in his chair at the mere thought. "I never met the man." He stayed bowed over, considering. "We do need someone to sound him out," he said. "See if he even knows what his job is here, and if he *doesn't* know, to tell him. I wonder—"

"Your daughter could do it," Mr Stock said daringly. "My niece," he added, because Tarquin seemed astonished by the idea. "If we could persuade him he needs a secretary – and he does, I don't doubt: he's used to several of them at that University, I'm sure – and then tell him we have the very person, wouldn't that suit?"

"It sounds a bit dishonest," Tarquin said dubiously.

"Not really. She's high-class stuff, our Stashe," said Mr Stock. "She could do the job, couldn't she?"

Pride caused Tarquin to sit straight again. "Degrees all over," he said. "She's probably too good for him."

"And too good for the Stables," Mr Stock prompted him.

"*Wasted* there," Tarquin agreed. "All right, I'll put it to her. Will Monday do?"

Bullseye! thought Mr Stock. "Monday it is," he said.

At almost the same moment, Mrs Stock said to her sister, "Now don't go putting ideas into Shaun's head, mind, but you can tell him he's really needed there. The place is crying out for someone to – ah – move furniture and so on. That man is really impossible as things stand."

"Can I give him a job description?" asked Trixie.

"Jargon," said Mrs Stock. "Anyway, *someone's* got to do something and my hands are full. We'll get on to it first thing Monday, shall we?"

In this way, plans were made for keeping Andrew under control. The trouble was, neither Mr nor Mrs Stock had thought very deeply about what Andrew was really like, or about what made Melstone such a special place, so it was not surprising that things took rather a different turn.

Mostly, this was because Aidan Cain turned up on Monday as well.

Chapter Two

idan Cain got off the train at Melton and joined the queue for taxis. While the queue shuffled slowly forward, Aidan fetched out the old battered wallet that Gran had given him just before she died, and cautiously opened it. By some miracle, the wallet had contained enough money for Aidan's half fare from London, plus a bacon sandwich and a chocolate bar. Now, the only things inside it were the two cash receipts for this food, a small one for the chocolate and a larger one for the sandwich. Gran had brought Aidan up not to cheat people, but the situation was desperate.

Still shuffling, Aidan took off his glasses and shut the wallet. Holding the glasses in his mouth by one sidepiece, he opened the wallet again and looked searchingly inside. Yes. The two flimsy receipts now looked exactly like a twenty-pound note and a ten-pound note. Aidan stared in at them for a moment with bare eyes, hoping this would fix them, and then put his glasses on again. To his relief, the two receipts still looked like money.

"I – I need to get to Melstone," he said to the taxi driver when his turn came. "Er – Melstone House in Melstone."

The taxi driver was not anxious to drive ten miles into the country for the sake of a kid. He looked over Aidan's dusty brown hair, his grubby sweatshirt, his shabby jeans and his worn trainers, his pale worried face and his cheap glasses. "That's twenty miles," he said. "It'll cost you."

"How much?" Aidan asked. The thought of walking twenty miles was daunting, but he supposed he could ask the way. But how would he know the house when he got there? Ask again probably. It would take all day. Enough time for the pursuit to catch up with him.

The driver tipped his face sideways, calculating a sum it was unlikely that this kid would have. "Thirty quid?" he suggested. "You got that?"

"Yes," Aidan said. In the greatest relief, he got into the taxi with his fingers crossed where the driver could not see them. The driver sighed irritably and set off.

It *was* quite a way. The taxi groaned and graunched through the town for so long that Aidan had to give up holding his breath for fear that the pursuit might stop it, but he only breathed easily when the taxi began making a smoother noise on a road between fields and woodlands. Aidan stared out at hedges laced with cow parsley and supposed he ought to be admiring the countryside. He had seldom been this far out of London. But he was too nervous to see it properly. He kept his fingers crossed and his eyes mostly on the meter. The meter had just clicked to £17.60 when they came to a village, a long winding place, where the road was lined with old houses and new houses, gardens and telegraph poles. Downhill they went, past a pub and a village green beyond it, with a duck pond and big trees, then uphill again past a squat little church surrounded by more trees. Finally, they turned down a side lane with a mossy surface and stopped with a croak outside a big pair of iron gates, overarched by a massive copper beech tree. The meter now read £18.40.

"Here we are," the driver said, over the panting of the taxi. "Melstone House. Thirty quid, please."

Aidan was now so nervous that his teeth were chattering. "The meter says – says eighteen pounds – pounds forty," he managed to say.

"Out-of-town surcharge," the driver said unblushingly.

I think he's cheating me, Aidan thought as he climbed

out of the taxi. It made him feel a little better about handing over the two cash receipts, but not much. He simply hoped they wouldn't change back too quickly.

"Don't give tips, eh?" the driver said as he took the apparent money.

"It – it's against my religion," Aidan said. His nervousness made his eyes blur, so that he had to lean forward to read the words 'Melstone House' deeply carved into one of the stone gateposts. So that's all right! he thought as the taxi drove noisily away on down the lane. He pushed open one of the iron gates with a clang and a lot of rusty grating and slipped inside on to a driveway beyond. He was so nervous now that he was shaking.

It all seemed terribly overgrown beyond the gate, but when Aidan turned the corner beyond the bushes he came out into bright sunlight, where the grassy curve of driveway led up to an old, old sagging stone house. A nice house, Aidan thought. It had a sort of smile to its lopsided windows and there was a big oak tree towering behind it. He saw a battered but newish car parked outside the front door, which was promising. It looked as if old Mr Brandon must be at home then.

Aidan went under the creepers round the front door and banged with the knocker.

When nothing happened, he found the bell push buried among the creepers and pushed it. It went *pongle-pongle* somewhere inside. Almost at once, the door was thrown open by a thin lady with an imposing blonde hairstyle and a crisp blue overall.

"All right, all right, I was coming!" this lady said. "As if I haven't enough to do— Who are *you*? I made sure you was going to be our Shaun!"

Aidan felt he ought to apologise for not being our Shaun, but he was not sure how to. "My – my name's Aidan Cain," he said. "Er – could I speak to Mr Jocelyn Brandon, please?"

"That's Professor Hope these days," the lady told him rather triumphantly. "He's the grandson. Old Mr Brandon died nearly a year ago." She didn't add, "And now go away!" but Aidan could see that was what she meant.

He felt a horrible sick emptiness and a double shame. Shame that he had not known Mr Brandon had died, and further shame that he was now bothering an even more total stranger. Beyond that he had the feeling he had run into a wall. There was literally nowhere else he could go. He asked desperately, "Could I have a word with Professor Hope then?" It was all he could think of to do.

"I suppose you *could*," Mrs Stock admitted. "But I warn you, he's got his head in that computall and probably won't hear a word you say. I've been trying to talk to him all morning. Come on in then. This way."

She led Aidan down a dark stone hallway. She had a most peculiar bouncing walk, Aidan thought, with her legs wide apart, as if she were trying to walk on either side of a low wall or something. Her feet slapped the flagstones as she turned a corner and threw open a low black door. "Someone to see you," she announced. "What was your name? Alan Cray? Here he is then," she added to Aidan, and went slapping away.

"It's Aidan Cain," Aidan said, blinking in the great blaze of light inside the heaped and crowded study.

The man sitting at the computer beside one of the big windows turned and blinked back at him. He wore glasses too. Maybe all professors did. For the rest, his hair was a tangle of white and blond, and his clothes were as old and grubby as Aidan's. His face struck Aidan as a bit mild and sheeplike. He seemed a lot older than someone's grandson had any right to be. Aidan's heart sank even further. He could not see this person being any help at all.

Andrew Hope was puzzled by Aidan. He knew very few boys and Aidan was not one of them. "What can I do for you?" he asked.

At least he has a nice voice, Aidan thought. He took a deep breath and tried to stop shaking. "I know you don't know me," he began. "But my gran – she brought me up – said— She – she died last week, you see—"

Then, to his horror, he burst into tears. He couldn't *believe* it. He had been so brave and restrained up to now. He had not cried once, not even that awful night when he had found Gran dead in her bed.

Andrew was equally horrified. He was not used to people crying. But he could tell real distress when he saw it. He sprang up and babbled. "Hey, take it easy. There, there, there. I'm sure we can do something. Sit down, sit down, Aidan, get a grip and then tell me all about it." He seized Aidan's arm and sat him in the only empty chair – a hard upright one against the wall – and went on babbling. "You're not from round here, are you? Have you come far?"

"L-London," Aidan managed to say in the middle of being shoved into the chair and trying to take his glasses off before they became covered in salty tears.

"Then you'll need something – something—" Not knowing what else to do, Andrew rushed to the door, opened it and bellowed, "Mrs Stock! Mrs Stock! We need coffee and biscuits in here at once, please!"

Mrs Stock's voice in the distance said something about, "When I've moved this dratted piano."

"No. *Now!*" Andrew yelled. "*Leave* the piano! For

once and for all, I *forbid* you to move the damned piano! Coffee, please. *Now!*"

There was a stunned silence from the distance.

Andrew shut the door and came back to Aidan, muttering, "I'd get it myself, only she makes such a fuss if I disarrange her kitchen."

Aidan stared at Andrew with his glasses in his hand. Seen by his naked eyes, this man was not really mild and sheeplike at all. He had power, great and kindly power. Aidan saw it blazing around him. Perhaps he could be some help after all.

Andrew tipped two computer manuals and a shower of history pamphlets off another chair and pulled it around to face Aidan. "Now," he said as he sat down, "what did your grandmother say?"

Aidan sniffed and then swallowed, firmly. He was determined not to break down again. "She – she told me," he said, "that if I was ever in trouble after she died, I was to go to Mr Jocelyn Brandon in Melstone. She showed me Melstone on the map. She kept telling me."

"Ah. I see," Andrew said. "So you came here and found he was dead. Now there's only me. I'm sorry about that. Was your grandmother a great friend of my grandfather's?"

"She talked about him a lot," Aidan said. "She said his

field-of-care was much more important than hers and she always took his advice. They wrote to each other. She even phoned him once, when there was a crisis about a human sacrifice two streets away, and he told her exactly what to do. She was really grateful."

Andrew frowned. He remembered, when he was here as a boy, his grandfather giving advice to magic users from all over the country. There was a distraught Scottish Wise Woman, who turned up once at the back door. Jocelyn sent her away smiling. But there was also a mad-looking, bearded Man of Power, who had frightened Andrew half to death by leering in at him through the purple pane at breakfast time. Old Jocelyn had been very angry with that man. "Refuses to hand his field-of-care on to someone sane!" Andrew remembered his grandfather saying. "What does he *expect*, for God's sake?" Andrew had forgotten about these people. They had been mysterious and scary interruptions to his blissful holidays.

Wondering if any of them had been this grandmother of Aidan's, he asked, "Who was your grandmother? What was her name?"

"Adela Cain," Aidan said. "She used to be a singer—"

"No! *Really*?" Andrew's face lit up. "I'd no idea she had a field-of-care! When I was about fifteen, I used to collect all her records. She was a wonderful singer – and wonderful-looking too!"

"She didn't do much singing when I was with her," Aidan said. "She gave it up after my mum died and I had to come to live with her. She said my mother's death had hit her too hard."

"Your mother was a Mrs Cain too?" Andrew asked.

Aidan found himself a little confused here. "I don't know if either of them were a Mrs," he explained. "Gran didn't like to be tied down. But she never stopped complaining about my mum. She said my dad was chancy folk and Mum should have known better than to take up with someone so well known to be married. That's all I know really."

"Ah," said Andrew. He felt he had put his foot in it and changed the subject quickly. "So you were left all alone in the world when your grandmother died?"

"Last week. Yes," said Aidan. "The social workers kept asking if I had any other family, and so did the Arkwrights – they were the foster family I was put with. But the – the *real* reason I came here was the Stalkers—"

Aidan was forced to break off here. He was not sorry. The Stalkers had been the final awful touch to the worst week of his life. Mrs Stock caused the interruption by kicking the door open and rotating into the room carrying a large tray.

"Well, I don't know what I've done to deserve this!" she was saying as she came face forward again. "It's a regular invasion. First that boy. Now there's Mr Stock and this one-legged jockey with that stuck-up daughter of his come to see you. And no sign of our Shaun."

Mrs Stock did not seem to care that all the people she was talking about could hear what she said. As she dumped the tray across the books piled on the nearest table, the three others followed her into the study. Aidan winced, knowing that Mrs Stock thought he was an intruder, and sat back against the wall, watching quietly.

Mr Stock came first, in his hat as usual. Aidan was fascinated by Mr Stock's hat. Perhaps it had once been a trilby sort of thing. It may once have even been a definite colour. Now it was more like something that had grown – like a fungus – on Mr Stock's head, so mashed and used and rammed down by earthy hands that you could have thought it was a mushroom that had accidentally grown into a sort of gnome-hat. It had a slightly domed top and a floppy edge. And a definite smell.

After that hat, Aidan was astonished all over again at the little man with one leg, who energetically heaved himself into the room with his crutches. *He* should have had the hat, Aidan thought. He was surely a gnome, beard and all. But his greying head was bare and slightly bald.

"You know my brother-in-law, Tarquin O'Connor," Mr Stock announced.

Ah, no. He's Irish. He's a leprechaun, Aidan thought.

"I've heard of you. I'm very pleased to meet you," Andrew said, and he hurried to tip things off another chair so that Tarquin could sit down, which Tarquin did, very deftly, swinging his stump of leg up and his crutches around, and giving Andrew a smile of thanks as he sat.

"Tark used to be a jockey," Mr Stock told Andrew. "Won the Derby. And he's brought his daughter, my niece Stashe, for you to interview."

Aidan was astonished a third time by Tarquin O'Connor's daughter. She was beautiful. She had one of those faces with delicate high cheekbones and slightly slanting eyes that he had only seen before on the covers of glossy magazines. Her eyes were green too, like someone in a fairy story, and she really was as slender as a wand. Aidan wondered how someone as gnomelike as Tarquin could be the father of a lady so lovely. The only family likeness was that they were both small.

Stashe came striding in with her fair hair flopping on her shoulders and a smile for everyone – even for Aidan and Mrs Stock – and a look at her father that said, "Are you all right in that chair, Dad?" She seemed to bring with her all the feelings that had to do with being human and warm-blooded. Her character was clearly not at all fairylike. She was in jeans and a body warmer and wellies. No, *not* a fairy-tale person, Aidan thought.

Mrs Stock glowered at her. Tarquin gave her a "Don't fuss me!" look. Andrew was as astonished as Aidan. He wondered what this good-looking young lady was *doing* here. He moved over to her, tipping another chair free of papers as he went, and shook the hand she was holding out to him.

"Stashe?" he asked her.

"Short for Eustacia." Stashe twisted her mouth sideways to show what she thought of the name. "Blame my parents."

"Blame your mother," Tarquin told her. "Her favourite name. Not mine."

"What am I supposed to interview you about?" Andrew asked, in the special, bewildered way he often found very useful.

"I've suggested her for your new secretary," Mr Stock announced. "Part time I suppose. I'll leave you to get on with it, shall I?" And he marched out of the room, pushing Mrs Stock out in front of him.

Mrs Stock, as she left, turned her head to say, "I'm bringing Shaun for you as soon as he turns up." It sounded like a threat.

Andrew grew very busy giving everyone coffee and some of the fat, soft, uneven biscuits Mrs Stock always made. He needed time to think about all this. "I have to deal with this young lady first," he said apologetically to Aidan. "But we'll talk later."

He treats me like a grown-up! Aidan thought. Then he had to balance his coffee on the bureau beside him in order to take his glasses off and blink back more tears. Everyone had treated him like a child, and a small one at that, after Gran died, the Arkwrights most of all. "Come and give me a cuddle like the nice little fellow you are," had been Mrs Arkwright's favourite saying. Her other one was, "Now don't you bother your little head with that, dear." They were very kind – so kind they were appalling. Aidan hurt all over inside just thinking about them.

Meanwhile, Andrew was saying to Tarquin, "You live in that cottage with all the roses, don't you?" Tarquin, giving him a wry, considering look, nodded. "I admire them every time I pass," Andrew went on, sounding desperate to say something polite. Tarquin nodded again, and smiled.

"Oh, you don't have to do the polite," Stashe protested. "Let's get on and talk business – or don't you approve after all, Dad?"

"Oh, I like him well enough," Tarquin said. "But I don't think the professor quite wants us. Bit of a recluse, aren't you?" he said to Andrew.

"Yes," said Andrew, taken aback.

Aidan hooked his glasses across one knee, drank his coffee and stared, fascinated. To his naked eyes, here were three strongly magical people. He had been right to think *leprechaun* about the brave, shrewd little man with one leg. He almost was one. He was full of gifts. But quite what that made Stashe into, Aidan could not tell. She was so *warm*. And direct as a sunray.

"Oh, *do* cut the cackle, both of you!" she was saying now. "I'd make you a good secretary, Professor Hope. I've every possible qualification, including magical. Dad's taught me magic. He's quite a power, is Dad. Why don't you take me on for a week's trial, no strings, no bad feelings if we don't suit?"

"I – er…" said Andrew. "I suppose I hesitate because I already have two strong-minded employees. And there's money—"

Stashe put her head back and laughed at the ceiling beams. "Those Stocks," she said. "Don't like change, either of them. They'll come round. Meanwhile, say yes or no, do. I've told you how much I'd charge. If you can't afford it, say no; if you can, say yes. I think you'll find I'm worth it. And then you can get back to this poor kid sitting here eating his heart out with worry."

All three turned to look at Aidan.

Tarquin, who had evidently been watching Aidan all along without seeming to look, said, "In several kinds of trouble, aren't you, sonny?" Stashe gave Aidan a blinding smile, and Andrew shot Aidan a startled look that said, "Oh dear. As bad as that." Tarquin added, "Who's chasing you, as of now?"

"Social workers, I suppose. They may have brought the police in by now," Aidan found himself answering. The little man was *really* powerful. Aidan had meant to stop there, but he seemed compelled to go on. "And at least three lots of Stalkers. Two lots of them had some kind of fight in the foster family's garden the night before last. The Arkwrights called the police, but the sergeant said it was probably cats. It wasn't though. We all saw shadowy sort of – people. They disappear by daylight. That's why I ran away at sunrise this morning."

There was a short silence, then Andrew said, "Aidan's grandmother died last week and told him before she died to come to Jocelyn Brandon if he was in trouble. And of course my grandfather is dead too."

After another short silence, Stashe said, "Have some more coffee."

"And give him another biscuit," Tarquin added. "Had any breakfast, did you?"

Aidan thought he was going to cry again. He managed to stop himself by saying, "I had money for a bacon sandwich."

"Good," said Tarquin. "These Stalkers. Haunts, were they? That sort of thing?"

Aidan nodded. "Three kinds. They seemed to know exactly where I was."

"Difficult," said Tarquin. "You can't really expect the police to be much help there. You need to hide, sonny, to my mind. My house has not got as much protection as this one has, but you'd be welcome to stay with me. I could use the help."

Before Aidan could say anything, Stashe gave her father a scornful look and bounced out of her chair. "Yes, Dad," she said. "I can just see you trying to fight a bunch of haunts by waving one crutch at them! We need a proper decision here. There must be a way to keep the kid safe. Is that today's paper I see there?"

Andrew, who was holding the biscuits out to Aidan and slowly coming to his own decision, looked vaguely round and said, "Mrs Stock did bring the paper in here I think."

Stashe was already pulling the newspaper out from under the tray. She tossed most of it impatiently on the floor among the history pamphlets and took out the sports section, which she spread out. "Where do they put the racing results in this rag? Oh, here, right at the end. Let's see. Kempton, Warwick, Lingfield, Leicester – lots to choose from. What won the first race at Kempton then? I always go to the first one they give."

Aidan and Andrew both stared at her. "Why do you want to know?" they said, almost together.

"Advice," said Stashe. "Predictions. I always use the racing results as an oracle. I do first race and last in the first track on the list, and then the last race in the last one."

"You can't be serious!" said Aidan.

"Works for her," Tarquin said, perfectly seriously. "I've never known her fail."

"Oh, look here!" Andrew said. "A horse that won yesterday, far away from here, can't have anything to do with—"

He stopped as Stashe read out, "The two-oh-five at Kempton: first, Dark Menace, second, Runaway, third, Sanctuary. That seems to outline the situation pretty well, doesn't it? Last race now. First, Aidan's Hope, second, Hideaway, third, The Professor. I think that settles it. Professor Hope, he has to stay here with you."

Andrew was sure that Stashe was making the names up. "I don't believe this!" he said and took the paper off her.

But they were all there, in print, just as she had read them out.

"Read out the last race at Leicester now," Tarquin said to him. "She uses that as the clincher."

Andrew moved the paper along and his eyes widened. He read out, in a fading, astonished voice, "First, Real Danger, second, Flight to Hope, third, Eustacia's Way. Look here," he said, "most horses have names like Bahajan King, or Lord Hannibal, or something in Arabic. What do you do when one of those comes up?"

"Oh, that's simple," Stashe said sunnily. "Depending if one of those without meaning comes first, second or third, they give you a question mark to the prophecy or advice. They say, 'This *might* work' or 'This is the best I can tell you' – things like that."

This girl is mad, Andrew thought. Barking. But I do need help with the computer.

"She's quite sane," Tarquin put in helpfully.

Andrew's mouth opened to contradict this. But at that moment Mrs Stock put her face round the door. "Here's our Shaun," she announced. "And you're employing him as handyman here. If you don't and you hire that Stashe instead, I'm leaving and you can just find yourself another housekeeper!"

Everyone stared at her. Trying not to laugh, Andrew

took his glasses off and slowly cleaned them with his handkerchief. "Don't tempt me, Mrs Stock," he said. "Don't tempt me."

Mrs Stock bridled. "Is that a jo—?" she began. Then it dawned on her that it might not be a joke. She gave Andrew a slanting, upwards look. "Well, anyway," she said, "this is our Shaun." She pushed a bulky young man into the room.

Shaun was probably about eighteen. It took Andrew – and Aidan too – only a glance to see that Shaun was what people in Melstone called "a bit in the head" or, Aidan thought, what the Arkwrights would call "mentally challenged". His face and body were fat in that way that showed that his body was trying to make up for his brain. His eyes looked tight round the edges. He stood there, perplexed and embarrassed at the way everyone was looking at him, and twisted his plump thumbs in his T-shirt, ashamed.

"He can do most things," Mrs Stock asserted, pushing her way in after Shaun. "Provided you explain them to him first."

Mr Stock had been prudently lurking outside the study windows to see how Stashe got on. Now he stuck his face, and his hat, through the nearest opening. "I am not," he said, "having that lummock-de-troll glunching about this place! Trod on all my tomatoes he did, last year."

And suddenly everyone was shouting at one another.

Shaun gave vent to a great tenor bellow. "Was not my *fault*, so!" Stashe shouted at her uncle to keep his nose out of things, and then turned and shouted at Mrs Stock. Mrs Stock shouted back, shriller and shriller, defending Shaun and telling Stashe to keep her bossy, managing face out of Professor Hope's business. Tarquin bounced in his chair and yelled that he was not going to sit there to hear his daughter insulted, while Mr Stock kept up a rolling boom, like a big bass drum, and seemed to be insulting everyone.

Aidan had never heard anything *like* this. He sat back in his hard chair and kept his mouth shut. Andrew rolled his eyes. Finally, he put his glasses back on and marched to his desk where he found his long, round, old-fashioned ruler, swung it back and banged it violently against the side of his computer. CLANG!

The shouting stopped. Andrew took his glasses off again, in order not to see the incredulous way they all looked at him.

"Thank you," Andrew said. "If you've all quite finished arranging my affairs for me, I shall now tell you what *I* have decided. Shaun, you can work here for a week's trial." He was sorry for Shaun and he thought a week wouldn't hurt anyone. "That suit you?" he asked. Shaun gave him a relieved, eager nod. "And you, Stashe," Andrew went on, "since you know your way around computers, you can come for a month's trial. I need a database set up and a lot of documents tapped in and something's gone wrong with this computer." Probably a lot more, he thought, now that he had hit the thing. "Is that OK?"

Mrs Stock glowered. Stashe, looking perky and triumphant, said, "I can do Tuesdays, Fridays and Mondays. When do I start?"

"She works down the Stables on the other days," Tarquin explained.

"Then start tomorrow," Andrew said. "Nine-thirty."

Aidan was greatly relieved. Up to now he had thought Andrew was the kind of person that everyone pushed about.

"Mr Stock," Andrew continued, "I'm sure you have work to do. And Mrs Stock, can you make up the bed in the front spare room, please? Aidan will be staying here until we can sort out what he ought to do."

"Oh, *thanks*!" Aidan gasped. He could hardly breathe, he was so relieved and grateful.

Chapter Three

Andrew was anxious to question Aidan further, but he had to leave that until the evening when Mr and Mrs Stock had left. Aidan fell into an exhausted sleep anyway, as soon as Mrs Stock had shown him to the spare room.

Downstairs, things were very unrestful. Mr Stock was enraged at the way Mrs Stock had thrust Shaun into the household. Mrs Stock could not forgive Mr Stock for producing Stashe. She was fairly annoyed with Andrew too. "I do think," she told her sister, "that with all I have to do, he didn't ought to have taken in that boy. I've no notion how long he'll be staying either. World of his own, that man!"

As always when she was annoyed, she made cauliflower cheese.

"I'll eat it," Aidan said, when Andrew was about to throw it away.

Andrew paused, with the dish above the waste-pail. "Not pizza?" he asked, in some surprise.

"I can eat that too," Aidan said.

Andrew, as he put the offending cauliflower back in the oven, had a sudden almost overwhelming memory of how much he had needed to eat when he was Aidan's age. This brought with it a flood of much vaguer memories, of things old Jocelyn had said and done, and of how much he had learned from the old man. But he was unable to pin them down. Pity, he thought. He was fairly sure a lot of these things were important, both for himself and for Aidan.

After supper, he took Aidan into the living room and began to ask him questions. He started, tactfully, with harmless enquiries about school and friends. Aidan, after he had looked round the room and realised, with regret, that Andrew did not have a television, was quite ready to answer. He had plenty of friends, he told Andrew, and quite enjoyed school, but he had had to give all that up when the social workers had whisked him off to the Arkwrights, who lived somewhere out in the suburbs of London.

"But it was nearly the end of term anyway," Aidan said

consolingly. He thought Andrew was probably worried about his education, being a professor.

Andrew secretly made a note of the Arkwrights' address. They were surely worrying. Then he went on to questions about Aidan's grandmother. Aidan was even readier to answer these. He talked happily about her. It did not take Andrew long to build up a picture of a splendidly quirky, loving, elderly lady, who had brought Aidan up very well indeed. It was also clear that Aidan had loved her very much. Andrew began to think that Adela Cain had been as wonderful as he had thought she was himself, in the days when he collected all her records.

Now came the difficult part. Andrew looked around the long, peaceful room, where the French windows were open on the evening sunlight. A fine, sweet scent flowed in with the sunset, probably from the few flowers Mr Stock had spared time to plant. Or was it? Aidan had taken his glasses off and looked warily at the open windows, as if there might be a threat out there, and then looked relieved, as if the scent was a safe one. Now Andrew remembered that there was *always* that same sweet smell in here, whenever the windows were open.

He was annoyed. His memory seemed to be so bad that he needed Aidan to remind him of things he ought to have known. He decided to treat himself to a small drink. It was so very small, and in such a small glass, that Aidan stared. Surely there was no way such a little sip of a drink could have any effect at all? But then, he thought, you did take medicine by the spoonful, and some of that was quite strong.

"Now," Andrew said, settling himself in the comfortable chair again, "I think I must ask you about those shadowy pursuers you mentioned."

"Didn't you believe me?" Aidan asked sadly. Just like the social workers and the police, he thought. They hadn't believed a word.

"Of course I believe you," Andrew assured him. He knew he would get nothing out of Aidan unless he said this. "Don't forget that my grandfather was a powerful magician. He and I saw many strange things together." They had too, Andrew realised, though he couldn't for the life of him think what they had seen. "When did you first see these creatures?"

"The night Gran died," Aidan said. "The first lot came and stood packed into our back yard. They were sort of tall and kingly. And they called my name. At least, I thought they were calling me, but they were really calling out 'Adam'—"

"They got your name wrong?" Andrew said.

"I don't know. A lot of people get it wrong," Aidan said.

"The social workers thought my name was Adam too. And I went charging off to Gran's bedroom to tell her about the Stalkers and—" He had to stop and gulp here. "That's how I found she was dead."

"What did you do?" Andrew asked.

"Dialled 999," Aidan said desolately. "That's all I could think of. The Stalkers vanished away when the ambulance arrived. I didn't see them again until they turned up outside the Arkwrights', with the other two lots that fought one another. That was two nights later. I suppose I'd mostly been sitting in that office, while people phoned about what to do with me, until then, and they couldn't get at me. They don't come indoors, you know."

"I know. You have to invite them in," Andrew said. "Or they try to call you out. And you weren't fool enough to listen to them."

"I was too scared," Aidan said. He added miserably, "The other two lots got my name wrong too. They called out 'Alan' and 'Ethan'. And the Arkwrights got it wrong too. They kept calling me 'Adrian' and telling me to forget all about Gran."

What a strange and unhappy time Aidan must have had of it, Andrew thought, full of strangers who couldn't even get his name right. And it did not sound as if Aidan had been given any time for grief, or even been invited to his grandmother's funeral. People needed to grieve. "Can you describe any of these Stalkers in more detail?" he asked.

But this Aidan found very hard to do. It wasn't just that they always appeared by dark, he explained. He just couldn't find words for how strange they were. "I suppose," he said, after several failed attempts, "I could try drawing them for you."

Andrew found himself glancing out of the windows at the red sunset. He had a very strong feeling that drawing the creatures was a bad idea. "No," he said. "I think that could be a way of calling them to you again. My grandfather kept his lands pretty safe, but I don't think we should take any chances." He put his tiny glass down and stood up. "Let's drop the subject until daylight now. Come and help me get rid of Mr Stock's punishment while we can still see." He led the way back to the kitchen.

Aidan could not really believe that vegetables might be a punishment, until Andrew led him to the pantry and pointed to the boxes. Then he believed all right.

"I've never seen so many radishes together in my life!" he said.

"Yes, several hundreds, all with holes in," Andrew said. "You carry them and I'll take the swedes and cabbages."

"Where are we taking them?" Aidan wanted to know, as they each heaved up a box.

"Round to the woodshed roof. It's too high for Mr Stock to see," Andrew explained. "I never ask what it is that comes and eats them."

"Must be a vegetarian – a *dedicated* vegetarian," Aidan panted. Radishes in such bulk were *heavy*. Then, as he staggered round the corner to the blank side of the house and saw the woodshed, a high and ramshackle lean-to, he added, "A *tall*, dedicated vegetarian."

"Yup," said Andrew, dumping his box on the ground. "But, as my grandfather always said, you *really* don't want to know."

But Aidan *did* want to know. While Andrew fetched the usual kitchen chair and stood on it on tiptoe to roll cabbages on to the woodshed roof, and then handfuls of radishes that came, many of them, pattering straight down on to the grass, Aidan felt quite scornful of someone who refused to find out about something as odd as this. Could the vegetarian be something that flew? No, because what Aidan could see of the grass, as he collected fallen radishes, was quite trampled here. A giraffe? Something like that. Andrew at full skinny stretch on the chair, with one arm up planting a swede up there, must measure a good fifteen feet. Or three metres, say.

"Where did your grandfather say this eating-creature came from?" he asked.

Andrew swung round and pointed with the big purple swede. "From over Mel Tump," he said. "Pass me the rest of the radishes now, will you?"

Aidan turned round. The garden petered out here, into a low hedge with wire in the gaps. Beyond were red-lit meadows, several of them, that stretched all the way to a sunset-pink hill about a mile away. The hill was all bristly with bushes and little stunted trees. Full of hiding places, Aidan thought, scooping up radishes. Didn't the professor ever go and *look*? Curiosity ran about inside him, like an itch. Aidan swore to himself that he *would* look, *would* solve this mystery. *Find out*. But not tonight. He was still dead tired.

He was so tired, in fact, that he went off to bed as soon as they were back indoors. The last thing Aidan remembered as he went up the dark, creaking stairs was Andrew saying from the hall, "I suppose we'll have to get you a few more clothes."

It was almost the first thing Andrew said the next morning too, when Aidan had sleepily found his way down to the kitchen where Andrew was eating toast.

"I need to go into Melton anyway," Andrew said. "You could do with something to keep the rain off at least."

Aidan looked to see if it was actually raining. And he saw, really saw for the first time, the coloured panes in the back door. While Andrew was putting more bread in the toaster and politely finding Aidan some cereal, Aidan took his glasses off and stared at the window. He had never seen anything so obviously magical in his life. He was sure that each different-coloured pane of glass was designed to do something different, but he could not see what. But the whole window did something else too. He itched with curiosity almost as strongly as he had last night. He wanted to know what it all *did*.

Andrew noticed Aidan taking his glasses off. He intended to ask Aidan about that. While they were having breakfast, Andrew wondered what magical talents Aidan had, and how strong these were, and how to put the question to Aidan in a way that was not nosy or offensive.

But just then he had to throw the cereal packet down on the table and rush to the door as Mr Stock's hatted outline appeared behind the coloured glass.

Mr Stock had thought carefully. He was still very angry with Mrs Stock and he wanted to annoy her by not producing any vegetables at all today. On the other hand, he was pleased with Andrew for giving Stashe a job – though why Andrew had to take in this runaway kid as well Mr Stock could not see. What the racing results suggested were just Stashe's nonsense to his mind.

So that morning, he marched into the kitchen without a

word, nodded to Andrew, but not to Aidan, and slapped down a very small baby's shoebox beside the cereal. The box contained a tiny bunch of parsley.

Andrew shut the door behind Mr Stock and burst out laughing. Aidan thought of all those radishes last night and got the giggles. They were still laughing on and off when Mrs Stock arrived, bringing the day's paper and carefully pushing Shaun in front of her.

"You have to explain to him carefully, mind," she said.

"Fine," said Andrew. "Just a moment. I want to look at today's racing results."

"I don't approve of betting," Mrs Stock said, taking off her coat and getting out her crisp blue overall.

"Wasn't that stuff about racing results all nonsense?" Aidan asked.

"Probably," Andrew said as he opened the paper. "But I want to test it out. Let's see. First race at Catterick—" He stopped and stared.

"What's it say?" Aidan asked, while Mrs Stock pushed Shaun out of the way as if he were some of the living room furniture and started to clear the table.

"First," Andrew read out in a slightly strangled voice, "Shaun's Triumph—"

"I *never*!" Mrs Stock exclaimed, in the middle of putting on bright pink rubber gloves.

"Second," Andrew read on, "Perfect Secretary, and third, Monopod. Third place means something with one leg. If you take that to mean Tarquin O'Connor, it all sounds surprisingly apt. I'm driving into Melford this morning, Mrs Stock. Can you write me a grocery list?"

Shaun cleared his throat anxiously. "What do I do, Professor Hope?"

Andrew had no idea of what Shaun should do, or *could* do. He toyed with the notion of getting Stashe to find work for Shaun when she arrived, but decided that this was not fair on either of them. He thought quickly. Where could Shaun do no harm? "Er – um. The old shed in the yard needs clearing out, Shaun. Think you can do that?"

Shaun beamed eagerly and made an effort to look clever. "Oh, yes, Professor. I can do that."

"Come with me then," Andrew said. Thinking that Aidan might have better ideas about what Shaun could do, he asked Aidan, "Like to come too?" Aidan nodded. Mrs Stock was going round the kitchen like a whirlwind, making him feel very uncomfortable.

The three of them went outside into a light drizzle of rain. They were just crossing the front of the house to get to the yard when a small car came hurtling up the drive and stopped, in a scatter of wet gravel. It was Tarquin's specially adapted car, with Tarquin driving it. The passenger door opened and Stashe leaped out. Andrew stared a little. Stashe had chosen to dress like an official secretary today. Gone were yesterday's wellies and body warmer. She was wearing a neat white shirt with a short dark skirt and high-heeled shoes. Andrew had to admit she looked pretty fabulous, particularly about the legs. Pity she was crazy.

"I'll get straight on with sorting that computer, shall I, Professor?" she called out, and went dashing through the rain and in through the front door before Andrew could answer.

Tarquin, meanwhile, was levering himself out of the driver's seat and assembling his crutches. "Can I have a short word with you, Professor, when you've a moment?" he said. "Short but important."

"Certainly," Andrew replied. The word would be something on the lines of Don't-you-go-messing-about-with-my-daughter, he thought. Understandable. It must be worrying having a beautiful, mad daughter. "Wait for me in the living room, if you would. I won't be a minute. I have to set Shaun to work."

Tarquin nodded and crutched himself to the front door. Andrew, Aidan and Shaun went on round to the yard where the broken-down old shed stood. Andrew always wondered what it had been built for. An artist's studio perhaps? It was old, built of bricks of a small, dark red kind that you hardly ever saw nowadays, with its roof in one slope. Someone had, long ago, given these bricks a thin coat of whitewash, which had largely worn off. The shed would have been big enough – just – for a stable or a coach house, except that it had no windows and only one small, quaintly arched door. Its roof leaked. Someone, long ago, had draped several layers of tarpaulins across the tiles to keep the wet out. Nettles grew in clumps against its walls.

Andrew forced the stiff door open on to a dimness stacked with bags of cement (When had his grandfather needed cement? Andrew wondered) pots of paint (Or those either?) and old garden seats. In the middle stood the huge old rusty motor mower that only Mr Stock had the knack of starting.

Shaun stumbled against the mower and barked his plump shin. "Ow," he said plaintively. "Dark in here. Can't see."

"One moment." Andrew went outside again, where he stood on tiptoe among the nettles and just managed to reach the corner of one of the tarpaulins. He dragged. The whole lot came down on his head in a shower of plaster bits, twigs and nameless rubbish.

Inside the shed, Aidan exclaimed and Shaun stood with his mouth open. There was a window there, slanting with the roof. It was made of squares of coloured glass, just like the top half of the kitchen door and obviously just as old. Unlike the glass of the back door, though, these panes were crusted with ancient dirt and cracked in places. Spiderwebs hung from them in strands and thick bundles, swaying in the breeze from the door. But it still let in a flood of coloured light. In the light, Aidan saw that the walls of the shed were lined with wood, old, pale wood, carved into dozens of fantastic shapes, but so dusty that it was hard to make out what the shapes were. He took his glasses off to investigate.

Outside the shed, Andrew trampled his way out from the tarpaulins and they fell to pieces under his feet. He took off his glasses to clean them, ruefully realising that he had just destroyed quite a large number of his grandfather's spells. Or his great-grandfather's. Possibly his *great*-great-grandfather's spells too.

"Come and look!" Aidan shouted from inside.

Andrew went in and looked. Oak, he thought. He patted the nearest panel. Solid oak, carved into patterns and flowers and figures. Old oak. The brick walls outside were just a disguise for a place of power. "My goodness!" he said.

"Cool, isn't it?" Aidan said.

Shaun, who had eyes only for the motor mower, said, "Church, this is."

"Well, not exactly," said Andrew, "but I know what you mean."

"Professor," Shaun said urgently, "I can mend this mower. Make it work. Honest. Can I do that?"

"Um," said Andrew. He thought of how jealously Mr Stock guarded his knack with this mower. But he had not the heart to disappoint Shaun. The lad was looking at him so eagerly and so desperately trying to seem cleverer than he was. "Oh, very well," he said. He sighed. This probably meant sixty-two cabbages tomorrow, but what did that matter? "Mend the mower, Shaun. And – listen carefully – after that, your work will be to clean up this place properly. Do it very gently and carefully and make sure you don't break anything, particularly that window up there. You can take days and days if you want. Just get it how it should be. OK?"

Shaun said, "Yes, Professor. Thank you, Professor." Andrew wondered if he had listened, let alone understood. But there was no doubt that Shaun was pleased. When he was pleased, he waved his hands about like a baby, with his fat fingers spread out in several directions, and beamed.

"Can I help him?" Aidan asked. He wanted to know what this shed really was.

"For ten minutes," Andrew said. "We're going into Melton to buy you some clothes, remember."

He left Shaun and Aidan to it. Beating dust and old spells out of his hair and slapping them out of his jeans as he walked, he went to the house to receive Tarquin's lecture.

Tarquin was sitting in a straight-backed chair with the stump of his leg propped across the piano stool. That stump, Andrew thought, must hurt him quite a lot.

"No, it doesn't," Tarquin said, just as if Andrew had spoken. "At least, the half that's still with me doesn't hurt at all. It's the *missing* half that gives me gyp. Most of the time it's pins and needles from the lost knee down. Just now, it's giving me cramp in the calf that isn't there. I can't seem to convince it that there's nothing there to give me cramp *with*. Stashe keeps telling me I ought to try hypnotism, but I don't like the idea of someone getting into my head and giving me, like, secret orders. The idea doesn't appeal at all, so it doesn't."

"No, I wouldn't like that either," Andrew agreed. He felt he could almost *see* the sinewy missing half of Tarquin's leg, spread out across the piano stool with its calf muscles in a tight, aching ball. Quite a telepathist, Tarquin. "What did you want to speak to me about?"

"Ah. That." Tarquin suddenly looked embarrassed. "Stockie and Stashe both seem to think I'm the best person to speak to you, the Lord knows why, and I thought I'd better do it before I lost my nerve for it. Forgive me for asking. Were you actually *here* when your grandfather died?"

Not what I expected! Andrew thought. "No," he said. "I was driving along a road quite near, not knowing he was dead, and I saw his ghost. Then I drove straight here."

Tarquin gave him an intent look. "And how did he seem – his ghost?"

"Rather urgent," Andrew said. "He was trying to give me a paper of some kind, with a big seal on it, but when I tried to take it, my hand went right through it. I thought it was his will, but that was quite a different shape when the lawyer produced it."

"Ah," said Tarquin. "We thought as much. You *don't* know. If you'll take my advice, you'll start looking for that document right now. It must be his field-of-care he was trying to hand on to you. It will tell you clearer than I can what you ought to do."

"What I ought to do about *what*?" Andrew asked.

Tarquin looked embarrassed again and wriggled on his chair. "That's what I don't truly know," he admitted. "I'm not a magician like Jocelyn Brandon was. I just have unofficial knacks, you might say – growing roses and knowing horses and such – but he was the real thing, Jocelyn, so he was, even if he had got old and a bit past it by the time I moved here. What I *do* know is that all round here, in a radius of ten miles or more, is strange. And special. And Jocelyn was in charge of it. And he was trying to hand the responsibility on to you."

"But I'm not a magician, any more than you are!" Andrew protested.

"But you could be," Tarquin said. "It seems to me that you could train yourself a little. You have the gift. And you need to find that document. I'll tell Stashe to help you look for it when she's sorted that computer. And you can count on me for any help you need – explaining or advising, or whatever. I'd be grateful to help, to tell the truth. I need my mind taken off my lost career sometimes, something cruel."

Tarquin meant this, Andrew could see. Though the life of a jockey was something Andrew could barely imagine himself, he could tell it had been as thrilling and absorbing as his own work on his book. And he wondered how he would feel if he had somehow lost both hands and couldn't write that book, or any other books, ever. "Thank you," he said.

"You're welcome," said Tarquin. "Now I'd better be going." He looked suddenly relieved. "Cramp's gone!" he said. "Virtual cramp, I should say. Cleared off like magic. So I'll be off now, but feel free to ask me anything about Melstone that you think I'll know."

Chapter Four

ndrew drove off to Melton with his mind full of what Tarquin had told him. Beside him, Aidan, who was not used to cars, was having trouble with his seat belt.

"Push until you hear it click," Andrew told him.

This added Aidan to his thoughts. And these Stalkers Aidan told him about. Andrew supposed he could protect Aidan from them and give him a holiday until the social workers arrived. Otherwise he was not sure what could be done. And meanwhile it seemed Andrew was supposed to be looking after his grandfather's field-of-care. Now he came to think of it, although he had always known there *was* such a thing, he had very little idea what a field-of-care was. He had never understood quite what it was that his grandfather did. Probably that document his grandfather's ghost had tried to give him would make all that clear. But where *was* the wretched thing? He had never set eyes on it while Jocelyn was alive. He would have to hunt for it, and it was going to interrupt the work on his book. *Everything* was going to interrupt him. Andrew's heart ached with his need to write his book. This was, after all, why he was employing Stashe.

And that brought his thoughts around to money. He was now employing two extra people and buying Aidan clothes, among other things. Luckily – and not entirely thanks to Mr Stock – Melstone House produced a lot of its own food; but that was a drop in the ocean, really, at the rate Aidan ate... Andrew began to wonder how soon he was going to be bankrupt.

Brooding on these things, Andrew drove past the new houses at the end of the village and past the football field, and on into the countryside. A couple of miles further on, there came the familiar little jolt, as if the car had for a second caught on some elastic. Aidan jumped.

"What was that?"

"We've just passed the boundary between the strange part my grandfather looked after and the normal places," Andrew told him.

"Funny," Aidan said. "I didn't notice it when I was coming."

"You probably had other things on your mind," Andrew said.

This was true, Aidan realised. He had been twitching all over, in case the Stalkers followed him, in case the taxi driver noticed about the money, in case old Mr Brandon couldn't help him. His whole mind and body had been roaring with nerves. Now his curiosity was aroused. "How big is this strange part?" he wanted to know.

"I'm not sure," Andrew said. "Tarquin O'Connor has just been telling me it has a ten mile radius, but I'm not sure it's that big, or not regularly. The boundary this side of the village is only two miles out. The boundary on the road to the University is probably five miles away, but that's all I know, I'm afraid."

"Don't you know where the rest of it is that's not on the roads?" Aidan asked.

"Not really," Andrew admitted. He remembered long hikes with his grandfather, but he rather thought they had all been inside the boundary. The area of strangeness – if this was Jocelyn's field-of-care – must actually be pretty big.

"You need a map," Aidan said. "It would be really interesting to walk all round it, not on the roads, and see where it goes."

Andrew thought. Tarquin had seemed to be saying that

it was Andrew's job to look after this area of strangeness in some way. "Not just interesting," he said. "I think it's necessary. Walking the bounds is something I'll need to do."

"I could help," Aidan said. "I could take a map and do it like a project for you, if you like."

He sounded as eager as Shaun. Andrew smiled. "We could make a start this weekend," he said. "You'll definitely need a raincoat." He turned the windscreen wipers on as the rain came down again.

Aidan sat quietly, thinking. Andrew was being amazingly kind. Clothes cost a lot. Gran was always complaining about how much clothes cost and how quickly Aidan grew out of them. Another of Gran's constant sayings was that one should never let oneself get into debt to anyone. "Debts get called in," she said. Yet here was Aidan relying on Andrew to buy him a raincoat and other things. He felt very guilty. Andrew owned a big house and a car – where Gran had never been able to afford either – and he had at least four people working for him, but Aidan looked across at Andrew's old zip-up jacket and his elderly jeans and could not help wondering if Andrew really was rich at all. And the only thing Aidan could do to pay Andrew back was to make a map of his field-of-care. That seemed pretty feeble.

It was still raining when they reached Melton and Andrew drove into the car park of the biggest supermarket. Aidan had another attack of guilt. Andrew was buying food for him too. Gran always worried about how much food cost. He felt so guilty that, in a weird mixture of hope and despair, he fetched out his old, flat, empty wallet and looked inside it.

He gasped. He went grey and dizzy with sheer surprise.

Andrew, in the act of getting out of the car, stopped and asked, "What's the matter?"

Aidan had whipped off his glasses to make sure this was real. He was holding the glasses in his mouth while he slid the big wad of twenty-pound notes out of the wallet. There was *masses*. And the money was still there to his naked eyes. "Money!" he mumbled round his glasses. "This wallet was *empty* just now, I swear!"

Andrew sat down again and shut the car door. "May I look?" he said, holding out his hand.

Aidan passed the wallet over. "Somebody must have filled it somehow," he said as he put his glasses on again.

Andrew felt the soft, old leather fizz faintly against his fingers. He remembered his grandfather explaining what this fizzing meant. "A fairly strong enchantment," he said, "worked in while the wallet was being made. How did you come by this?"

"Gran gave it me," Aidan said. "Last week, a couple of days before she – she died. She said I might as well have it, because it was the only thing my dad had ever given my mum – apart from me, of course."

"And when did your mother die?" Andrew asked, slowly passing the miraculous wallet back.

"When I was two – ten years ago," said Aidan. "Gran said that my dad had vanished off the face of the Earth before I was even born." He took the wallet back and removed his glasses again to count the money.

"So would you say," Andrew asked, thinking about it, "that the wallet fills with money when you need it?"

"Um." Aidan looked up, surprised. "Yes. I suppose. I know it was empty when Gran gave it me. But it had my trainfare in it the night before I came here. And then the taxi money. Bother. I lost count." He went back to counting twenty-pound notes.

"Then it looks as if you're required to buy your own clothes," Andrew said, in some relief. "Tell me, do you always take your glasses off to count money?"

Aidan lost count again. "No," he said irritably. *Must* Andrew keep interrupting? "Only to see if something's real – or magical – or real *and* magical. Or to keep it there if it's only magical. You *must* know how it works. I've seen you do it too."

"I don't think I— How do you mean?" Andrew asked, startled.

"When you're working with magic," Aidan explained. "You take your glasses off and clean them when you want people to do what you say."

"Oh." Andrew sat back and let Aidan get on with counting. The boy was right. Times out of mind, he remembered himself cleaning his glasses while he forced that Research Assistant to do what she was told for once. He had got treats out of his parents the same way. And – he could not help grinning – he had once passed a French oral exam by cleaning his glasses at a particularly terrifying examiner. He supposed that was cheating really. But the man *had* frightened him into forgetting English as well as French. The real question was, how did it *work*?

Thinking about how, Andrew took a trolley and went into the supermarket with Mrs Stock's list, in that state of mind that caused Mrs Stock to say, "Professors! World of his own!" Aidan also took a trolley and went to the other end of the store where the clothes were.

Aidan was expecting to have the time of his life. He had never bought clothes on his own before. He had never had this much money before. He was all prepared to lash out. But, to his surprise, he found himself almost passionately spending the money as economically as he could. He hunted for bargains and things that said "Two for the price of one". He did sums frantically in his head as he went round the racks and shelves (it did not help that most things were So Many Pounds, ninety-nine pence). He saw the perfect pair of trainers and he painfully did not buy them because they cost too much of his money. He took ages. He put things in his trolley and then took them out again when he found something cheaper. He almost forgot pyjamas. He had to go back for some, because he knew he would need them when he sneaked outside tonight to see what it was that ate the vegetables. He bought a fleece to go over the pyjamas and a zip-up waterproof for warmth. He nearly forgot socks. He ended up with a high-piled trolley and just two pence left in the wallet. Relief! He had got his sums right. Pity about those perfect trainers though.

It was just as well he took so long. Andrew took longer. He spent much of the time standing in front of shelves of bacon or sugar, either staring into space, or taking his glasses off and putting them on again to see if the bacon or sugar looked any different. They looked blurred, but that was all. But whoever heard of enchanted bacon anyway? So how did it work? Was it, Andrew mused, that bacon to the naked eye had the *possibility* of being enchanted? Would this make it the real world? Then when you put your glasses back on, maybe you could see more clearly, but the glasses blocked out the reality. Was that it? Or was it something else entirely?

By the time Andrew had finally managed to put all the things Mrs Stock needed into his trolley and then pay for them, Aidan was waiting outside in the drizzle, wondering if he had found the right car.

The drizzle stopped while they drove back to Melstone, but Andrew was still more than usually absent-minded. He really *was* a professor, Aidan thought, looking across at Andrew's creased forehead and intent stare. He hoped they didn't hit anything.

They turned into the driveway of Melstone House and nearly hit Shaun.

Shaun was standing just beyond the bushes, doing his baby arm-waving thing, with his fingers out like two starfish. Shaun probably never realised how near he came to death. Andrew slammed on his brakes so hard and so quickly that Aidan looked at him with respect.

"What is it, Shaun?" Andrew asked, calmly leaning out of his window.

"I did it, Professor! I *did* it!" Shaun said. "She sings. She sings sweet. Come and see!" He was red in the face with pride and excitement.

Realising that Shaun must be talking about the motor

mower, Andrew said, "Move out of the way then, and I'll park the car."

Shaun obediently backed into the bushes and then ran after the car. As soon as Andrew and Aidan had climbed out, he led them at a trot to the strange shed. Inside it, the motor mower was standing under the coloured window in a ring of rust. Shaun seemed to have polished it.

"Pull the starter. Hear her sing," Shaun pleaded.

Dubiously, Andrew bent and took hold of the handle on the end of the starter wire. Normally, this felt as if you were trying to pull a handle embedded in primordial granite. On a good day, you could pull the handle out about an inch, with a strong graunching noise. On a bad day, the handle would not move however hard you pulled. On both good and bad days, nothing else happened at all. But now Andrew felt the wire humming out sweetly in his hand. When it reached the critical length, the engine coughed, caught and broke out into a chugging roar. The mower shook all over, filling the shed with blue smoke. Shaun had worked a miracle. Andrew felt total dismay. He knew Mr Stock would be furious.

"Well *done*, Shaun," he said heartily, and tried to calculate how long it would be until Mr Stock felt moved to mow the lawns. "Er…" he bellowed above the noise of the mower, "how long is it until the Melstone Summer Fête? How do I turn this thing off?"

Shaun reached forward and deftly twitched the right lever. "Two weeks," he said in the resounding silence. "Not for two weeks. I thought everyone knew that."

"Then we should be safe from the Wrath of Stock until then," Andrew murmured. "Good work, Shaun. Now you can get on and clean this shed up."

"Can't I mow the grass?" Shaun pleaded.

"No," Andrew said. "That would be most unwise."

Shaun and Aidan were both disappointed. Aidan had thought that taking turns with Shaun at chugging about with the mower would have been fun. Shaun looked sadly around the rubbish in the shed. "What do I do with the cement bags?" he said.

The cement bags had been there so long that they had set like a row of hard paper-covered boulders. "Better bury them," Andrew said over his shoulder as he pushed Aidan out of the shed. "Come on, Aidan. We have to unload the car."

As they crossed the front lawn to the car, Aidan looked meaningly at the grass. It was all tufts and clumps. It had a fine crop of daisies, buttercups and dandelions, and several mighty upstanding thistles. If ever a lawn needed mowing...

"Don't ask," Andrew said. "Mr Stock will be busy full

time until the Fête, stretching beans and pumping up potatoes. He collects First Prizes. He also prides himself on being the only one who can start that mower. I hope, by the time the Fête's over, that the mower will have reverted to its old form. Otherwise I shall get mountains of dead lettuce."

"I understand," said Aidan. "I think."

"And yard-long carrots," Andrew said bitterly.

They unloaded the groceries and took them to the kitchen. Then Aidan went back for his own bulging bags. While he was hauling them up to his room, he heard a noise that sounded like the mower. Shaun must have disobeyed Andrew, he thought, looking out of the landing window. But the noise turned out to be Tarquin O'Connor's adapted car arriving to take Stashe home for lunch. Good! Aidan thought. There was a huge electric torch on the windowsill of Andrew's study. Once Stashe was out of the way, Aidan intended to go in and borrow it. He was going to need it for tonight.

Aidan liked the room he had been given. He liked its size and its low ceiling and its long, low window that showed that the walls were three feet thick. He wondered if that window had at one time been several arrow slits. Melstone House was certainly old enough. Above all, Aidan was charmed by the way the creaky wooden floor ran downhill to all four walls. If he put the marble he happened to have in his pocket down in the middle of the room, it rolled away to any one of the walls, depending how he dropped it.

To his dismay, Mrs Stock was in the room, tidying repressively. Being forbidden to move the living room furniture, Mrs Stock was taking out her feelings on the spare room. She glowered at Aidan and his carrier bags.

"Moving in for a long stay, are you?" she said. "You've got enough for a lifetime there. I hope you're grateful to Professor Hope. He isn't made of money, you know."

Aidan opened his mouth to tell her he had bought the clothes himself. And shut it again. Andrew didn't like cauliflower cheese. If he annoyed Mrs Stock, she would make cauliflower cheese for supper and that would annoy Andrew. Aidan most desperately needed *not* to have Andrew annoyed, in case Andrew sent him back to the Arkwrights. Aidan was not sure he could bear that.

"Yes, I am," he said. "Very grateful." He went over to the window and unloaded the packages of clothing on to the three-foot-wide sill.

"Those go in the chest-of-drawers," Mrs Stock pointed out.

"I want to put some of them on now," Aidan said

meekly. "Did you know Shaun worked a miracle on the lawnmower?"

"And bring all that plastic down to the bin— *Did* he now?" Mrs Stock said.

"Yes. Professor Hope was really amazed," Aidan said artfully – and just about truthfully. "Mr Stock can mow the lawn now."

Mrs Stock's glower phased into a malicious smile. "Ho ho, *can* he?" she said. "It's about time that veggie-freak did some of the work he's paid to do! Good for our Shaun!" She was so pleased at the thought of Mr Stock being dragged away from his Prize Vegetables, that she rushed off to find Shaun, only saying over her shoulder as she scooted off, "Lunch on the dining room table in half an hour. Plastic in the bin."

Aidan whoofed out an enormous breath of relief.

Downstairs, Andrew put his face round his study door to tell Stashe that her father had arrived. Stashe looked round at him from a screenful of hurrying letters, signs and figures. "Tell Dad I'll be another half hour," she said. "I have to leave this so that I know where I am with it. What did you *do* to this machine? Put Dad somewhere where he won't be in your way. He won't mind. He's used to waiting around for important horse people." She backed up this command with a dazzling smile.

Andrew retreated from his study feeling as if that smile had shot him in the chest. Though Stashe didn't strike him as quite so mad today, he was still not sure he liked her. She was, as Mrs Stock said, bossy. And Tarquin might be used to waiting around, but Andrew was not an important horse person and he was *blowed* if he was going to dump Tarquin in a corner somewhere.

He found Tarquin balancing on his crutches in the hallway. The missing leg was cramping again, he could see. "Stashe says she'll be another half hour," Andrew said. "Come into the living room and make yourself comfortable."

"Hit a snag or three in the computer, has she?" Tarquin commented, swinging himself along after Andrew. When he had got himself into the living room and was arranging himself and his stump along a sofa, he said, with a bit of a gasp, "Leg's always worse in wet weather. Pay no attention."

"Is that what stops you having a false leg – prosthetic, or whatever it's called?" Andrew asked.

"Something to do with the nerves, so it is," Tarquin agreed, "but I never understood what. It was all doctor-talk. I'm used to it now."

Tarquin's small, bearded face looked to Andrew to be showing agony. But he reminded himself that the man had been a jockey and that jockeys were used to pain. To take both their minds off it, he said, "About this field-of-care. You implied it was roughly circular and maybe twenty miles across, but I don't think it's that big or that regular—"

"No, more like a ragged egg-shape," Tarquin agreed. "I think you need to make sure of the boundaries."

"I will," Andrew said. "I've discovered that young Aidan can feel the boundaries almost as well as I can, so I'm going to take him with me and walk all round them. But what I really want to know is what happens *inside* these boundaries. What makes it different? What happens in Melstone that doesn't happen in Melford, for instance?"

"Well, as to *that*," Tarquin said eagerly, "I have my own theories. Have you noticed yet that every person living in Melstone has a knack of some kind? Stockie grows vegetables. Trixie Appleby – Mrs Stock's sister, that is – does hair better than any London hairdresser, they say. There's five boys and two girls up the road shaping to be football stars, and one of those boys plays the cornet like an angel. Rosie Stock up at the shop bakes cakes to die for. And so on. Probably even Trixie's Shaun has a knack if only he could find it—"

"Oh, I think he has," Andrew said, amused. He could hardly take his eyes off Tarquin's missing leg, lying throbbing along the sofa. It was awful. And so unfair.

"And I myself discovered I could grow roses as soon as I came to live here," Tarquin went on. "Not to speak of cook, and I'd never had much talent that way before. It strikes me that this area is further into the occult than most other places. Stuff comes welling up – or out – from somewhere, so it does, and it was Jocelyn Brandon's job to cherish it and keep it clean, so that it does no harm. Mind you, it may be more complicated than that—"

Andrew took his glasses off and cleaned them. He simply could not bear the sight of that throbbing leg. "Yes, but have you any idea what my grandfather *did* to cherish or control this… this occult stuff?" he asked. "I never saw him do anything unusual while I stayed here as a boy."

"Nor I. There was just a power in him," Tarquin said. "And yet I am sure there were things he must have done. Now why am I so sure?" Thinking seriously about this, forgetting the pain and forgetting that he had only one leg, Tarquin swung himself up off the sofa and started to pace up and down the room. "Always think better on my feet," he said. "I—"

He stopped talking and stood in the middle of the room, swaying a little. Below the folded-up right leg of his jeans, Andrew could clearly see the missing leg, transparent and sinewy, and the strong, strong muscles in its calf.

"What have you done?" Tarquin asked quietly.

Used Aidan's method without thinking, Andrew thought guiltily. He flourished his glasses. "I'm not sure. It was so much still *there* that I could practically *see* it hurting you."

"It's not hurting now," Tarquin said, looking down at where his foot should be, "but I can't see it. Can you?" Andrew nodded. "How long will it last?" Tarquin asked.

Probably just until I put my glasses on again, Andrew thought. Very slowly and cautiously, he eased his glasses back on to his nose. The transparent leg vanished. But it was obviously still there. Tarquin did not sway or fall down. He stood steadily in the middle of the room, without his crutches, looking a little dazed. "Keep your crutches within reach," Andrew said. "I really don't know how permanent this is."

"Just half an hour will do me!" Tarquin said devoutly. "You've no idea the relief! But I shall look very odd, walking on one invisible leg, so I will. It feels funny, so it does, with one bare foot."

"You could let that trouser leg down," Andrew suggested, "and wear a shoe."

"I could," Tarquin agreed. "And who would know? But is it likely it'll vanish away into a stump again if I go over into normal country?"

"I really don't know," Andrew confessed. "But if it

does, then come to me and I'll put it back again." He could see Tarquin was almost in tears, and that embarrassed him.

Meanwhile, Aidan sped downstairs feeling cool, cool in some of his new clothes. Naturally he had forgotten to bring the plastic wrappings to put in the bin. He was simply thinking of that torch. Assuming that Tarquin had now taken Stashe away for lunch, he crashed merrily into Andrew's study.

"Hi there." Stashe turned round from the computer with a beaming smile.

Aidan stopped dead. The smile made him feel totally defeated. He would have preferred Stashe to tell him to get out.

"I'm having dreadful trouble here," Stashe continued. "I thought at first that he'd got faulty software – and I wish it was that simple. But goodness knows *what* he's done! In the end I've had to strip it right down and start again from scratch. Do you know anything about computers?"

Aidan felt very shy. He was not used to pretty ladies treating him like a friend. What he wanted to do was to go away and come back for the torch later. He could see it sitting on the windowsill beyond Stashe, as big as an old-fashioned lantern. "We did a bit in school," he said. "They were always going wrong."

"Then you know how I feel," said Stashe. "I'm going to be all day fixing this one. *Then* I have to set up this database he wants. I'd hoped to make a start on sorting old Mr Brandon's papers, but that's just not on. Would you like to help me go through those when I get round to them?"

Her friendly manner made Aidan want to help her, even though he knew that going through papers was bound to be boring. "I might," he said. Meanwhile, what about that torch? Stashe was not to know why he wanted it. He settled for walking boldly over to the window and simply picking up the torch.

Stashe gave him another friendly smile as he walked past her. "New clothes?" she said. "Pretty cool."

"Thanks," Aidan said. He gave her a flustered smile and scudded away. Safely upstairs, he hid the torch under his bed and, after a second's thought, the big heap of plastic clothes-wrappers too. Then he galloped down again.

In the hallway, he came upon the astonishing sight of Tarquin O'Connor carrying both crutches under one arm and walking on one real leg and one invisible one. Andrew was with him. Aidan had to stop and stare. Both men were beaming all over their faces. They greeted Aidan like a long-lost friend.

"I hear I've you to thank for this, lad," Tarquin said.

"Your trick with your glasses," Andrew explained.

Aidan was astonished. He had not realised that such a simple thing could be so powerful.

Chapter Five

Aidan spent the rest of the day exploring the house and its grounds. Andrew, leaning attentively over Stashe and the computer, and trying to take in what she was telling him, watched Aidan pass and repass the study windows and was reminded of himself at Aidan's age. Things at his grandfather's house had seemed so magical in those days.

No. Correction. Things *had* been magical then. It was quite possible they still were. Watching Aidan scoot away across the tufty lawn, Andrew began, at last, to remember some of the very odd things that had happened while he stayed here as a boy. Hadn't there been a werewolf that was nearly shot for chasing sheep? His grandfather had rescued it somehow. Andrew had told his mother about that when he came home and she had told him angrily to forget all Jocelyn's silly nonsense.

"Are you listening, Professor?" Stashe asked. She was using a special *kind* voice on Andrew and his ignorance.

Andrew jumped. "Yes, yes. It's just that my Research Assistant used to handle all this for me. Double-click on the right-hand button here, you said. And do, please, call me Andrew."

"Or use this function key," Stashe said, pointing to it. "Honestly, P- er... Andrew, until today I didn't believe there *were* such things as absent-minded professors. I know better now."

Aidan had been up to the attics, where there was no proper floor. He had stood on the joists and looked up at the cobwebby holes in the roof. It was queer that no rain had come in. Aidan took off his glasses and saw why. The apparent spiderwebs were really thin, old enchantments holding the roof together. Emboldened by what Andrew had done to Tarquin, Aidan tried to see the cobwebby spaces as proper roof tiles. And, as he stared at the spaces, the attics slowly became dark, dark and musty, too dark to see much in.

Pleased with himself, Aidan felt his way from joist to joist – because it wouldn't do to mend the roof and then put a foot through a bedroom ceiling – and went down to explore the grounds. They were wonderfully bushy and wild. But the amazing thing about them was that they felt utterly and securely safe, safe the way Gran's rented house had been until she died. Aidan knew that no Stalkers could get near him here. He went everywhere.

There were Beings living in the safety of these grounds. Things that Aidan could feel but not see seemed to lurk at the corners of his eyes, in the orchard particularly, but also among the laurels by the gate. There was a sort of grotto near one of the back walls, where water trickled and ferns grew. Something definitely lived there, but even without his glasses, Aidan had no clue what kind of entity it was.

One of the times he crossed the lawns, he encountered Shaun. Shaun had a bag of cement in each hand. He looked lost. Aidan was astonished at how strong Shaun must be. He had tried to lift one of those stone-hard bags himself and hadn't been able to budge it.

"Professor said to bury these," Shaun said. "Would here do?"

They were right in the middle of the main lawn. "No, I don't think so," Aidan said. "You'd better find somewhere with bare earth."

"Ah." Shaun nodded. "Easier to dig."

He trudged off one way and Aidan went another.

After a while, Aidan worked round to Mr Stock's particular, privileged walled vegetable garden. It was so orderly and clean and square that it was more like a room that had lost its roof than a garden. Aidan could see Mr Stock's hatted head moving about inside the greenhouse in one corner. He veered off towards the opposite corner and tiptoed around a bed of broccoli that seemed to be trying to grow into oak trees, hoping not to be seen. He didn't want to get Andrew punished again. But, my goodness, things grew huge in this garden! There were strawberries the size of pears and a vegetable marrow, reposing in a rich, black bed of its own, that reminded Aidan of a small dinosaur; then he thought, No, what it is, is an ecological zeppelin. Beyond it, runner beans half a metre long trailed from tall, tall peasticks.

Beyond these, Aidan came upon Shaun busily digging in another rich, black bed, with the cement bags waiting on the path to be buried.

Oo-er! Aidan thought. Crisis! "Er…" he said. "Shaun…"

Shaun just grinned at him. "Good place," he said and went on digging.

Aidan could think of only one way of stopping Shaun. He ran to find Andrew. When he put his face round the study door, Stashe was alone in there. She gave Aidan one of her hundred-watt smiles. "What's up?"

"I need Professor Hope," Aidan said. "Urgently."

"In the living room," Stashe said. "I overloaded him and he went to play the piano."

Aidan tore off there. But by the time he got to the living room, and Andrew had looked up from sorting music out of the piano stool, it was already too late. Mr Stock's voice crashed like thunder in the distance.

"My *sparrowgrass!* That hulking, brainless looby of yours is DIGGING UP MY SPARROWGRASS BED!"

And the voice of Mrs Stock shrieked back, sharp as daggers, "And what if he is? I don't know what you grow it for! Not *one stalk* of asparagus have you brought into this kitchen *ever*!"

"It's for the *Fête*, you stupid cow! GO AND TELL HIM TO STOP!"

"*You* tell him. It's *your* asparagus!"

"Oh dear!" Andrew said. "Is that what you were coming to tell me about?" Aidan nodded. He was thoroughly out of breath. "I think," Andrew said, "the only thing to do is to keep our heads down. Why—?"

"You told Shaun to bury those bags of cement," Aidan panted. "And then *I* told him not in the middle of the lawn."

Andrew grinned. "Then it's too late to do anything but make bets on what our punishment's going to be."

Aidan discovered that he really, really liked Andrew. Up

to then, he had been too shy of him to know. He grinned back. "He's got some broccoli like little oak trees."

"No, rhubarb," Andrew said. "I bet on rhubarb. He's got some that's taller than you are."

In fact, what they got was asparagus. Only minutes after Mrs Stock had collected Shaun and stormed off in a dudgeon, the asparagus was sitting on the kitchen table in an enormous box half filled with earth.

"Double punishment," Andrew said cheerfully. "Mrs Stock didn't even wait to make cauliflower cheese. Do you like asparagus?"

"I've never had any," Aidan said. "How do you cook it?"

"You can steam, roast or boil it," Andrew said, picking about in the box. "My grandfather used to love it because you're allowed to dip it in butter and eat it with your fingers. But I'm afraid that Mr Stock has let this lot get too big and woody. Let's just wash it and put it on the woodshed roof. Someone might like it."

Yes, and I can't wait to see *who*! Aidan thought.

Andrew took the usual kitchen chair out and stood on it, while Aidan passed him dripping green bundles of asparagus they had washed in the biggest iron pan in the kitchen.

They had hardly started when Stashe came hurrying

around the corner, staggering a bit in her elegant shoes. "It's all fixed and I'm just off now," she was saying, but she stopped and giggled when she saw what they were doing. "Oh, do you have a visitor too? Ours takes stuff off our outdoor table. But only meaty bits. Dad says it must be a fox. What do you think yours is?"

Andrew paused in laying asparagus carefully along the dips in the corrugated roof. "I'm not at all sure. Is the computer ready to use now?"

"Perfectly," said Stashe. "And I'm hurrying off now so's I can walk home and save Dad the drive. You wouldn't believe the muddle he got in this lunchtime! He kept forgetting the car was adapted to drive with his hands."

She beckoned imperiously. Andrew found himself bending double on the chair to bring his ear near her mouth. Bossyboots! he thought. But Stashe certainly had a way with her. He couldn't help laughing.

"*Thank* you for what you did for Dad!" she whispered. "He was so depressed I was getting worried. How did you *do* it?"

"Um – his leg was almost still there," Andrew said. "I just brought it back."

"And will it *last*?" Stashe asked urgently. "I don't think he could bear to lose it again."

"I can always bring it back," Andrew said, much more

confidently than he felt. "Keep telling him that."

"I will," said Stashe. "Now I must fly. See you!"

She went rushing off at a smart stagger round the house. Andrew waved goodbye with the bunch of asparagus he was holding and almost fell off the chair. "A right fool I look!" he said to Aidan. "Next bunch, please."

By the time they had finished, the woodshed appeared to be thatched in asparagus. Aidan could hardly wait to see what came and ate it. It was a good thing there was so much of it. He would have plenty of time to get downstairs with the torch as soon as he heard munching.

Aidan went to bed early, saying he was tired again, which was far from true. Upstairs, he propped all his bedroom windows open as far as they would go by wedging them with new packets of socks. He put on new pyjamas, new fleece and the new waterproof over those. Then he fetched the pillows from the bed to make the windowsill comfortable and settled down there with the torch to wait and listen. The woodshed was just round the corner. He ought to hear munching easily.

An hour later he was freezing, in spite of the new fleece, but nothing else had happened. Aidan had heard an owl hooting, cars on the road and people laughing in the distance down by the pub. But those were all ordinary sounds. An hour later still, when it was quite dark, he began to wonder if the mysterious visitor might be magically silent. Aidan was going to sit here all night and not hear a thing.

The idea panicked him and he saw that the only way to be *sure* of seeing anything was to go outside and wait beside the woodshed. He sprang up, clutching the torch, and tiptoed across the creaky floor, up the bulge in the middle and down to the bedroom door. He creaked the door open. Bother. Stupid. He should have oiled it. There was a can of WD40 in the kitchen, but he had not thought to borrow it like the torch. He crept along the corridor and down the stairs. They creaked too. Was there any way to oil stairs? Probably not. Things creaked when they were old. It was a relief to get down to ground level, where the floors were stone. Aidan scudded across the flagstones and along to the kitchen.

Andrew, sitting reading in the comfortable chair in the living room, heard light footsteps fleeing down the passage, and looked up. Aidan? Up to what? Hungry again probably and going to find the biscuits they had bought this morning. Not to worry. Andrew looked back to his book and, as he did, he heard the faint, distant sound of the back door being carefully opened and shut. Then he knew just what Aidan was doing. He swore and flung down the book.

Aidan tiptoed through the dewy grass, gasping at how cold it was. He should have put shoes on. Rather late for that now. He came to the corner of the house and, very cautiously, put his shoulder against the stones of the wall and sidled round.

The visitor was already there. It was enormous. There was a fitful moon that was rushing through smokelike clouds and Aidan could see the visitor against the sky, towering over the woodshed, stooping and strange. It reached out a piece of itself...

The Stalkers in London came instantly back to Aidan's mind. For an hour-long minute, he was even more terrified than he had been then, paralysed with horror, while the great shape unfolded upwards and made mysterious movements. Then there was a crunch, followed by very large munching.

It's a vegetarian, Aidan reminded himself. It's eating the asparagus. He managed to take a deep breath. He lifted up the big torch, aimed it at the creature and switched it on. It made a fan of dazzling white light.

The visitor gave a yelping grunt and tried to hide its eyes with the bunch of asparagus in its huge hand. It said, quite distinctly, "Don't do that!"

Aidan automatically said, "Sorry," and switched the torch off. Then of course he could see nothing. He opened and shut his eyes to clear the dazzle off and thought about what he had seen. For a moment, he thought he had been looking at Shaun. But Shaun at least four times the usual size, almost five metres tall and wide with it. Shaun with wild hair tangling down on to his thick shoulders. But the grimy face up among the hair had not been padded with the fat of stupidity, the way Shaun's was. No, it was not Shaun. It was something else.

"Let's face it," Aidan found himself saying aloud. "You're a giant."

"Not yet," the visitor answered discontentedly. He ought to have had a deep, rumbling voice, but in fact his voice was quite high, rather like Shaun's. "I grow slow," he said. "Who you? You got windows on your eyes, but you not the usual boy. That one had hair like straw."

"I'm Aidan," Aidan said. And he thought, He must mean Professor Hope, when he was a boy! So Andrew *did* go and look! "And what's your name?"

The visitor took a big bite of asparagus and answered as he munched.

"Pardon?" said Aidan. No one's name could be *crunch*.

At that moment, Andrew said from the corner of the house, "Hallo, Groil."

"H'llo, h'llo!" the visitor replied excitedly, waving two bunches of asparagus against the faint light of the sky. He waved just the same way that Shaun did when he was excited. "Who *you*? Not the usual old man, are you?"

"No," said Andrew. "I'm Andrew."

"Andrew! *You* grew quick!" the giant exclaimed. He swung a fistful of asparagus towards Aidan. "Then he—?"

"Staying here," said Andrew. "Like I used to do. I hope Aidan isn't disturbing you at your supper. My grandfather used to get very cross with me—"

At this, Aidan looked nervously from Andrew to Groil, but Groil simply crammed both bunches of asparagus into his mouth, crunched mightily, swallowed with the sound of a drain being unblocked and said, "Nah, nah." In the grey, gusting light from the moon, he seemed to be smiling. After another drain-like swallow, he said, "Still wearing the jumper you gave me. See?" He plucked proudly at his chest.

Aidan was seeing quite well now. The thing Groil was plucking at might have been a jumper once, but now it was mostly holes, like a dark, irregular string vest, stretched very tightly across his great chest. Below that, he wore a loincloth that *could* once have been a bath towel.

"Aren't you cold like that?" Aidan asked before he could stop himself.

"Sometimes," Groil admitted. "In winter." He picked up another fistful of asparagus and pointed it at Andrew.

"He gave me clothes, see." He stayed pointing the asparagus at Andrew. Aidan could see his big eyes shining rather sadly in his big face. "Then he grew. Everyone grows so quick except me. You look like the old magician now. Where is he?"

"He's dead, I'm afraid," Andrew said.

The eyes, dimly, blinked. Then they looked at Aidan for help. "What is dead?" Groil asked.

Aidan and Andrew both spoke at once. Andrew said, "Gone for good."

Aidan said, "Not here any more," and gulped back misery.

"Ah." Groil munched asparagus for a while, thinking. "And then you ate him?" he suggested. "I ate a gone-for-good squirrel once. I didn't like it much."

"Well, no," Andrew said. "Not quite. More like the squirrel before you ate it. He left me in charge here. Let's change the subject. Do you like the asparagus we put out for you?"

"This?" Groil scrabbled up another bunch of asparagus from the roof and held it into the moonlight. "Very tasty. Crunchy. A little bitter. It tastes green. Sparrowgrass, is it?"

Aidan thought of Mr Stock and tried not to laugh.

Groil grinned at him. Big flat teeth caught the

moonlight. "I heard him shouting about it in the garden," he said. "It's a new word I know."

So Groil must lurk about Melstone House somewhere, Aidan thought. "What do you do in the winter when it's cold?" he asked.

"I curl down," Groil said. "Under stuff. Earth keeps you quite warm."

"Wouldn't you like some more clothes?" Aidan asked.

Groil thought about it. "Something looser?" he said, plucking at the strands of wool across his chest.

"Then I'll see if I can find you some," Aidan said.

Andrew coughed. "Aidan, I think we should leave Groil to his supper now. My grandfather was always very strict about this. And you should be in bed. Don't forget to bring the torch."

"Oh." Groil was not quite a vegetarian, Aidan realised. Someone who could think of eating dead grandfathers might not draw the line at living boys. "Oh, I— Goodnight then, Groil. See you."

"See you, Edwin," Groil said happily. His teeth closed on more asparagus with a snap and a great crunch.

Aidan, as he bent and groped about for the torch that he had put down in the grass somewhere, wondered crossly why it was that *nobody* could get his name right. He muttered about it as he followed Andrew round the house and into the warmth beyond the French windows. "I don't want to go back to bed yet," he said once they were indoors. "I'm too excited. Do you mind if I stay in here and make Groil some clothes?"

Gran would have said No and sent Aidan off to bed at once. Andrew simply asked agreeably, "How do you propose to make clothes?"

"I'll show you." Aidan put the torch on the piano and pelted off upstairs to his room. He came back with his old clothes – clothes he had worn for the best part of last week – and spread them out on the worn, patterned carpet. He took his glasses off. "Like this," he explained to Andrew, who was now sitting in the good chair with his book again. "If I take my glasses off, things go larger anyway. I think I can make them go *really* larger."

Andrew answered, in his polite way, "It's certainly worth a try. I remember, when I was your age, getting pretty distressed at how cold Groil must be. When I first met him he had no clothes on at all."

And how had he forgotten that? Andrew wondered. He had forgotten Groil completely. All he had remembered was that it was very unwise to try to see what, or who, ate the food on the woodshed roof. And he *ought* to have remembered. He had been in trouble with his grandfather about spying on Groil, and in trouble with Mrs Stock over stealing the bath towel. Then, when he got home, he had been in trouble with his mother about the missing jumper. She had knitted it herself for Andrew to wear in Melstone. All that was enough to make a person remember, you would have thought. But he had forgotten because when he was older, he knew that adults didn't believe in naked giants at midnight.

Then there was the puzzling way that Groil looked so like Shaun. Andrew thought that he had probably given Shaun a job because Shaun looked familiar somehow. He had a dim feeling that his grandfather had talked about this kind of resemblance. It was another of the magical things Jocelyn had told him about. He suspected that, one way or another, his grandfather had prepared him quite thoroughly for this field-of-care thing. And Andrew had forgotten every bit of it.

"Did Groil remind you of anyone?" he asked Aidan.

"Yes," said Aidan. "Shaun."

Aidan was having trouble. The clothes were stretching, but very slowly and unevenly, and going spiderweb thin in places. Andrew took his glasses off and looked across at Aidan crouching on the carpet, staring, staring at a pair of jeans with one leg longer than the other. A couple of years ago he would have thought Aidan was mad.

"Try taking them back smaller, and then thinking of each thread as longer and thicker," Andrew suggested. "Like looking at cloth under a microscope."

"Oh, yes, but— Thanks," Aidan said, flustered.

There was a pause, during which the sweatshirt grew at last and the jeans shrank.

"You know," Aidan burst out in his frustration, "I do hate my name!"

"Why is that?" Andrew asked.

"No one gets it *right*!" said Aidan. "Not even Groil! And it's an awful name anyway. Aidan's a saint and Cain was the first-ever murderer. What a mixture!"

"Well, most people are that kind of mixture," Andrew said.

"Yes, but they don't have names that *say* so!" Aidan said disgustedly.

"True," Andrew agreed. "But has it occurred to you that if those Stalkers of yours had called you by the right name, you might have gone out to them?"

"Oh!" Aidan was much struck by this. "Do you think I would have?"

"Yes. Names are powerful things," Andrew told him. "It could even have saved your life that they got yours wrong. Besides, neither of your names means what you think they do. Here. Let me show you."

Sick of brooding on things he could maddeningly not remember, Andrew sprang up and went to the bookshelves. Aidan distrustfully watched him seize two fat books and spread them open on the piano. Being a professor again, Aidan thought.

"Yes, here we are," Andrew said. "Aidan is a diminutive – that means a smaller version or a pet name – of an Irish name that means 'fire'. You are 'young fire'. Think of yourself as crackling and throwing up long yellow flames. Sparks too. And Cain…" He turned to the other book. "It says here that Cain as a surname has nothing whatsoever to do with the first murderer in the Bible. It means either 'war zone' or 'son of a warrior'. You can think of yourself as 'Young Fire, Son of a Soldier'. Does that make you feel better?"

"Let me see," Aidan said, jumping up. Andrew obligingly pushed the books towards him. Aidan bent over them and discovered that what Andrew said was quite true – except that Andrew had somehow made the meanings more colourful than the books did.

When he turned back to the garments on the floor, he found they were growing nicely all by themselves. They were now slightly larger than Groil-size and took up most of the carpet. No matter. Groil said he was still growing. "*Stop!*" Aidan told them, and they did. Aidan turned to

Andrew, grinning with relief. "Quite a learning curve!" he said. "Spells and names."

"The two things are often the same," Andrew said. "But I do think that when people say 'a learning *curve*' they make a mistake. Learning to me always seems to go in a straight, ignorant line and then, every so often, takes a jump straight upwards. Wouldn't you agree?"

Aidan considered this, and nodded. You always learned things suddenly, mostly because people came and told you things. He was beginning to think that Andrew was impressively wise.

"Now go to bed," Andrew said. "Or I'll tell Groil you want him to eat you."

Chapter Six

idan went to bed, where he slept sweetly. Andrew, on the other hand, had a disturbed night, full of restless dreams, in which he was constantly searching for the things his grandfather had told him. In the dreams, he was always looking for his grandfather to ask him and his grandfather was never there. Once or twice he found Stashe instead, but she just said airily, "It's all on the computer," and went away. So then, Andrew dreamed, he looked on the computer and found information that was like coloured smoke and, like smoke, the knowledge escaped through his fingers when he grasped at it. At one point he half woke himself up, saying, "I suppose I have to work this out myself then." This annoyed him, because it was going to interfere with his book. He finally woke up into a warm, grey morning, relieved that the night was over.

In the normal way, Andrew would have got down to work on his book. But he needed Stashe, in order to start, and Stashe was not coming that day. Andrew grumbled to himself over breakfast, "Wasted day, wasted day."

"Why don't we take a map and walk the boundary then?" Aidan suggested.

"Good idea!" Andrew said.

Since Mrs Stock was late that day – if she was coming at all after her row with Mr Stock – Andrew and Aidan made themselves sandwiches and left Mrs Stock a note. Andrew discovered that he and Aidan took the same size in shoes – Aidan was obviously going to end up pretty tall – so Andrew, rather grudgingly, lent Aidan his second-best walking boots. They took waterproofs, found the map and set off across the damp, grey fields towards Mel Tump.

Aidan enjoyed it hugely. He had not expected to, being a city boy and not used to rough walking. In fact, when they crossed the ragged hedge opposite the woodshed, he was certain he was not going to enjoy this. Entering the first field gave him a queer, nervous feeling.

"It doesn't feel nearly so safe out here," he said to Andrew.

"No, it probably isn't," Andrew said. "I think I remember my grandfather saying that Melstone House and its grounds are a sort of safety zone. But don't let that worry you. He owned – and I own now – all these fields, and the hill, and that wood over there. I rent them out for pasture, but they're all still mine."

Aidan wondered what it felt like to have a spread of land like this that actually belonged to you. Rather good, probably.

He did not enjoy the next bit either, when they met Wally Stock, the farmer who pastured his cows and sheep in Andrew's fields. Wally was short and red-faced and gloomy. He wore a flat, gloomy hat and he was a great talker. Aidan stood impatiently by while Wally tried to persuade Andrew to take a whole sheep for his freezer as part payment for renting Andrew's fields. Andrew knew this was a tax dodge and he was not willing; but then he looked round at Aidan, fidgeting beside him, and thought about how much Aidan ate. He agreed to the sheep and tried to walk on. But Wally was by no means finished.

"You heard about the shenanigans on the Fête Committee?" he asked. Andrew said No, he hadn't. "Proper row," said Wally. "That Mrs Fanshaw-Stock throwing her weight around over the bouncy castle until two of the committee walks out. No one knew what to do at first. But then they bring the vicar in, proper enough, to make up the numbers, and the vicar says to ask Mr Brown—"

"Mr Brown?" Andrew asked.

"Mr Brown down at the Manor," Wally explained. "Proper recluse, he is, worse than you are, Professor. Surprised the hell out of everyone when Mr Brown agreed. Nobody knows what good he'll be, but there you go. At least we've got a proper celebrity to open the Fête. Well known. Cooks all over the telly. He'll draw people in all right. With any luck, we'll make a profit this year, provided we get good weather. Weather's been terrible this year. Fit to ruin me, what with the price of milk being so low and the supermarkets paying peanuts for lamb."

"He always says he's being ruined," Andrew said to Aidan when Wally had promised to deliver the sheep next month and they were at last able to walk away.

"Oh, hey!" Wally called after them.

Andrew turned back, hoping Wally had not overheard him. Aidan sighed.

"I heard," Wally said, "from that Stashe – working for you now, ain't she? – that her dad's got him a false leg after all. Went to a new specialist, I heard. Did you hear that?"

Andrew said he had heard. "Honestly!" he said, when Wally finally allowed them to walk away. "Does everyone in Melstone know everything we do?"

They walked across two fields and through a gate on to Mel Tump. It was here that Aidan truly began to enjoy the walk. Mel Tump, close to, was a fascinating mass of little green paths running this way and that among strong-scented bushes. Aidan got a feeling that people had been very busy here. Perhaps Groil was one of them. Aidan looked and looked as they climbed, in case Groil was curled up somewhere, under a bush or in one of the surprising grassy hollows, but there was no sign of him. There were rabbits and birds, but nothing out of the ordinary. From the top of the Tump, you could look out over the winding stretch of the village and over Melstone House, half hidden by its two great trees, the oak tree and the copper beech. There was even a glimpse of the distant chimneys of Melstone Manor, where the reclusive Mr Brown lived. Looking over the other way, you saw mile after mile of deep green countryside.

"There's no way you can see the boundary," Aidan said, putting his glasses on after experimenting with them off.

"You never can," Andrew said. "We'll have to do it by trial and error."

They went down the hill and across country to the one piece of the boundary Andrew was sure of: the dip in the road where he had met old Jocelyn's ghost. When they came to it, warmed by walking and cooled by the slight, moist wind, Aidan was thinking, This is the life! He felt rather let down to find just an ordinary road with occasional cars rushing along it.

When there were no cars coming either way, Andrew led the way down the bank, to cross the road just beside the dip where the ghost had been. Going as slowly as he dared, in case someone was speeding, he wove up and down the slight rise in the road, until he had it fixed in his mind what the boundary felt like. The side where the field-of-care was felt like what he now thought of as normal: deep and slightly exciting. The other side—

"Oh!" Aidan exclaimed. "It's all boring and dangerous this side! Like standing on a runway in the path of an aeroplane. Flat, but you're lucky you're not dead."

"Right. We look for that feeling. Then we know we're just outside the boundary," Andrew said.

There was a gate in the hedge opposite. Beyond it was a field of nearly ripe wheat with the remains of a cart track running beside it.

"It looks," Andrew said, "as if there was once a path here. If there's a path all round the boundary, that will make it all much easier."

It was not that easy. There *was*, or had been, a path most of the way, but whoever owned the land there had ploughed the path up, or taken out the hedges to make larger pastures, and in these places it was truly difficult.

Aidan, as he swerved from deep-and-exciting to flat-and-dangerous, hoped no one was watching them. They must look mad, the two of them carefully zigzagging across a wide green meadow. Andrew was more worried that some farmer would see them swerving about in the field of maize they came to next, madly rustling through and trying not to spoil the crop.

They came to a small river, where there had been a bridge. But it was broken, and the whole river was fiercely fenced off with barbed wire and thick bushy trees.

"It almost looks as if someone doesn't want us to do this," Aidan said.

"It does rather," Andrew agreed, wondering if his grandfather had had enemies he did not know about. "Let's eat the sandwiches."

They ate lunch sitting on the bank of the river, further up into flat-and-dangerous, where there was a sandbank that Andrew thought might help them cross the water. While Aidan cheerfully munched his way through more than half the sandwiches, Andrew got out the map and marked in the boundary as they had found it so far. It was surprisingly regular, a steady curve that seemed to be the beginning of a large oval emanating from Melstone House near its centre. He was tempted to mark in the rest of the oval by guess and go home. But that felt like cheating. He was, now he was doing it, quite convinced that his responsibility to the field-of-care meant that he had, personally, to walk every step of its boundary. All the same, he pencilled in where he *thought* it went on the map. It would be interesting to see if it did as he predicted.

They crossed the river by jumping from the sandbank and got rather wet doing it. Then they walked downriver to the broken bridge and went on from there.

On this stretch, the path must once have run between two hedges and then been forgotten. They now had to struggle through the middle of a hedge, where brambles tore at their clothes, branches whipped their faces, crab apples clouted their heads and nettles tried to sting through to their legs. The pair of them forced their way on for miles, hot and out of breath, while their hair filled with seeds, until Aidan's new fleece no longer looked new and their boots were heavy with mud.

Then it was suddenly different. They staggered out into a proper lane with a fence on the other side of it. A notice fixed to the fence said:

PRIVATE GALLOPS
KEEP OUT

"What does that mean?" Aidan gasped. He took his fleece off and shook seeds out of it.

"It's where they exercise the racehorses," Andrew said. He leaned on the fence and looked at the long stripes of green turf running from right to left across their way. "You know," he said, "this boundary must be very old. I can see I'm supposed to look after half these gallops, but not the other half. They must run right across our boundary. That wouldn't make sense unless the gallops are much newer." He climbed the fence and swung over on to thick, thick cushiony grass. "Come on, Aidan. We'll have to do a bit of trespassing."

Aidan quailed. Suppose someone called the police…

"I'm sure it's all right," Andrew told him. "They only ride the horses out in the early morning, I know that. I'll be surprised if we see anyone at all."

He strode off, dropping divots of seed-filled mud from his boots as he went. Aidan followed him, cringingly. The green spaces were only divided from one another by lines of longer grass full of wild flowers. They spread out over the hillside roughly in the shape of a bunch of bananas, so open and exposed that Aidan expected the two of them to be seen and shouted at any second. And, in a way, he was right.

The boundary curved more abruptly here towards the

end of the village, making the narrow end of the oval Andrew had predicted. They traced it up a steep hill and slantwise down again, to where they could see red brick buildings that were obviously the Stables and the big house that went with those, down among trees in the distance. Here someone on a horse came thundering up the turf towards them. Aidan turned round and looked desperately about the empty grass for somewhere to hide. He wondered whether to throw himself flat.

But Andrew was waving cheerfully at the rider. The rider waved back and thudded happily up to them. The horse gave a protesting sort of snort as it was pulled up. Stashe, on its back, looking surprisingly glamorous in a hard hat, smiled down at them.

"Hello, you two," she said. "Lost? Or just doing a bit of trespassing?"

"The latter," Andrew said in his most professor-like way. "We're tracing the boundary of my field-of-care." He was terribly pleased to see Stashe so unexpectedly, but not quite sure how to show it.

"Oh!" said Stashe. "Is *that* what it is? It sort of plucks at you, doesn't it? All in a slant across the gallops. If you need to walk every inch of it though, I'm afraid you've got problems. It goes right through Ronnie Stock's house. Dad says Melstone Grange must have been built long after the

Brandons set up their field-of-care. But not to worry," she said quickly, seeing how dismayed Andrew looked. "There's race meetings all over today. Ronnie and Mrs Ronnie *and* the assistant trainer are all away at them. Meet me by the big gates and I'll see what I can do. But I must give poor Flotsam a *bit* of exercise first!"

She shouted the last sentence over her shoulder as the horse galloped off. Andrew shrugged. "We might as well go on," he said.

It became a little dreamlike for Aidan after that. They followed the boundary down the hill, then out of the gallops into a beautifully cared for garden, where it went through one corner of a rose bed. They had just reached tall iron gates that seemed to open on to the stable yard, when Stashe came galloping up on the other side of the garden wall. She hitched the horse to a ring in the wall there, gave it a lump of sugar and – Aidan winced – a kiss on its great nose, and slipped through the gate to join them.

"This way," she said, and led them into the large, well-kept house. "Do you think you could carry those boots of yours?" she said as they went. "I don't think Ronnie would appreciate all that mud on his carpets."

So they traced the boundary in their socks. It was better like that, Aidan found. The boundary fizzed under his feet from beneath Ronnie Stock's carpets. They were obviously very expensive carpets. Aidan thought they were hideous – which, he decided, *proved* they must be good carpets, in the way that nasty things *were*, like white of egg being good for you. But it felt very queer to be following the fizz through someone's majestic living room, and then into a big hall, resplendent with chandeliers and more nasty carpets. And then to come to a dead end in a downstairs cloakroom.

"Oh dear," Aidan said, hard up against a toilet with blue flowers all over it.

"Use it while we're here," Andrew said. "The boundary must run under the wall. We'll pick it up again outside." He looked, rather irritably, at Stashe. She was in fits of laughter.

"You – you've got half of a floral loo in your care!" Stashe managed to say. That made Andrew laugh too.

They went through the grand front door and sat on the imposing front steps to put their boots on again. Stashe said cheerfully, "I must see to Flotsam. See you the day after tomorrow," and shut the front door behind them.

After this, the boundary took them down the broad curve of a gravel drive, almost to the front gates of Melstone Grange. But there it curved off again into fields and moorland on the other side of the village. Andrew looked that way, satisfied. It was almost exactly the line he had pencilled in on the map. But he could see Aidan was quite tired.

"I think we'll leave the rest for another day," he said, "and walk home through the village."

Aidan was glad to agree. He felt as if he had walked for a week. And he suspected it was still a long way through the village to Melstone House.

He was right. Melstone was a long, thin village. It looked very fine in the late afternoon light, with its rows of cottages alternating with bigger houses built of old red brick, and the occasional newish bungalow squeezed in between. One of those bungalows belonged to Mr Stock, Andrew said, but he wasn't sure which. Aidan sighed. It was becoming just a long, long road to him.

Talking of Mr Stock made Andrew think of vegetables. "My feeling is that we owe ourselves a slap-up supper tonight," he said. "Are you any good at cooking?"

"Not bad," Aidan said. "Gran always said she didn't hold with helpless males who couldn't even boil an egg. She made me learn cooking when I was quite small. I can do most ordinary things."

"Good!" said Andrew. "Then you can do some tonight."

Oh dear. "When my legs stop aching," Aidan said

swiftly, and looked around for something to take Andrew's mind off cooking.

The road was winding them downhill towards the dip where Melstone House lay. And there, on the next corner, stood the perfect thatched cottage, one of those that had snuggled itself down into the land over the centuries, so that it looked as if it had grown there rather than been built. Flowering creepers grew round its diamond-paned windows and its slightly sideways front door, and its front garden was a mass of roses, roses of every possible colour.

"Hey!" Aidan said craftily, but meaning it too. "That's a nice house! I like it better than that place of Ronnie Stock's."

"Who wouldn't?" Andrew agreed. "It's idyllic."

Someone was bobbing about in the garden, tending the roses. As they came closer, they saw it was Tarquin O'Connor – Tarquin walking on two legs, but very carefully, as if he didn't quite trust his new, non-existent leg not to disappear suddenly and dump him in a rose bush.

Tarquin saw them at the same time. He came limping to his front gate with a delighted smile above his little beard. "Hello there!" he called out. "I wondered if you'd be along. Come on in and have a cup of tea. I've just made some biscuits, so I have."

Relief! thought Aidan.

The biscuits were some of the best shortbreads Aidan had ever tasted. Tarquin's teacups were the kind Gran had kept in a glass-fronted cupboard and never used. Aidan hardly dared drink out of his. He stared round Tarquin's rambling, comfortable room while he listened to Tarquin confessing to Andrew, with a rueful smile, that his non-existent leg was still there, but he just didn't *trust* it.

"It's the way my fingers go through it when I put my socks on," he explained.

Andrew took his glasses off and examined the leg. Aidan looked at the polished furniture and the low ceiling with black beams in it, and then at Tarquin's old, glowing, Oriental rugs.

"Oh, I like your carpets much better than Ronnie Stock's!" he exclaimed.

"And so you should!" Tarquin said, laughing. "Ronnie never did have any taste. As long as something costs a lot, Ronnie thinks it's good. But how come you saw inside his house?"

"Stashe took us in," Aidan said. He and Andrew described the way the boundary of the field-of-care ran through the middle of Melstone Grange, including the downstairs cloakroom.

Tarquin laughed at that, just as Stashe had. "Ronnie will have it," he said, "that the Grange is ever so old. He was always telling me so when I used to ride for him. So I went to the County Record Office and looked the place up. And it was built in 1832, so it was. That makes it Victorian, more or less. This cottage goes back three hundred years before that – and maybe more, but there's no records for earlier than that. And I'll bet that your field-of-care goes back as far as my house does at least, or it wouldn't have the Grange built across it. By the way, did Stashe tell you of the great row there's been on the Fête Committee?"

"No," Andrew said, still staring at Tarquin's leg. "Wally Stock did."

"Him! He *would*!" Tarquin said. "I swear that man knows things before they happen! But it's true, so it is, that for a while there it looked as if the whole Fête was off. I was thinking that Stockie – your Mr Stock – might be likely to cut his own throat with nowhere to show his veg at. But now it turns out that they've brought in Mr Brown and all's right again, so it is."

Andrew put his glasses on again to say, "I've not met Mr Brown."

"Him down at the Manor? Really not?" Tarquin said. And he added, just like Wally Stock, "Recluse and a bit of a scholar, just like you, Andrew. I'm surprised you don't know him."

His grandfather, Andrew remembered, had always said,

"Mr Brown is not for us, Andrew, but we have to be very polite to him." He said thoughtfully, "No. My grandfather didn't seem to get on with him."

"Doesn't surprise me," Tarquin said. "*Nobody* knows the man. That makes it all the more surprising he's going to run the Fête, so it does. Anyway, what do you make of this leg of mine?"

"I think I can harden it up," Andrew said. "But slowly, bit by bit. Drop in to see me as often as you can, and I'll get it more solid gradually."

"Thank you kindly," Tarquin said gratefully. "It was a bit embarrassing this morning when Stockie dropped by to see me – having a rave about the Fête being cancelled, so he was – and I caught my trouser leg on a nail. I walked off in one direction and my trouser leg went in another. Stockie stared a bit."

"You'd think he'd be used to such things," Andrew said, "working for my grandfather all these years. Oh, well. Are your feet rested, Aidan? We'd better be going."

Chapter Seven

Mrs Stock had gone home when Andrew and Aidan arrived back at Melstone House. There was, quite inevitably, a dish of caulifower cheese in the middle of the kitchen table. There was a reproachful note under it that said, *Our Shaun dint know what to do so he went in that old shed. If he done wrong you should a been here.*

Andrew simply laughed and set about cooking steak from the freezer. Andrew did most of it, to Aidan's relief. Aidan didn't know where saucepans were kept or how the stove worked, but he helped. And all the time, he kept looking at the huge clothes for Groil that he had brought downstairs and hung over a kitchen chair, hoping that it wouldn't rain, so that they could put the clothes out on the woodshed roof after supper. Those clothes were Aidan's very first big magical project and he wanted it to *work*.

I can't *wait* to see if they fit! he kept thinking.

While Aidan was thinking this for at least the fortieth time, his grandmother's voice came into his mind, saying what Gran always said when Aidan said he couldn't wait. *Aidan, don't wish your life away!* Usually Aidan took this to mean that he wasn't to waste present time by longing for something in the future. But this time he remembered how big Groil was and how Groil was not *strictly* a vegetarian. Gran's words took on quite a different meaning then. Aidan thought Oh! and felt rather small.

All the same, he watched Andrew toss the big clothes up on to the woodshed roof at sunset. Then Aidan found he had not the slightest desire to know if they fitted or not. He went to bed. He was quite tired after all that walking and he went to sleep at once.

Around midnight, he was woken by a rattling bang from his window. Wind, Aidan thought sleepily. The bang happened again. He heard the window shake. He'll break it! Aidan thought and got out of bed fast, up the floor and down again to the window. Rather like last night, he could see a bulging white moon hurtling through a thin smoke of clouds. As he got to the window, moon and clouds vanished behind a great dark fist. BANG. The window leaped about.

Aidan climbed cautiously on to the three foot wide sill

and opened the window. He knelt there and looked out at Groil's fist, just stopping itself from hitting the glass again. Below that, Groil's huge face was turned up to him, foreshortened, so that Groil looked more like Shaun than ever. The face broke into a vast smile as Aidan leaned out, showing two rows of extremely big square teeth. Below that, Groil was wearing the clothes. Aidan had actually made them too big. Groil had had to turn the sleeves up and roll up the legs of the jeans. Aidan could see the pale cuffs of them above Groil's bare feet – which still looked enormous, even from this height.

"Oh, good! You found the clothes!" Aidan said.

Groil nodded vehemently, his eyes all creased up with his smile. "You made them?"

"Yes," Aidan said.

"Thought so," said Groil. "They smell of you. A smell of good magics."

"And you like them?" Aidan asked anxiously.

Groil nodded again and smiled blissfully. "Cosy," he said. "Warm. Smart too. I shall sleep well, come the winter days. And room to grow. No one can laugh at me for being bare now. You are very kind. I shall praise you to the High Lord. Might even ask someone to mention you to the King."

"That's all right," Aidan said, wondering who this High

Lord and this King were. "You're very welcome."

"I had a bit of trouble with the not-buttons though," Groil said. "Did I get them right?" He backed away, so that Aidan could see the zip on the jeans and the one at the neck of the sweatshirt, and gestured to them. "You pull them up shut? Right?"

Both zips were properly closed. Groil was no fool, Aidan thought, even though he had probably never seen a zip in his life before. "Yes," he said. "Zips. You got both zips right. You look good."

"Zips," Groil repeated. "I look good. I feel good. I got *clothes!*" He whirled away, waving his arms Shaun-fashion, and began to dance around the dim, moonlit lawn. "I got *clothes!*" he sang in a grating tenor voice. "I look *good!* I got *zips*, I got *clothes*, I look *good!*" He leaped. He cavorted. He flung his legs up in extravagant high kicks. He jumped. Once or twice Aidan was sure Groil came down on a thistle, but didn't appear to notice. His feet must have been like leather. "I got *zips!* I got *clothes!*" Groil roared out, and leaped like a ballet dancer, twizzling round in mid-air.

After a moment or so, Aidan caught Groil's rhythm and leaned out of the window and clapped in time to the dance. His hands were quite sore by the time Groil finally danced himself round the corner of the house and out of sight.

Even then, Aidan could hear him singing in the distance. He went back to bed, rather astonished at how easy it was to make someone that happy. Gran had always said you made yourself happy too, but Aidan had never really believed her until now.

"Groil liked the clothes," he reported to Andrew in the morning.

Andrew grinned over the bacon he was frying. He seemed to be making breakfast earlier than usual. "I heard him singing," Andrew said. "*Not* one of the world's great tenors."

"He danced too," Aidan said.

"I felt the ground shaking," Andrew replied, turning the bacon and fried bread out on to two plates. "Eat up. Today we're going to follow the boundary round the other way, to the left of the dip in the road. And it looks like rain, so I want to get going as soon as possible."

It started drizzling slightly as the two of them set off, and it was decidedly colder. Groil would be glad of the clothes, Aidan thought as he trudged past Wally Stock's cows on the way to the road. Come to think of it, Aidan was glad of his own new zip-up waterproof. I got zips! he thought to himself, and couldn't help grinning.

The boundary on this side was nothing like as regular as Andrew had thought. It took a great bulge away from the wood and Andrew's fields, out into unknown meadows, where it ran beside the road for a space, until the road swerved away towards Andrew's former University. Here they lost the line of the boundary for a while. In fact, Aidan wondered if they had lost themselves too. They waded through a marshy field full of tall rushes, where they could not even see the village, although they could hear the church clock striking somewhere in the distance behind the wood. Eleven o'clock, Aidan thought. Already.

Here the rain came down properly, white and pelting. The rushes bent and hissed with it and the distant wood was almost cancelled out by grey rods of rain. They could hardly see where they were walking, let alone find the boundary. They were soaked in seconds, with hair streaming into their eyes and their glasses nearly useless.

Andrew made two sloshing, sucking strides in what was probably the wrong direction, and stopped. "This is no good," he said. "Let's make for the wood and shelter there until this stops. It can't rain this hard for very long."

Aidan took his glasses off and could then just about see the wood, dark green behind the rain. It was much further off than he had thought. They floundered and squelshed towards it, each of them trying, from time to time, to wipe wet glasses on Andrew's handkerchief. Aidan had forgotten, in his shopping orgy, that he might need handkerchiefs. He was cursing himself about it by the time they finally stumbled through a bramble thicket and in under the trees.

"It's just as wet here," he said disgustedly.

"Yes, but in a different way," Andrew said.

This was true. The leaves on the trees held the rain up, so that they could at least see where to walk. But every so often a tree would become too full of water and it would all come down, twenty minutes' worth of heavy rain, and tip itself on their heads. Up above, they could hear the rain hissing steadily on to the tops of the trees, while all around them one tree after another unloaded cold water with a wet crash.

"I think we're going to drown," Aidan said miserably.

Andrew looked at him. City boy. Not used to this. Aidan's face was wet and white, and he was shivering. Come to that, Andrew was not too happy himself. "All right," he said. "Let's go back to the house and wait until the rain stops."

They tried to do that. But, by this time, neither of them was quite sure where the house was. After some muddling about – during which time a vast tree tipped several tankloads of rain, mixed with twigs, caterpillars and leaves, straight down on their heads – Andrew set off firmly in a straight line. The wood was not that large. He knew they had to come out of it soon. Aidan followed, wriggling his shoulders and morbidly wondering if the squirming down his back was just water or in fact a large, legless critter that had somehow got in under his hood.

They found themselves in front of a wall.

It was not a large wall. It was about knee high and built of old crumbly bricks covered with moss. But the slightly sinister fact about it was that someone had filled in the gaps and low places in it with very new-looking barbed wire. It seemed to run right across the wood for as far as they could see either way.

"I don't remember *this*!" Andrew said. "And why the barbed wire? It's all my property. I never agreed to let anyone wire part of the wood off."

With a bit of a grunt, he heaved one wet boot up and put it down on the other side of the wall. It went *crunch* on the dead leaves there.

As if this were a signal, there was more crunching from further along the wall. A large man in a grey knitted hat and a wet navy-blue jacket came marching up beside the wall in big rubber boots. He was carrying a gun. And there was a dog with him on a lead. An unpleasant-looking dog it was, rather like a bull terrier, with a smooth, bloated face and mean, pinkish eyes. Andrew, looking from the man's face to the dog's, thought that the faces were remarkably alike, right up to the mean, pinkish eyes. All the same, the man reminded him strongly of someone else. Take away the bloating, he thought—

"Get that foot out of there," the man growled at Andrew, "or I set the dog on you. Beyond this wall you're trespassing."

Andrew felt idiotic, caught astride a wall like this, but he said, "No, I'm not. I own this wood. I'm Andrew Hope. Who the devil are you?"

"Security," growled the man. The dog growled too and strained on its lead towards Andrew's leg.

Andrew, as haughtily as he could, took his leg back rather quickly to the other side of the wall. "Security for whom?" he said.

"For Mr Brown of course," the man snarled. "This side of the wall and the wood's all his. He don't allow anyone on his property."

"Nonsense!" Andrew said.

"You don't believe me, go and ask Mr Brown," the man said. "He has it all down in black and white. So get the hell out. Now." Here the dog put its front feet on the bricks and snarled fruitily at Andrew. Drool draped its big yellow fangs.

Andrew backed away. "This is a complete fabrication!" he said angrily. "You've no right to turn me off my own land! I shall certainly speak to your employer. Tell me your name."

"Security," the man said. "That's all the name you'll get. Speak to whoever you like, but you get the hell out of this wood first, before I take the dog off the lead." He reached to where the lead was fastened to the dog's collar. "Scarper," he said. "Both of you. Now."

There seemed nothing for it but to go. White with anger, Andrew swung round and marched away. He was so angry that he had no memory of having been lost in this wood a moment ago. He simply turned towards Melstone House and marched there in long, angry strides, with Aidan trotting beside him to keep up. Sure enough, rain-whitened green meadow appeared between the trees moments later. Andrew strode in among Wally Stock's sheep, fulminating.

"That wood is *mine*!" he said. "It belonged to my grandfather. It's marked on the deeds. I shall phone my lawyer. This Brown has absolutely no *right* to fence half of it off, let alone employ a man to threaten us!"

Aidan glanced up at Andrew's glaring white face and was impressed. This was the first time he had seen Andrew look dangerous. He wondered what Andrew was going to do.

When they reached the house, Andrew dashed to his

study and hauled out the dusty yellow package that contained the deeds of Melstone House.

"What are you both doing, dripping water all over the house?" Mrs Stock wanted to know.

Andrew ignored her and spread the deeds out on the table, regardless of rain plopping on to them from his hair. "There you are!" he said to Aidan, impatiently brushing water off the map. "Just as I thought. That line marks the edge of the property and it goes *right round* the whole wood. The Manor land only comes up to the edge of it. Set a dog on me, would he!"

He snatched up the phone and furiously punched in his lawyer's number.

"And are you going to be in for lunch now?" Mrs Stock asked.

"Not now," Andrew said, with the phone to his ear. "I'm too angry to eat. Hello? Can I speak to Lena Barrington-Stock, please? Urgently."

"Did you hear me? Lunch?" Mrs Stock demanded.

A voice in Andrew's ear was telling him that Mrs Barrington-Stock was out of the office just now, but would get in touch if Andrew would leave his name and telephone number. He scowled at Mrs Stock. "Aidan will be having lunch," he said. "I'm busy."

"Pardon?" asked the phone.

"Andrew Hope, Melstone House, Melstone," Andrew said. "You've got my number in your records. I've forgotten it. Go away, Mrs Stock." He rang off, snatched up the telephone directory and feverishly turned to the Browns.

"I'm not used to being treated like this," Mrs Stock said. She flounced off.

Knowing there would be pages and pages of Browns, Aidan left Andrew to it and went quietly away to get into dry clothes. He came back to find Andrew still at it. And swearing.

"I've been through all the Browns twice now," he told Aidan, "and there's no Brown of Melstone Manor *in* here! The wretched crook must be ex-directory. He *would* be!"

"You could have lunch after all," Aidan suggested.

"No, no," Andrew said. "I'm getting angrier every minute." He flung the directory down and went storming away upstairs.

Aidan loitered on in the study, well aware that Andrew had offended Mrs Stock very severely indeed and wondering how he could avoid going near her. Cauliflower cheese, he thought. In bucketfuls. He was still loitering in the study when Andrew stormed back in there to look at the map. Andrew was wearing much neater clothes than usual – if you didn't count the leather patches on the elbows of his tweed jacket – and was actually putting on a tie.

"I'm driving round to see this Mr Brown," he said, fetching the map out of his rucksack. "Ah. Here we are. I knew getting to the Manor was tricky. You'd better keep out of Mrs Stock's way. You could eat the sandwiches in my rucksack for lunch." He yanked the knot of his tie angrily tight and rushed away through the hall.

"And where are you off to now?" Aidan heard Mrs Stock say.

Andrew's voice replied, "It's none of your business *whose* neck I want to wring!" This was followed by the front door heavily slamming. Shortly after, Aidan heard the car start up and a great scattering of gravel as Andrew roared away down the drive.

The rain seemed to be slackening. Aidan decided he would go out as soon as it stopped. In the mean time, he ate the sandwiches and then went into the living room, thinking he might play chopsticks on the piano. But Mrs Stock was there, vengefully moving the piano into the dark corner again. Aidan retreated hastily. Since the rain was now only a drizzle, he put his wet waterproof on again and went out. Anything seemed better than staying in the house with Mrs Stock.

Aidan had become used to the not-quite-as-safe feeling

beyond the grounds of Melstone House. He decided he would explore the other end of the village. So, at the end of the lane he turned right and went downhill, past the church among its trees and then past the green and the pub. There were quite a few other children about there. The local school – wherever that was – must have broken up for the holidays. Since he didn't know any of them, Aidan went on, uphill now, past the shop and the hairdresser, towards the new houses at the end of the village. Just before he reached them, he came upon the football field. There was a big notice fixed to the hedge there announcing MELSTONE SUMMER FÊTE HERE NEXT SATURDAY and giving the date as the Saturday after next. Slightly mad, Aidan thought. He went nosily in through the gate to investigate.

There were no goalposts up, but this had not stopped eleven boys – no, two of them were girls – starting a game of football on the wet grass, with the goals marked by heaps of their clothes. The side with six players was winning. They scored two goals while Aidan watched.

Aidan went elaborately casual and sauntered over. Another goal was scored against the side with five players just as he got there. "I can be in goal for you if you like," he offered, as if he didn't care.

They accepted his offer at once. Aidan zipped his glasses

into his waterproof, put it to mark the goalpost with the other garments and joined in gladly. An hour or so later, the scores were even and Aidan had eleven new friends.

In this way, both Aidan and Andrew missed the incident that was The Last Straw for Mrs Stock that caused her to collect Shaun and leave early. She had left a note in which her feelings seemed to have got the better of her spelling:

You still dint give Shaun any work. There was some woman prowelling round the house gouping in windows, I went out and gave her a peace of my mind. Mr Stock run out of collyflours so I did you potato cheese. We sent her packing.

Chapter Eight

You got to Melstone Manor by taking the narrow road behind the church, although you had to be careful not to take the *other* narrow road with the signpost that said MELFORD. Most days, Andrew might have made this mistake. But that day his fury drove him into the right, unlabelled road and then jouncing and bumping down what proved to be an unpaved lane. This lane suddenly became a potholed track through parkland and fine trees. A herd of deer bolted out of his angry way. He swept round a corner and came to the Manor.

The Manor was highly Elizabethan. It had tall chimneys, lots of black beams on the outside and large numbers of big, dim, diamond-paned windows. It had gables enough to supply several manor houses.

"Just like a ghost movie!" Andrew said between his teeth. "A bad B movie! Absurd!"

He parked in front of the mighty black oak front door, marched through the drizzle and up the brick steps, and hauled on the large brass bell ring. A dim jangling sounded somewhere inside.

Andrew waited, hoping very much that he had arrived in time to interrupt Mr Brown's lunch. He was just about to haul on the bell pull even harder, when the door opened with the most impressive creak. A short, fat man in morning dress looked up at him. "Yes, sir?"

The butler, Andrew thought. There *would* be a butler. There was something about the man's little plump face that struck him as familiar, but he was too angry to wonder about it. "I want to see Mr Brown," he said. "Now."

"Yes, sir. What name shall I say, sir?" the little man asked.

This seemed too easy. Andrew refused to be put off by it. "Tell him Professor Hope," he snarled. Everyone here thought he was a professor. He might as well make use of it. "From Melstone House," he added menacingly.

"Yes, sir. Please to follow me, sir." The butler waved Andrew into the house and shut the door behind him with another impressive creak. Then he went pattering away into the gloomy interior, past carved oak panelling and across acres of red tiles.

Andrew followed. The fact that he was being let in without question made him angrier than ever. The butler didn't even seem to notice he was angry. Trying to take the wind out of my sails! he thought. There was a strong smell of roast beef in the air. It led Andrew to hope that he was about to burst in on Mr Brown feeding, probably with a napkin under his chin and a decanter by his fat elbow.

But it seemed that lunch at the Manor must be over. The butler led him to a dark and cushy library-place, where leather-bound books glimmered on the walls and red leather chairs with buttons on stood about on a deep fawn carpet. A small fire flickered at the bottom of a vast, arched chimney-piece with a coat of arms on its leaded front.

"A Professor Hope to see you, sir," the butler said, holding open the fat linenfold oak door. "From Melstone House, he tells me."

"Come in, come in, Professor," said a pleasant, silvery voice. A tall silvery gentleman in a very smooth pinstriped suit stood up from beside the fire and advanced with his hand out. "I'm very pleased to meet the tenant of Melstone House. Can I offer you a drink?"

"No, thank you," Andrew said, glad that he was not much of a drinker. "And it's not *tenant*. It's *owner*." He managed to avoid shaking hands with Mr Brown by taking his glasses off and cleaning them. To his naked eyes, the man looked even taller, and impossibly slender. There seemed to be a sort of silvery haze around him.

Mr Brown took his hand back. He seemed perplexed. "But surely, my dear sir, your name should be Brandon if you're not a tenant?"

"Jocelyn Brandon was my grandfather," Andrew said. "And I'm sorry to make your acquaintance on an unfriendly note, but I've come to complain."

"Dear, dear," said Mr Brown. "Well, if you won't have a drink, at least take a seat and unburden yourself."

He waved Andrew to the red buttoned chair opposite the one he had been sitting in himself. Andrew had always thought that this kind of chair was probably acutely uncomfortable. He sat down warily and found he was quite right. The thing was all slippery knobbles. Deep instinct caused Andrew to keep his glasses off. On the pretext of finding a smear on the left lens and then on the right one, Andrew managed to keep his eyes naked for most of what followed.

He watched Mr Brown sink his silvery length into the chair opposite and pick up the glass he had been drinking from. The drink was rose-coloured. From time to time it even looked, blurrily, as if Mr Brown was actually sipping at a real rose. The decanter Andrew had imagined earlier was there, on a table at Mr Brown's slender elbow. In fact, there were several decanters. One contained an oddly pulsing blue liquid. Another was yellow, with a dazzle to it that made Andrew's naked eyes water, and a third was violently green. None of them was rose-coloured. Andrew was extremely glad he had refused a drink. He gave silent thanks to Aidan for showing him this trick with your glasses.

"Mr Brown," he said, "an hour or so ago I was walking in my wood – Melstone Wood, it is called on the deeds to *my property* – and I found half of the wood fenced off and patrolled by an extremely unpleasant fellow who said he was Security for you. He ordered me off with threats. Now, whoever he is—"

Mr Brown gave a graceful shrug. "I'm afraid I can give you no other name for him but Security," he said.

"—I object very strongly," Andrew went on, "to being ordered off my own property."

"But look at it from my point of view," Mr Brown said, calm and soothing. "There are creatures in that wood that I wish to protect."

"I can perfectly well protect my own squirrels!" Andrew retorted. "The fact remains that you have absolutely no right to fence off half my w—"

"We are not talking of squirrels," Mr Brown cut him off, placid and silvery. "We are talking of my personal privacy, which is mine to protect, not yours."

"Nobody goes in that wood anyway," Andrew snarled, "except me, and I *own it*, Mr Brown! *All* of it."

"As I said," Mr Brown continued, as if Andrew had not spoken, "you must see it from my point of view, Mr Hope. As a scholar and, I presume, a gentleman, you can surely see both sides of a question. I came back to live in this Manor last year, sorely in need of privacy. My two former wives are, both of them, moving against me. Naturally, until I can destroy the lever they have against me, I need somewhere well defended to live. Unfortunately, that lever is proving rather hard to locate and, until I *can* locate him, I must insist on my privacy."

"I fail to see," Andrew snapped, "what your love life has to do with this! We are talking about my legal rights!"

Mr Brown shook his silver head and gave a pitying smile. "Ah, Mr Hope, you must be younger than you look if you have never yet had trouble with grasping women. And I must point out to you that my position would have been a great deal more comfortable if you had made the slightest effort to keep to our covenant."

"What covenant?" Andrew said. "I never met you till today."

"Yes. That was why I assumed you were merely renting Melstone House," Mr Brown said, placidly crossing his pinstriped legs and sipping at his blurred rosy glass. "If you have indeed inherited that property, then you are under an obligation to protect me and mine, by covenant signed by your ancestors. Do not think that the fact that you are not called Brandon excuses you from this, Mr Hope. I have legal rights too."

"No, you don't!" Andrew said, so angry now that he scrambled out of the uncomfortable chair and stood glaring threateningly down on Mr Brown. "You're simply trying to distract my attention from what you've done. I repeat, Mr Brown, you have *no right* to fence off half my wood!"

Mr Brown did not seem to feel threatened at all. He smiled calmly up at Andrew. "I have," he said, "naturally to put my point of view to you. It is far more important than yours. Because you had made no attempt to abide by the covenant, I had no choice but to protect myself. My enclave here is now unsafe. Your so-called grandfather was as negligent as you are. When I came back here to avoid my wives, it was clear from the number of counterparts in your field-of-care that my realm has been leaking for years. You should correct this, if you please."

"I don't know what you're talking about," Andrew said. "Your enclave, as you call it, is Melstone Manor and its grounds. And nothing more. *You* have done the leaking."

Mr Brown, with an indulgent smile, shook his silvery head. "Go home, Mr Hope. Go home and consult your covenant. You will find it clearly states that counterparts are not to occur."

"What do you mean – counterparts?" Andrew demanded. His thoughts went, uneasily, to the ghostly paper with the black seal that his grandfather's spirit had tried to give him. But that's got nothing to do with this fellow blandly trying to steal half my wood! he thought. "I haven't the foggiest idea what you mean," he said.

"I see you are very ignorant," Mr Brown said, sighing. "Very well. I shall, just this once, excuse you on those grounds. That, and because I can see my Security has annoyed you—"

"*Annoyed* me!" Andrew almost screamed.

"—and I shall order him to eject you more politely in future," Mr Brown went on. "Also I will enlighten your ignorance by explaining to you, as if to a child, what counterparts are. Counterparts are people within your field-of-care who strongly resemble – in appearance *and* in powers – people who belong to my realm. You must order all these counterpart folk to leave Melstone, Mr Hope. Or..." Here Mr Brown, still smiling, seemed to turn from silvery to steely. "Or I shall have to assume that you are trying to set yourself up with a powerbase against me. And we wouldn't want that, would we, Mr Hope?"

For a second or so, Andrew could not think of a word to say. *Order* people to *leave*! Was Mr Brown mad? Or were he and Mr Brown simply on two different wavelengths? In which case, Mr Brown's wavelength seemed to Andrew quite sinisterly occult. Andrew was not his grandfather. Occult magic was something he knew nothing about. He settled for giving an uneasy little laugh. "Of course I'm not setting up a powerbase," he said. "I wouldn't know how. And if this is all you can say, you'll be hearing from my lawyer very shortly."

"When I do hear, I shall of course apologise politely for the bad manners of my Security," Mr Brown said placidly. "I am sure we can be civilised about it. I think you should leave now, Mr Hope."

"So do I!" Andrew said through clenched teeth. He put his glasses on with a flourish. "Good afternoon!"

He slammed out of the library-place and strode to the massive front door so swiftly that the little butler had to patter madly over the red tiles after him in order to open the door and bow him out into the weak sunshine beyond.

"You know, sir," the little butler said, "it would have

been far better if you had accepted that drink. Most of your ancestors did."

"I don't drink!" Andrew snapped and stormed down the brick steps to his car.

He drove off with a roar and, until he got to the main road, he could do nothing but gibber with rage at how politely rude Mr Brown had been. As he turned towards Melstone House, it did occur to him, in gaps, that some of the things Mr Brown had said were pretty queer. Telling him to make people leave Melstone, for instance. That *had* to have been a joke. Yes, it was probably a joke, designed to take Andrew's mind off Mr Brown's takeover of half the wood. Mr Brown had been *playing* with him! Andrew's rage enlarged. His lawyer would soon sort *that* out. Silvery, smooth *crook*!

He burst into Melstone House, wanting nothing so much as to tell someone about the extraordinary things Mr Brown had had the gall to say. Stashe would have been the perfect person to tell, but Stashe would not be here until tomorrow. Mrs Stock had left. Andrew found her note and threw it aside with an angry laugh. He had half a mind to throw aside the big sloppy bowl of potato cheese too, but then he remembered Aidan and how much Aidan ate. He left the bowl on the kitchen table and stormed round the house, looking for Aidan to tell him what Mr Brown had said. There was no Aidan either. Andrew stormed to his study and phoned his lawyer again.

This time he got someone who seemed to know a bit more than the first person. This voice told him that Mrs Barrington-Stock was away on holiday, but would be in touch the moment she was back. Andrew hurled the phone down in disgust and wondered whether to look for Aidan again. But, by this time, he had cooled down just enough to decide that he ought not to burden someone Aidan's age with all that strange stuff. No. The urgent thing was to dig out old Jocelyn's papers and see if he could discover this contract, or covenant, or whatever Mr Brown thought it was.

Mrs Stock, he remembered, had bundled all old Jocelyn's papers into three large cardboard boxes. "I've not thrown anything away," she had told Andrew, "not even his pipe cleaners. I don't know what's important." And she had put the boxes somewhere until Andrew had time to look through them.

Andrew could not find those boxes. They were not in his study, or in the hall cupboard, or the cupboard under the stairs, and they were certainly not in the living room – where he was furious to find Mrs Stock had moved the piano *again*. The boxes were not in any of the bedrooms, or in the attics, or anywhere else Andrew could think of.

By the time he had searched the house, Andrew had simmered down enough to notice he was hungry. He made himself a pot of tea and some bread and honey. Then he felt calm enough to move the piano. By this time, his anger had gone into the background of his mind and stuck there, hard and black and unforgivingly.

When Aidan finally came back, he found Andrew in the living room, reading a book about glass-making in early Victorian times. "Did you see Mr Brown?" Aidan asked.

"Yes," said Andrew.

"My friends playing football said he was scary," Aidan said.

"He's a smooth, silver crook," Andrew said, with what struck Aidan as truly dreadful calm.

"Do you think he's a gangster?" Aidan asked, interested.

"Probably," Andrew said. "Whatever he is, he claims to have had some kind of contract with my grandfather. But I'll have to wait for Mrs Stock before I can find it."

"Can I eat that potato cheese?" Aidan said.

Mrs Stock was slightly later than usual that Friday. Her sister Trixie came with her. The two of them were tenderly leading Shaun between them. Shaun had a new hairstyle. Aidan couldn't take his eyes off it. The top of Shaun's head was all flaxen tips, with touches of red, and the red-and-flaxen gathered together at the back to make a kind of starburst of hair with a parting down the middle of it. Aidan had never seen someone with a parting at the *back* of his head before. He stared until Shaun looked self-conscious.

Andrew stared too. Trixie was as fat as her sister was thin, smoothly and pinkly overweight, and obviously many years younger than Mrs Stock. Nevertheless, the two of them were so alike that they could have been twins. They had the same fair hair in the same elaborate hairstyle, and the same shaped face with the same slightly bulging, shrewd blue eyes. They even walked in the same way, as if their feet were on either side of a small wall. Here Andrew remembered Mr Brown's Security again and swallowed rage. Despite this, he wondered what Trixie was here for. He knew a deputation when he saw one and he wondered what this one was about.

The truth was that Mrs Stock had remembered Andrew's not-quite-joke the day Aidan arrived. She might have been furious with Andrew, but she was also afraid of losing her job. Her aim was to distract Andrew into some kind of reconciliation.

"You're not *really* angry with Shaun, Professor," Trixie said warmly. "He was only doing what he thought right."

"And how was he to know Mr Stock was growing asparagus?" Mrs Stock added. "He's kept that pretty secret, I can tell you!"

Andrew had entirely forgotten the matter of the asparagus. "No, no. Not at all angry," he said.

"You see, you have to tell Shaun just exactly what to do," Trixie said earnestly. "Then he'll do it, no problem."

"And you haven't told him a thing what to do these last two days," Mrs Stock put in, reproachfully and according to plan.

"They say you're going to give me the sack, Professor," Shaun said anxiously.

Andrew lost patience with this manoeuvring. "Of *course* I'm not going to give you the sack!" he said to Shaun. "I told you to clean out the old shed. You've been doing that, haven't you?" Shaun nodded vigorously, so that his hairstyle glittered in the coloured light from the back door. "Then you run along and keep doing that," Andrew said. "That's your job."

Shaun cried out, "Wey-*hey*!" and did his arm-waving thing. Both Andrew and Aidan thought, Just like Groil! And Andrew thought, Counterparts? and felt uneasy. Shaun was not a giant, but no one could deny he was well built.

Trixie grinned triumphantly at her sister. "Told you it

would be all right." She waddled over and patted Andrew's shoulder. "You're a good man to look after my Shaun," she told him. "Any time you want your hair cut free, you come to me. I've got a lovely product that'll tint you up those grey sides there too. It'll take ten years off you, Professor, if you let me do that."

Her fat hand patted gently at the side of Andrew's head. Andrew squirmed. He could feel his face heating up and see Aidan trying not to laugh as Aidan imagined Andrew with a hairstyle like Shaun's.

Fortunately, the back door opened at that moment and Stashe breezed in. Andrew felt boundless relief. Joy! Now he could get on with his book. Stashe was like a gust of fresh air, driving Trixie away from his head. She was looking lovely too, in a short green dress that showed off those fine legs of hers. He found he was smiling before she was halfway into the room.

"Morning all," said Stashe. "Hi, Trixie. I was going to phone you. Can you fit me in for a hair appointment late on Wednesday? Ronnie Stock needs me until five."

"Can do," Trixie said cheerfully.

Stashe turned to Andrew then. "Professor—"

"Oh, please remember to call me Andrew," Andrew said. Aidan looked shrewdly from him to Stashe and thought, If those two get together, they won't want me around. He sighed, thinking of the Arkwrights.

"Andrew," Stashe corrected herself. "If you're not needing me to take notes or do letters, I'll make a start on old Mr Brandon's papers for you."

"Yes, do. But I don't know where the papers are," Andrew said.

Mrs Stock tut-tutted. "World of his own! I *told* you, Professor. They're in the little room off your study that used to be the pantry when your study was the kitchen." She said to Stashe, "Men!"

Stashe said, "Good. Then I'll be nearby if you need me – er – Andrew."

Trixie said, agreeing with her sister, "Men. I'll be off then. Wednesday, late then, Stashe. Now, Shaun, you be good and work *careful*, see." Shaun nodded humbly.

"Right." Stashe took hold of Aidan by one shoulder. "Come on, my lad. You promised you'd help me go through those papers."

"Oh – I…" said Aidan. "I said I'd play football—"

"With Jimmy Stock. I know," said Stashe. "But you promised *me* before you even met Jimmy, and it's wrong to break promises, you know that."

Aidan sighed and went away with Stashe. Trixie left. Shaun departed, grinning joyously. Mrs Stock took herself to the living room, where she gave all the furniture a sort of tweak towards the traditional places, just to show she had not forgiven Andrew.

Left to himself, Andrew picked up the newspaper Mrs Stock had brought and turned to yesterday's racing results. He knew he was being as superstitious as Stashe, but he could not somehow resist. There turned out to have been only one racecourse that had not been flooded by yesterday's rain, and the winner of its first race had been Parsnip's Pleasure. Meaningless. I knew it! Andrew thought. The second horse home was called Dogdays and the third, Heavy Queen.

"That proves it's all nonsense," Andrew said. He threw the paper aside and was just in time to jump up and hold the back door open as Mr Stock stalked in and dumped a box down on the newspaper.

"You still letting that looby work for you?" Mr Stock said. "Don't let him come near my veg, or I won't answer for what I'll do." He stalked out again.

Andrew looked into the box. It contained two gigantic parsnips, each of them big enough to have been Tarquin's missing leg.

"Oh," Andrew said.

Chapter Nine

Helping Stashe, Aidan discovered, involved a lot of running about. He had to find Stashe a rug to kneel on while she sorted through the three boxes in the bare little room. Then he had to find more boxes, one for throwing stuff away in, one for things that *might* need throwing away after Andrew had seen them, and several more to hold things to be kept. Aidan thought carefully about this mission – "using his noggin" as Gran would have said – and decided there was going to be a need for extra boxes when Stashe invented more categories. He went daringly to Mr Stock's box store in the garden shed and brought Stashe as many as he could carry.

"Nice one," said Stashe, kneeling on the rug and looking rather daunted. The boxes to be sorted through were huge.

Three of Mr Stock's finest, Aidan thought. Expect earth in the bottoms of all three.

When Stashe started on the actual sorting, she said, "What did he keep all these paid bills for? This one goes back twenty years! Throw away, Aidan."

Aidan obediently stuffed several hundred paid bills into the rubbish box. He yawned.

Stashe caught him in mid-yawn when she said, "*All* his pipe cleaners! *Layers* of packets! You want them? You can make models out of them." And when Aidan managed to shut his mouth and shake his head, "No?" said Stashe. "Rubbish box then. Now what's this layer? Oh, he seems to have written notes to himself. The prof— *Andrew* will definitely want to look through these. Give me a special box, Aidan."

Aidan brought up a clean, empty box and helped Stashe pack scores of little tattered notes in it. The notes were written on pieces torn off letters, old magazines and even raggedly torn pieces of new paper. Old Mr Brandon's writing was black and crotchety and full of character. Aidan noticed one that said, *If Stockie brings me any more carrots, I'll pull his head off!!!* Another said, *O. Brown is talking <u>nonsense.</u> Counterparts <u>not</u> dangerous.* And a third said, *Trouble in London again. Sigh.*

Then they were down to ordinary letters from different

people, all of them pitched anyhow into the box in a great slithering heap. Stashe scooped up a sheaf of them and held them to the light, frowning. "New box," she said.

Aidan slid a new box forward, congratulating himself on bringing so many, and looked into the big box to see if this box was large enough. Half the letters in the heap were in his grandmother's writing. Aidan would have known her writing anywhere, neat and light and slanting, with dashes instead of any other kind of punctuation. Gran always said, "I've no patience with commas and full stops and things. Folk have to take me as they find me."

Aidan's heart banged heavily. His eyes suddenly felt hot and full. He found he had to stand up.

"What's the matter?" asked Stashe.

"Those letters," Aidan said, pointing. "They're from my gran."

Stashe had no trouble knowing how Aidan felt. After her mother had died – when Stashe herself was not much older than Aidan – there had been times when small, silly things – like Mum's favourite egg cup, or just a whiff of Mum's perfume – had brought her loss back to her as if Mum had died only yesterday. At those times, Stashe had had to be alone. Usually she had locked herself into her bedroom, often for hours and hours.

"You want to go away?" she said to Aidan. "Go on. I won't mind."

Aidan nodded and stumbled away to the door with tears pouring out from under his glasses. Stashe surprised herself by starting to cry too.

Aidan raced for the living room as the nearest way outside. "My goodness!" said Mrs Stock, as Aidan fought his way out through the French windows. "What's up with *you*?"

Aidan didn't feel like answering. He stumbled out on to the lawn and then round past the woodshed and through the hedge into the fields beyond. He took his glasses off, but that didn't help. His nose ran as well as his eyes, and he still didn't have a handkerchief. He could still see Gran, just as she had been, coming out with her clipped little sayings and usually – unless the saying was a grim one – grinning as she said them. He could smell her, feel the shape of her on the rare occasions when she hugged him. He could hear her voice...

And he was never going to hear, feel or see her again.

Aidan could not forgive himself. He had been behaving just as if he was on holiday, having fun, noticing new things, playing football, exploring, living on the surface of himself, and almost forgetting he had lost Gran forever. He had never even told her how much he loved her. And now he couldn't ever tell her anything ever again. He had lost her for good.

"Oh, Gran, Gran!" he sobbed, stumbling among Wally Stock's cows and hardly noticing them. When he had walked this way with Andrew, he had, to tell the truth, been quite alarmed by the size of those cows and the way they stared. But they stared now and he couldn't care less. Gran was dead. Gone. Lost.

Aidan was not sure where he went after barging past those cows. He wandered for hours in his misery, just wanting to be alone. When his sorrow began to slacken a little, he made for Mel Tump and wandered among the bushes there. "Groil?" he called out after a while. "Groil?" He couldn't bear to meet anyone else, in case they sympathised with him. But he thought Groil probably wouldn't be sorry for him. He could bear Groil.

But, as before, there was no sign of Groil. Aidan wandered down the hill and off towards the wood, thinking that, to be fair, Stashe hadn't sympathised with him. Nor had Andrew really. But they had both understood how he felt and had been careful not to upset him. Aidan badly wanted someone who didn't *understand*. Someone who couldn't care less. His football friends? No, they would be like Stashe or Andrew and – worse! – embarrassed with it.

He wandered along the edge of the wood. Suppose he went in as far as the broken-down wall and deliberately ran into Security? Security was not likely to be understanding. Nor was his dog. There was quite a chance they would kill him. They were both pretty scary. On second thoughts – and third and fourth thoughts – Aidan was not sure he wanted to be killed. He supposed he ought to be hungry, though he felt as if he'd never want to eat again, and he turned away from the wood. Oh, Gran, Gran!

There were eager crashing noises from inside the wood.

Aidan whirled round. A big, dim shape was bouncing and charging towards him among the trees and bushes. Help! It's a *lion*! Aidan thought. It certainly looked like one. The animal was the right colour for a lion, sort of yellowish. But then the creature uttered a glad yelp and Aidan realised it was only a dog. It bounced and crashed its way through the last of the trees and came lolloping towards Aidan on long legs that flopped all over the place, ears flying, big pink tongue draping out of its mouth and its tail passionately wagging.

Really just a puppy, Aidan thought.

The dog bounced up to him, panting out glad little whimpers, put its paws on Aidan's chest and tried to lick his face. Aidan turned his face away and couldn't help laughing. Its large, feathery tail didn't so much wag as go round and round like a propeller. Aidan found himself laughing at that too. After that, in the most natural possible way, Aidan found he was kneeling in the grass with his arms round the beast, stroking its silky ears and talking all sorts of nonsense to it.

"What's your name then? No – don't answer that. I think it's Rolf. You look like a Rolf. You're big, aren't you? Does your tail always windmill like this? Who do you belong to? Where have you come from?" The dog had no collar, yet it was clear it had run off from someone. Whoever it belonged to must have looked after it quite well. Though its yellow coat was full of burrs and goosegrass, it shone with health. The dog's big black nose that it kept dabbing at Aidan's cheek was cool and wet and its teeth were white and perfect. Its big brown eyes, staring gladly at Aidan, were clear and bright.

It wanted to play.

Aidan went to the edge of the wood to look for a stick to throw. The dog dashed past him in among the trees and came back with an elderly tennis ball. It dropped the ball by Aidan's feet, where it went down on its fringed elbows and encouraged Aidan with a bark. Well, here was someone who wasn't sympathetic or even understanding, Aidan thought. That's a relief! He picked the ball up and threw it. The dog dashed off after it delightedly.

They played fetch-the-ball up and down the edge of the woods for what seemed hours, until Aidan was quite tired. By that time Aidan's sorrow for Gran had gone down to a sore place some distance back in his brain somewhere. It still hurt and he knew it would always be there, but it did not cause him the frantic sadness he had been feeling earlier. He looked up and around and realised that he and the dog *had* played for hours. The sun was behind the wood, making long shadows of trees stretch across the field towards Melstone House. The sight turned Aidan quite hollow inside. He had missed lunch. He might even have missed supper too.

"OK," he said to the dog. "Time to go home." He hurled the ball far into the wood and, as soon as Rolf rushed off after it, Aidan set off for Melstone House.

Here his troubles began. Aidan had gone barely ten steps before Rolf was beside him again bouncing, wagging and whining, obviously determined to come too.

"Oh no," Aidan said. "You can't. You don't belong to me." He pointed sternly at the wood. "Go on home!"

Rolf swerved away towards the wood and then stood there, looking desolate.

Aidan pointed to the wood again, and again said, "Go *home*!"

Rolf lay down, whining miserably. And as soon as

Aidan turned and began to walk towards the house, Rolf was beside him, strutting bouncily, pretending to be *so* glad that Aidan was taking him too.

"*No!*" Aidan said. "You don't *understand*. You belong to someone *else*. Go back to your owner. Go *home!*"

The trouble was, Aidan was sure that Rolf *did* understand, perfectly. He just preferred Aidan to whoever he belonged to.

This happened ten more times. Aidan would turn round, point and sternly tell Rolf to "Go home!" and Rolf would sheer off, looking miserable, and then chase after Aidan as soon as Aidan was walking again. It was worse if Aidan ran. Rolf was after him in a flash. He threw himself down in front of Aidan's feet and gazed at him with big brown, pleading eyes.

By this time they were halfway across the field. Wally Stock's sheep ambled sedately out of their way, quite unworried by Aidan's efforts, or Rolf's. They were not afraid of Rolf in the least. Rolf was treating Aidan like a sheep, Aidan realised, herding him towards the house. Clever, Aidan thought. He really was a superb dog.

"Oh, *honestly!*" Aidan said, as Rolf threw himself at Aidan's feet yet again. "I *told* you. You don't *belong* to me!"

This time, Rolf's reply was to turn round and round. Chasing his tail, Aidan thought. Round and round, dizzily, so fast he became a yellow blur. Then he was a yellow fog, billowing beside Aidan's shoes. Aidan backed away a little. This was really strange. He took off his glasses, but Rolf was still a yellow fog to his naked eyes. Then, watched by a ring of placid, interested sheep, the fog hardened into a different shape and stood up as a small boy. Aidan put his glasses back on and Rolf was still a small boy. His hair was a pelt of gold curls, the same colour as the dog's coat, and he was wearing a sort of romper suit made of golden velvet. He stared beseechingly at Aidan with the dog's soulful brown eyes and threw both arms around Aidan's legs. He looked about five years old.

"Oh, *please* take me with you!" he said. His voice was much gruffer and lower than you would expect from a five-year-old. "Please! I haven't got a home. I ran away when they tried to put a collar on me and make me into Security. Please!"

"You're a *were*-dog!" Aidan said. He supposed this did make a difference.

The small boy nodded. "I'm Rolf," he said. "You knew my name. Nobody else did. Let me come home with you."

Aidan gave in. It was those yearning brown eyes he supposed. "OK," he said. "Come along then. But be very polite to Mrs Stock. I think the others will understand, but I don't think she will."

Rolf gave a cry of joy and dissolved into yellow fog again. Next second he was a large golden dog, far more comfortable as a dog than a boy, Aidan could tell, as Rolf tore round and round Aidan, frisking, cavorting and giving little barks of delight. Every so often he tried to lick Aidan's hands and feet. Aidan had to keep pushing him off all the way across the field.

Andrew, meanwhile, was trying to get on with his book. With the computer working and Stashe in the room next door, where he could call on her for help at any time, conditions seemed ideal for work. He was getting out all the stuff he would need when it occurred to him that he ought to check up on Shaun first, in case Shaun was up to anything that would result in more large parsnips. He got up and went round to the yard.

The first thing he saw was the lawnmower. It had been pushed into the middle of the yard and surrounded by old paint tins, broken garden chairs and two halves of a stepladder. Good. That seemed to mean Shaun was at work where he should be.

The next thing Andrew saw was Groil. Groil was

leaning over the shed roof, carefully cleaning the coloured panes in the window there. He looked like an optical illusion at first in Aidan's enlarged clothes: a very large boy cleaning a very small shed. Andrew blinked at the sight. Then Groil was a giant cleaning a normal-sized shed.

"Good God, Groil!" Andrew exclaimed. "I didn't expect *you*!"

Groil turned round. The roof creaked as he leaned one hand on it. He gave Andrew a huge, shy grin. "I can reach the window, see," he said.

Shaun heard their voices and came to the shed door. "I got a friend to help me," he said. "Don't mind, do you?"

Both he and Groil gave Andrew the same half-proud, half-guilty grins. Looking up at Groil and downward at Shaun, Andrew had no doubt that the two of them were what Mr Brown had called counterparts. Apart from their size, that was, and Shaun's new hairstyle. Groil's hair was a shaggy mop. The other differences were that Groil seemed cleverer than Shaun, and Shaun seemed older than Groil. Odd that. Groil was, to Andrew's knowledge, at least as old as Andrew was himself, but he looked a child still.

Andrew's mind shied away here from whatever this had to do with Mr Brown. "No, of course I don't mind," he said heartily, "so long as you remember to be specially gentle with the cracked panes, Groil. And there'll be a parsnip for you later."

He pushed Shaun gently aside and took a look at the interior of the shed. It was full of the smell of wet grime, where Shaun was in the middle of washing down one of the carved walls.

"They polish up lovely when they're dry," Shaun said, pointing to a large tin labelled Best Beeswax Polish. "Auntie give me the rags to work it in with. But…" He pointed to the window in the roof with all its dangling spiderwebs. "…Groil has to do that."

"How? Can he get inside here?" Andrew asked.

Shaun grinned. "He, like, squinges up," he said. "He can go smaller than me when he wants. But then he gets all heavy."

"Oh," said Andrew, thinking, You live and learn. "Fine. You're both doing fine, Shaun. Keep at it."

He went back to his study and started up his computer. He assembled the stuff for his database. He made sure all his closely-written notes were propped on a lectern. Then he sat staring at the screen saver wondering about counterparts instead. How and why did they happen? Why was Mr Brown so much against them? Why did he blame Andrew for not stopping them? As if Andrew *could*! Shaun had been born years before Andrew came back to

Melstone. The more Andrew thought about this, the more he thought that the best way he had of getting back at Mr Brown for his politely rude orders was to *encourage* counterparts. If only he knew how.

He was still staring at his screen saver making coloured, diving patterns an hour later, when Stashe came in carrying a cardboard box. "Your grandfather wrote at least a thousand little memos to himself," she said. "I've sorted out all the ones I've found so far and I think you'll have to look through them. Some of them look important, but they're far too cryptic for me."

"Put them over in that corner," Andrew said. "I'll look at them later."

He watched Stashe with pleasure as she carried the box to a free space on the floor and put it down. She really looked marvellous in that brief green dress.

"By the way," she said, "Aidan's gone out, poor kid. A whole lot of letters in the box I'm on turned out to be from his gran. That really upset him. I think he wanted to be alone for a while – you know how it is."

Andrew nodded. His parents had both died while he was a graduate student. He knew how that felt. He sighed. "Let me look at those letters too, will you?"

"I'm going now to sort them into the order they were written in," Stashe said. "Someone's just bundled them into that box anyhow, and they're all mixed up."

She was on her way to the door when Andrew said, "You haven't come across a folded paper with a black seal on it, have you?"

"No," Stashe said. "Important, is it?"

"Very. I think," Andrew said. "If you do find it, let me see it at once."

"Right," said Stashe. "Priority for the black seal then."

"Oh, and Stashe," Andrew said. Stashe stopped with her hand on the doorknob. "Do you know anything about counterparts here in Melstone?"

"Not really," Stashe said. "But you'll find a lot of your grandfather's memos are about counterparts. He seems to have been in a major row about them with Mr Brown down at the Manor. To do with power, it looks like. Dad might know. Ask him."

"I will," Andrew said. "Is he likely to be coming here today?" But he found he had said this to the closed door after Stashe had gone. He sighed and clicked off the screen saver. Work.

The phone rang.

The caller was his lawyer's secretary explaining all over again that Mrs Barrington-Stock was away and would contact him as soon as she came back next month.

"And what good is next month?" Andrew asked the air.

"I want Mr Brown put in his place *now*." He turned back to his computer and found that the screen saver had come on again. He was just about to click it off once more, when Mrs Stock put her face round the door.

"That woman's back," she said. "At the front door this time, wanting you."

"What woman?" said Andrew.

"The one that prowled yesterday," said Mrs Stock. "Changed her hairstyle but she still looks the same. Thinks I don't know her by her walk, doesn't she? I told her to wait outside. I don't trust her."

Sighing, Andrew got up and went to the front door.

The fat woman standing on the doorstep glowered at him. She was wearing what was, possibly, a uniform. But the main thing Andrew noticed about her was that she was remarkably like Mrs Stock's sister Trixie, that is if you imagined Trixie hot and bad-tempered and smelling quite strongly of armpits.

"Are you in charge here?" she demanded.

"I own this house, yes," Andrew said cautiously. Without thinking, he took his glasses off and cleaned them. The woman looked even more like Trixie to his naked eyes, right down to her blonde hairstyle. Her face was the same shape and so were her prominent blue eyes, but her mouth was pursed with bad temper and there were lines of ill nature all over her fat face. The word "counterpart" came into Andrew's mind and made him very cautious indeed. "What can I do for you?" he asked her politely.

The woman snatched a card out of her breast pocket, waved it quickly at him and put it away again before Andrew had a chance to see what the card was. "Mabel Brown," she announced. "I'm looking for Andrew Craig. I'm his social worker."

A social worker would surely have Aidan's name right, Andrew thought – if it *was* Aidan she was after. And *did* social workers wear a uniform? This uniform was old and tight. The almost official-looking jacket must have taken major traction to button up. It strained over Mabel Brown's massive bosom.

"There is no one called Andrew Craig in this house," Andrew told her truthfully. "I think you must have come to the wrong address."

Mabel Brown lowered her blonde eyebrows and half-shut her bulging eyes. The result was a poisonous glare, full of anger and suspicion. She kept the glower on Andrew while she hauled at a tight lower pocket and fetched out a crumpled notepad. She turned the glower on one of its pages. "Alan Craike," she read out. "Adrian Gaynes, Evan Keen, Abel Crane, Ethan Gay. He could have given any one of those names. Is he here or not?"

"No," Andrew said. "No one by any of those names is here. My name is Andrew Hope and I think you must have confused someone else with me. As you can see, I have no need for a social worker. You have come to the wrong house, madam. Good morning."

He shut the front door crisply in Mabel Brown's face and stood there cleaning his glasses all over again, while he waited for signs that the woman was going away. He heard muttering on the other side of the door. It sounded like swearing. At length, after what felt like ten minutes, he heard heavy footsteps crunching away down the drive. Andrew dodged to the narrow hall window to be sure. And there, to his relief, was the large back view of Mabel Brown plodding away from him, looking as if her feet were on either side of a wide plank.

"Phew!" Andrew said, putting his glasses on again as he went back to his study.

"Who was that?" Stashe asked brightly, dodging out of the box room full of curiosity.

"Someone looking for Aidan – I think," Andrew told her. "She said she was his social worker, but I don't think she was. I shouldn't think they trust people that unpleasant to look after children. At least, I hope they don't. And she couldn't even get Aidan's name right."

He went into his study, where his computer gave a whining sort of sigh and went blank.

"*Stashe*!" he shouted.

Stashe came and had a look. She leaned over Andrew – which he found very pleasant – and tried this, then that. Eventually the screen saver reappeared. "At last!" said Stashe. "I don't know – it seems to have had some sort of power surge."

"That woman—!" Andrew said.

They stared at one another, almost nose to nose. Andrew had to struggle not to grab Stashe and kiss her.

"Then she *definitely* wasn't a social worker," Stashe said. "With the amount of protection your grandfather had round this place, it would take someone hostile a huge surge of power to even get inside to the driveway. Put some more wards up." Then, to Andrew's disappointment, she went away.

Andrew got back to work, trying not to think of Stashe. Mabel Brown went out of his mind so completely that he did not even try to remember how to put up wards. He had dim memories of Jocelyn telling him more than once how this was done, but he was too busy with other thoughts even to try to recall what his grandfather had said.

A couple of hours later, Mrs Stock put her head round the door again.

"It's a policewoman now," she said. "And me in the middle of cooking your lunch. Something's going to burn if you don't get rid of her quickly."

The policewoman was short, stout and grim. The hair under her cap was brown and so were her eyes. "Mr Hope?" she said. "WPC92. I'm looking for a twelve-year-old boy called Adam Gray. Five foot two, brown hair, wears glasses, no other distinguishing marks. We have reason to believe he came to this house."

Andrew snatched off his glasses. The face of WPC92 blurred. So did her uniform. It became much too tight for her and lost some of its policewomanishness. Inside the blur of her face, Andrew could just pick out a shape that reminded him of Trixie. He was almost certain that Mabel Brown and WPC92 were the same person. There was even the same smell of armpits.

"No one called Adam Gray has ever come to this house," he said.

"Are you sure?" the policewoman demanded. "It's against the law to harbour a criminal."

"Criminal?" Andrew said. "What crime?"

"The boy absconded from London with a wallet containing at least one hundred pounds," WPC92 replied, in a toneless, official voice.

Stashe spoke up suddenly from behind Andrew. "What

are you *talking* about? We don't harbour criminals here. Your computer's gone down again," she added significantly to Andrew.

"And I'll thank you to get off my clean doorstep and stop pestering the professor!" Mrs Stock said. She came up on the other side of Andrew, swinging a large iron ladle.

WPC92 winced back from the ladle. "You'll be in trouble," she said, "threatening a member of the police force in pursuance of her duty."

Stashe said sweetly, "Then if you go away, she won't need to threaten you, will she?"

Large boots clumped noisily from either side of the house. Shaun loomed up from the yard, saying, "Is it lunch yet, Auntie? Something wrong?"

And from the garden side of the house came Mr Stock, walking much more loudly than usual. "What's going on here? Need some help, Professor?"

"I think so," Andrew said. "This person claims to be a policewoman, but I'm pretty sure she's a fraud."

"Now *that's* against the law," Mr Stock said. "Impersonating the police."

The blurred face of WPC92 turned a fierce red. "I am here," she intoned, "to arrest Adrian Cork for the theft of a wallet containing an estimated hundred pounds."

"Oh, for God's sake, woman!" said Mrs Stock. "Don't

you use that toneless official voice at me! It won't make you any more real."

"Or your nonsensical accusation!" added Stashe.

Shaun's face wrinkled under his hairstyle as he tried to make sense of this. "I know what," he said, unwrinkling. "I can run her off for you, Professor."

"You dare!" said WPC92.

"I'm stronger than you," Shaun pointed out. "So's Mr Stock. He's all, like, wires. And Auntie's got an iron ladle."

WPC92 eyed the ladle nervously and backed away from the doorstep. As she moved, Tarquin O'Connor came up the drive behind her, helping himself speedily along with his one crutch. Andrew nearly laughed. It was ludicrous the way everyone seemed to have turned up to help him. But he was impressed – almost honoured – all the same.

Tarquin took in the situation with one piercing look. "You'd better leave," he said to WPC92, "before things get ugly. It took you quite a push to get in here, didn't it? I felt it from my car. So now you get out, before we all push back."

WPC92 tossed her head. "I'm going to prefer charges against all of you," she said haughtily, "for obstructing the police when in hot pursuit."

"You do that," Tarquin said. "But you just do it as far away from here as you can get."

They all watched WPC92, so called, turn and stump away down the drive. Mrs Stock said, "I don't like that strange way she walks, feet apart. It's not natural."

Chapter Ten

arquin had arrived, it seemed, in hopes that Andrew could firm his missing leg up before he took Stashe home to lunch. "Got her some real delicacies today," he said. "I do love to cook. What was that woman after? Aidan?"

Andrew nodded.

"Thought so," Tarquin said. "She's one of those that don't use iron. Funny how you can tell. I've thought all along that it was those kind after the boy. You'd better give your wards a boost. You can do it on the computer these days. Get Stashe to show you how. She did it for Ronnie a while back when there was talk of someone trying to nobble his horses. Where is Aidan anyway? Did the woman get a sight of him?"

Andrew shook his head, concentrating on Tarquin's leg.

"He went out. I think his grandmother's death has just hit him and he wanted to be alone."

"Poor lad." Tarquin propped his missing leg up along a sofa and chatted cheerfully away. "Grief's a funny thing, so it is. I swear Stashe didn't seem to notice her mother was gone for good until two weeks later when she ran across an egg cup my wife liked to use. Hidden in a cupboard it was. Then there was no consoling her. I thought she'd never get over it, to tell the truth."

He chatted on. Shortly he was telling Andrew of further problems in the Fête Committee. It seemed that the famous cooking celebrity who was supposed to open the Fête had cancelled. "Got invited to go to America and it seemed he liked that idea better," Tarquin said. "Left them all in the lurch, so he did. Looking everywhere for a replacement, they were, until someone said that Ronnie Stock was enough of a celebrity these days to do the job. So they asked him. And Ronnie's that vain," Tarquin said, "he's agreed like a shot. It's York Races that weekend and he's got horses running at Bath and Brighton too, but he's so darned flattered to be asked to open our little tinpot Fête that he's sending his wife off to York in his place. Madness! Needs his head examined. But then, it always was a little swelled. Are you going to tell Aidan that these people have traced him here?"

Andrew nodded absently, although he was not sure at all. For one thing, he knew it would scare Aidan horribly. For another, Mabel Brown and/or WPC92 had sown seeds of doubt in Andrew's mind. Aidan, according to Aidan's own story, *had* absconded from London and *did* possess a wallet. It could well be that it was through this wallet that Mabel WPC92 had traced Aidan. It must give off a fair surge of power when it filled itself with money. So there was no doubt that *someone* was after Aidan. But there was no way of knowing who was in the right and who was in the wrong. Andrew had only Aidan's word for most of it. He *thought* Aidan was honest, but he didn't *know*. It seemed to Andrew that he might have been rather too trusting. He decided to ask Aidan a lot more questions when Aidan came in for lunch.

But when Aidan did come in it was nearer teatime than lunchtime, and he was accompanied by a large, gladsome dog, with a tail like a propeller that knocked things down all over the house. Everything everyone was doing had to stop while Mrs Stock made her feelings plain.

"I have enough to do without picking up after a great dirty dog!" she said, over and over. "I'm not *used* to dogs. Hairs and muddy feet! I can't be *doing* with it! Is it house-trained? *Is* it? And you expect me to feed it, do you?"

Mixed in with this were Mrs Stock's complaints about the time Aidan had come in. "*And* your lunch thoroughly spoilt! The nicest plate of liver and bacon you ever did see completely spoilt! Ruined! Look at it! *Look* at it!" She wagged the offending lunch under Aidan's nose. It looked like a black shoe sole and some dog chews. "Just look at it!" Mrs Stock proclaimed.

"Rolf can eat it," Aidan suggested.

"What a waste!" Mrs Stock retorted. "Feeding it to stray dogs because you treat the professor's house like a hotel and come in at any time you please! And is he house-trained? *Is* he?"

By this time, Andrew and Stashe had arrived in the kitchen and Shaun and Mr Stock were looking in through the window over the sink. Aidan began to hope that there would be a severe earthquake soon, to open a hole in the floor and swallow him and Rolf up. He knelt down in front of Rolf. "*Are* you house-trained?" he whispered urgently. Rolf stared pleadingly and gave a very slight nod. "He *is* house-trained," Aidan said. But his voice was drowned out by the others'.

Shaun said, "It's a *lovely* dog, Auntie."

Stashe said, "I know he isn't wearing a collar, but he's in beautiful condition. He must belong to someone. You simply can't keep him, Aidan."

And Mr Stock said to Mrs Stock, "Oh, stop your noise, woman. Old Mr Brandon had his two spaniels for years. You never minded those dogs, not like I did. Used to bury their bones under my tomatoes, both of them. *You* used to give them the bones."

Mrs Stock objected so loudly at this that Andrew took Aidan and Rolf out of the clamour and shut his study door behind the three of them. "Now look here, Aidan," he said, "I know this is a lovely dog, but he almost certainly belongs to someone else and—"

"He doesn't," Aidan said. "He's not a dog. Show him, Rolf."

Rolf nodded, shook himself and briefly chased his tail. Next moment he was a billow of yellow mist swirling across a pile of history pamphlets, and the moment after that he was a small boy, staring at Andrew with big, anxious dog eyes. "Please keep me!" he begged in his growl-like voice.

Andrew took his glasses off and stared back. "Oh," he said. "I suppose that does make a difference."

"He's a were-dog," Aidan explained. "He can't belong to anyone because he's a person really. But he wants to stay here and I want to keep him. Please?"

"Do you prefer being a dog or a boy?" Andrew asked Rolf.

"Dog," said Rolf. "It's easier." He dissolved into mist again and became a dog, pleadingly scraping at Andrew's leg with one large, damp paw.

Well, Andrew thought, dogs were easier to explain than boys. He remembered suddenly that the second horse in the racing results had been called Dogdays. They were probably fated to have Rolf. And the third horse, Heavy Queen, had to refer to Mabel WPC92. Stashe's method of foretelling really worked! "All right," he said, resigned to Rolf. "I'll go and settle Mrs Stock. If I can."

Half an hour later, Rolf was allowed to eat Aidan's spoilt lunch, which he seemed to enjoy very much, while Aidan himself ate most of a loaf with honey. Mrs Stock stayed only long enough to make Andrew cauliflower cheese from an old cauliflower that had been forgotten at the back of the pantry, before collecting Shaun and going off to complain to Trixie.

"Wish he was mine," Shaun said wistfully over his shoulder as Mrs Stock hauled him away.

Mr Stock wagged an earthy finger under Rolf's nose. "Any bones in my veg," he said, "and I come after you with a spade. Understand?" Rolf nodded humbly, slightly cross-eyed from the finger.

Andrew then explained matters to Stashe. If anyone had told him a month ago, he thought, that he would be seriously telling a lovely young secretary that they now had a were-dog staying here, he would have been utterly scornful. And even more disbelieving that Stashe took the information quite calmly. She turned to Rolf. "Does this explain why our visitor always eats the meaty bits from our barbecue?" she asked. Rolf lowered his eyes bashfully and did not deny it. "So it wasn't a fox after all," said Stashe. "Well, you're not living rough now. So behave."

After that, Rolf and Aidan shared the cauliflower cheese. Stashe went home and Andrew was left contemplating the two immense parsnips.

"Did your grandmother ever teach you how to cook parsnips?" he asked Aidan rather plaintively.

"Oh, yes," Aidan said, collecting empty dishes. "Creamed parsnip's lovely. You boil them, then you put them in the mixer with pepper and salt and lots of butter and cream. Shall I show you?"

"Please do," said Andrew. "Think of it as the way you earn Rolf."

So Aidan washed the parsnips – which, he thought, was rather like giving someone's legs a bath – and set one of them aside for Groil. Then he found Mrs Stock's sharpest knife and tried to cut the other parsnip up. On the first cut, the knife sank into the parsnip and stuck. Aidan pulled and wriggled at the knife but it refused to move. "Can you help me?" he asked Andrew. Then, rather forgetting that Andrew might not understand things the way Gran did, he explained, "I seem to have excalibured this knife."

"So I see." Andrew pulled his glasses down to look. "The Sword in the Parsnip. It doesn't sound quite as romantic as the King Arthur story, does it?" As soon as he said it, Andrew was hit with the knowledge that he had just said something highly important. He stood very still, thinking about it.

Aidan laughed, delighted that Andrew understood things the way Gran had.

Andrew continued to think, all through the hour it took them to cut up and tame the parsnip – which turned out to be delicious when they ate it – and went on thinking all through the evening and far into the night. He gave up the idea of asking Aidan any questions yet and he did not even mention Mabel WPC92 to him. Aidan was very occupied anyway, rolling about on the floor with Rolf. Andrew watched them and brooded.

There was something quite special about Aidan. Andrew blamed himself for not finding out what this was. He knew he should have made enquiries straight away. He should, at the very least, have *told* someone where Aidan was. Mabel WPC92 had made Andrew realise that social workers – real ones – must be looking for Aidan all over

London. People *worried* when a child disappeared. Andrew blamed himself for simply letting Aidan be. He had, he knew, been behaving as if Aidan was one of his students. If one of his students had decided to go to Hong Kong or San Francisco in their free time, Andrew would not have worried at all – provided they came back with an essay written – and Andrew had been vaguely thinking of Aidan in the same way. He knew this would not do. No wonder Mrs Stock went round muttering, "World of his own!"

Long after Aidan had gone off to bed, Andrew reached a decision. He would have to go to London tomorrow and make some cautious enquiries. The question was, should he tell Aidan? Yes, he decided. It was only fair. He went upstairs and put his head round the door of Aidan's room to find it full of moonlight. Aidan and Rolf were both asleep in Aidan's bed, back to back with both their heads on the pillow. Rolf had all four legs braced against the wall, in a way that suggested he would have pushed Aidan out on to the floor before morning. Andrew had not the heart to disturb them. He grinned and went downstairs to leave a note on the kitchen table, saying simply that he had gone to London.

In the morning, he drove into Melton and caught the London train.

He bought a newspaper at the station. As the train moved off, he unfolded it to the racing results, thinking, I'm getting as superstitious as Stashe! He smiled at the thought of Stashe and then stared. The winner of yesterday's first race at distant Catterick was called Confirmation. The horse that came in second was Careful Careful and the third was Ouch. Knowing he was being very silly to believe in this, Andrew still resolved to be very cautious indeed.

In London, he took a taxi to the street where Aidan said he had been boarded with the Arkwrights. As he walked slowly along to the right house, he tried to discount the feeling you got outside the boundary of his field-of-care, of this world being at once very flat and very dangerous. They were such very normal houses, large and semi-detached, each with false beams on its front gables and different well-kept gardens. But the feeling of danger grew. By the time Andrew was passing Number 43, he had such a strong sense of being watched that the hair was lifting at the back of his head. As he passed Number 45, the feeling was so strong that he was tempted to turn round and go away. But he told himself that this was silly, now he had come all this way, and went on to the right house, Number 47. As he lifted the latch on its front gate, it felt as if the invisible watchers said, "Ah!" and concentrated all their attention on him.

I was a fool to come here! Andrew thought. His skin came out in gooseflesh all over, shuddering with it, as he walked up the front path and pressed the bell at the ordinary front door.

The bell went sweetly *pongle-pongle* inside. A comfortable middle-aged lady, with nicely done grey hair and a floral apron on her comfortable front, opened the door and looked at him enquiringly. She was so completely normal that Andrew told himself he was being a *fool* for feeling so uneasy.

"Mrs Arkwright?" he asked. She nodded. "Good morning," Andrew said. "I'm sorry to disturb you. I'm looking for a boy called Aidan Cain. I'm a distant cousin of his and I understood he might be here. My name's Hope. Andrew Hope." He passed her one of his old business cards that still happened to be in his wallet.

Mrs Arkwright took the card and looked at it, evidently dismayed. It said DR A. B. HOPE and gave his address as that of his old University. Mrs Arkwright seemed to find this all too much for her. She turned half round and shouted, "Father! Father! You'd better come here!"

They waited. Andrew wondered who to expect. Mrs Arkwright's old dad? Or priests were often called Father, weren't they?

A door behind Mrs Arkwright opened and a middle-aged man shuffled out. He was wearing slippers and an old zip-up cardigan. He did not look well. Andrew saw at once that he must be Mrs Arkwright's husband and neither her parent nor a priest. He and she probably supplemented Mr Arkwright's sickness benefit by fostering children. The hall behind Mr Arkwright was filling with interested children. They were of several different races and assorted sizes, but they were all, without exception, years younger than Aidan. Poor Aidan! Andrew thought. He must have towered over them.

"What is it, Mother?" Mr Arkwright quavered. Though his voice was weak and wavery, he seemed very much in charge.

"There's a University doctor here, come about Adrian," Mrs Arkwright said helplessly.

"Ask him in then, Mother. Ask him in," quavered Mr Arkwright. He turned to the watching children. "Back you all go," he told them kindly. "In there and watch the telly again. This is grown-up business, so don't come in the kitchen till we've done. Just keep in the lounge."

"Please come in Mr – er – Dr Hope," Mrs Arkwright said. "This way."

She shut the front door behind Andrew and led him across a front hall smelling of bacon and air-freshener, while the children crowded away in front of them. As Mrs Arkwright led Andrew into the kitchen, he had a glimpse of all the children settling one by one in a row on a long sofa, facing a television on which a silent space battle was taking place. A Chinese boy of about eight grabbed for the remote control. A smaller Indian-looking girl grabbed it too and wrestled him for it for a moment, before giving in. The Chinese boy pressed a button. The room filled with roars, whistles and explosions.

Andrew shuddered. He never could stand television. He was glad when Mr Arkwright firmly shut that door and shuffled after him into the spotless, air-freshened kitchen.

"Please take a seat," Mrs Arkwright invited, pulling a stool out from under the big plastic-covered table. "Can I get you a coffee?"

"Only if you're having some too," Andrew said cautiously. He was particular about his coffee. Mrs Arkwright looked more of a tea person.

"Oh, Father always has one about now," she assured him cheerfully, and bustled away somewhere behind, where Andrew, perched on his stool, could not see her. He was not sure what she did there, but he feared the worst about that coffee. Mr Arkwright settled into a majestic oak chair, lined with cushions, and stared at Andrew with a polite sort of keenness.

"Now, sir," he said to Andrew, "perhaps you'd like to explain how you come to be here."

By lying, Andrew could not help thinking. That business card was really a lie, as well as pretending to be Aidan's cousin. Shame. These were kind, well meaning people and it went against the grain to lie to them. But after the way he had felt something watching him outside, he was sure he had to avoid at all costs telling them where Aidan actually was. "I live and work in a university," he began, "and I'm sure you know that universities are ivory towers. So it wasn't until – uh – yesterday that I learned that my distant cousin, Adela Cain, had died. I—"

"And just how did you learn that?" Mr Arkwright asked.

Fair enough, Andrew thought. Mr Arkwright is no fool. "Oh, a colleague showed me her obituary in the paper," he said. "She used to be quite a well-known singer—"

"And fairly famous in her day," Mr Arkwright agreed. "Not that I hold with crooners and such, but I did hear her name when I was younger. And?"

"Well," Andrew invented, "I knew of course that Adela's daughter was dead and Adela had had sole charge of her grandson, and I realised that I must be the child's only surviving relative. So—"

"And how did you get on to us?" Mr Arkwright asked shrewdly.

Um, Andrew thought. How *did* I?

Luckily at that moment Mrs Arkwright put down in front of Andrew a mug with THIS IS A HAPPY HOME painted on it. "Milk? Sugar?" she asked cheerfully.

The mug was full of a pale brown liquid that smelt, quite strongly, of old scrubbing brushes. Andrew found himself bending over it incredulously. How could anyone call this coffee? "No thanks," he said bravely. "I'll take it just as it is."

Another mug was put down in front of Mr Arkwright, who was waiting patiently for Andrew's answer. Mrs Arkwright sat cosily on another stool. "Coffee does things to my poor stomach," she explained.

I'm not surprised! Andrew thought. By this time some distant, inventive part of his brain had come up with an answer for Mr Arkwright. "I went on the internet," Andrew told him. "Then of course I checked with the police," he added, in case the first answer sounded too improbable.

To his relief, both the Arkwrights seemed to accept this. They nodded and looked at one another unhappily. Mr Arkwright said gravely, "Your information is a little out of date, I'm afraid. Adrian's not here any longer. We had to ask the social workers to take him somewhere else. We had a little trouble with him, you see."

"How do you mean?" Andrew asked.

Mrs Arkwright looked at Mr Arkwright. Both of them seemed quite uncomfortable now. During the silence this caused, Andrew distinctly heard a slight shuffling outside the kitchen door. It sounded as if not all the children were obediently watching the space war.

"Well, it wasn't as if Adrian wasn't a *good* boy," Mrs Arkwright said.

"Aidan," Andrew corrected her.

"Adrian," Mrs Arkwright agreed, as if that was what Andrew had said. "But he was a bit *strange*. Know what I mean? You'd think someone whose granny had just passed on would be glad of a little cuddle. I kept asking him for a cuddle, but he always said no. Said no and went away. I was quite hurt, to be honest. And then… Shall I tell the rest, Father? Or do you want to?"

"I will." Mr Arkwright looked straight and seriously at Andrew and pronounced weightily, "Poltergeist activity."

"I *beg* your pardon!" Andrew said.

"Yes," said Mr Arkwright. "What I said. Poltergeist activity. You being a university man might know all about it, but I had to read up on it. That's what it was. Teenagers in a distressed state of mind, the book said, can cause strange energies to be released. Things fly through the air, strange noises are heard. They can cause a lot of damage. They don't know they're doing it of course."

"*Did* things fly through the air?" Andrew asked.

"No, that would have come next," Mr Arkwright told him. "We didn't wait for that. What we got was bad enough – strange noises all round the house outside, yelling and caterwauling and such, the garden gate banging, over and over. And the children kept saying they saw strange flitting shapes. We couldn't have that."

"We had to get rid of him. He was frightening the children," Mrs Arkwright explained. "So we asked for him to be taken away."

"So," Andrew was beginning to wonder what was going on here, "when did Aidan actually leave?"

"Last Monday, nearly a week ago, wasn't it, Mother?" Mr Arkwright said.

"And where is he now?" Andrew asked.

Both Arkwrights looked puzzled. Mrs Arkwright suggested, doubtfully, "You could ask at the police station. *We* didn't need to know, you see."

"But you saw him leave?" Andrew said.

They looked even more puzzled. "I suppose we did," Mr Arkwright said. "But kids come and kids go, here. You know how it is. I don't exactly recall, to tell the truth."

Something *very* odd was going on here. Andrew took one brave swig from his mug. The so-called coffee tasted like it smelt. He put the mug down and stood up. "Thank you very much for your help," he said heartily. "It was good of you to spare me the time. I have to be going now."

Going where? he asked himself as he let himself out of the Arkwrights' front gate. The only thing that was clear was that something peculiar had happened here, to someone who might have been called Adrian. Andrew wondered whether to go and ask the police. He supposed he had better, or he would have told a lot of lies for nothing—

The feeling of being watched came back, intensely, as soon as he was outside in the street.

I shall go home, Andrew decided, with the back of his neck pricking. And this time he would ask Aidan a *lot* more questions. He strode towards the main road, where there was more chance of finding a taxi.

A shrill voice behind him cried out, "Hey! Mister!"

Andrew whirled round in time to see the small Chinese boy leap down from the Arkwrights' wall and chase after him. He was followed by the smaller Indian-looking girl. After her came a small black girl. Both girls had their hair done up in bright red ribbons that streamed and flapped as they pelted after the boy. "Mister! Mister, wait a moment!" they screamed.

All three came panting up to Andrew and stared at him urgently. "What is it?" he asked.

"They told you a lot of crap," the boy panted, "about Aidan. There were *real* things round the house in the night. Three lots of them."

"After Aidan," said the Asian girl. "They kept shouting out 'Adrian!' Everyone gets his name wrong, but it was Aidan they wanted."

"They were aliens," added the black girl. "One lot had, like, aerials on their heads. Two long bits poking up that wobbled."

"And they didn't like each other," said the Asian girl. "They fought."

"Thank you," Andrew said gratefully. "Thank you for telling me." All three children were beautifully clean and well cared for. Mrs Arkwright obviously did a splendid job when it came to physical needs. "Were you very frightened? Mrs Arkwright said you were."

"Sort of," said the boy. "It was more exciting than anything. Mrs Arkwright was the one that was *really* scared."

"Mai Chou was scared," the black girl said scornfully.

"But she's little. And stupid," said the other girl.

"*But*," said the Chinese boy, firmly sticking to the point, "they told you wrong about Aidan going too. They didn't send him away. He ran off."

Both girls nodded, ribbons fluttering. "He told us he was going," said the Asian girl. "He said not to worry and if *he* went, the aliens would leave the house alone. And they did."

"*Aidan* was scared," said the black girl. "His mouth was shaking."

"Well it was him they wanted to kill," the boy said. "And the police thought it was only cats fighting!"

"Did Aidan tell you where he was go—" Andrew began.

He stopped. A strange tall figure was standing in front of them, out of nowhere it seemed. It was nearly eight feet tall and clearly not human. Its slender body was covered in what looked like golden armour, with – possibly – a gauzy purple cloak hanging from its shoulders. Or could the cloak actually be wings? Andrew found himself wondering. He stared at the being's tall, oddly-shaped head, topped with golden curlicues and with golden sidepieces curling up on to its narrow cheeks, and wondered if this was a helmet or the creature's natural head. Odder still, the face staring out from the curly gold was exactly like Mr Stock's, thin and wry and bad-tempered.

Another counterpart? Andrew wondered, thoroughly shaken. Here? In London?

All three children had hurled themselves behind Andrew. He could feel them hanging on to the back of his jacket, while Andrew himself looked frantically around for help. There was no one walking on the pavements. Cars were going up and down the road, but none of the people in them glanced his way.

Nothing to do then but tough it out, Andrew thought. He took his glasses off. The creature looked weirder still to his naked eyes. It was like a golden skeleton surrounded in a silvery nimbus, although he still could not decide if the cloak was wings or not. "Now what do *you* want?" he asked severely.

The creature leaned towards him. It spoke, in a deep voice with an echo behind it. "Tell," it said. "Tell us where Adrian is."

Andrew felt a truly intense pressure to tell this being that Aidan was in Melstone. In fact, if the creature had said "Aidan" and not "Adrian", he was fairly sure he would have told it at once.

"That's one of them," the boy said from behind Andrew, as if the pressure had forced him to speak. "Those lot stood by the wall and laughed."

"So you were fighting in the Arkwrights' garden, were

you?" Andrew said. The pressure did seem to force you to say *something*.

The creature stood up to its full, tall height. "Not I," it echoed out scornfully. "I do not fight such as those. I am a King's man."

"What King would that be?" Andrew asked.

"Oberon of course," the creature answered haughtily.

Weirder and weirder, Andrew thought. *Stunningly* weird. An alien being stood in a London street and calmly announced itself a follower of the Fairy King. "This is mad," he said. "Why would that make you want to kill – uh – Adrian?"

"For being the only living son of my King," the creature answered, as if this was the most natural of reasons. "The King will not abide to be forced from his throne."

Andrew could think of nothing to say but, "Well, we live and learn. Are you *sure*?"

"So tell," the creature repeated, leaning forward again. The pressure seemed to squeeze at Andrew's skull.

"We *can't!*" the Chinese boy shrilled from behind Andrew. "Aidan didn't *say*. He said if he didn't tell us, we couldn't tell."

"So go away and stop frightening us!" shouted one of the girls.

"Yes, do go," Andrew said. He could feel the children

shaking. It made him angry. What business had this creature to try to terrorise three children who had only happened to be where Aidan was? In a powerful surge of rage, he waved his glasses towards it and thundered out, "Go *away*! Get *gone*!" A look of astonishment came over the creature's narrow face. Andrew was irresistibly reminded of Mr Stock, the time Andrew had told him to mulch the roses. It made him realise that he was in the right here too. "I mean it!" he yelled. "*GO!*"

To his surprise, the creature went. It seemed to compress into itself from both silvery misted sides, so that it became a gold and silver streak that squeezed away into empty air. The pressure to speak, and the feeling of being watched that had hung heavily in the street all along, went too, quite suddenly.

"And don't come back!" Andrew added to the empty pavement.

"That was *good*, Mister!" the boy said admiringly.

One of the girls said, "I knew he was good."

The other said, "Let's get back in, or they'll notice."

The three of them went racing away, back to the space war.

Andrew walked on, to what proved to be a dreadful journey home: almost no taxis, trains delayed, trains cancelled and the train that Andrew did eventually catch breaking down three stations away from Melton. It was almost as if that creature had ill-wished him. Yet Andrew hardly noticed. He spent the entire journey thinking, I don't believe this! I do not *believe* this!

The trouble was, he *did* believe it. He felt he could hardly blame the Arkwrights for inventing their own version of things.

Chapter Eleven

When Aidan came yawning down to the kitchen that morning, with Rolf eagerly following, he found Andrew's note on the table. It never occurred to him that Andrew's journey to London had anything to do with him. He wondered whether to leave the note for Mrs Stock. He knew it was the kind of thing that would make Mrs Stock say, "World of his own!" and start making cauliflower cheese, but he thought she ought to know where Andrew had gone. So he decided to leave it, but make sure he was not in the house when she found it. Meanwhile, he was rather glad that Andrew was not here to see how much cereal he and Rolf were eating between them.

Then, as Mrs Stock had still not arrived, Aidan took his glasses off and examined the old, old coloured glass in the kitchen door. This was something he had been itching to do, but not in front of Mrs Stock or even Andrew. It struck him as very ancient and secret.

At first, all he could tell was that the glass was quite powerfully magic. He had a feeling that you could use it for something, either pane by pane, or in various combinations – red with blue, blue with green, and so on – or you could use all the colours together, rather powerfully. But he still had not the least idea what you might use it *for*.

Rolf, seeing Aidan so interested, put his paws on the lower half of the door and reared up to look at the glass too. Aidan could see Rolf's reflection, dimly, in the yellow pane in the middle at the bottom. The glass was so old and foggy that things reflected in it only faintly, as if you were not really seeing them at all.

"Have you any idea what this window *does*?" Aidan asked Rolf.

Rolf's paws slipped. He landed on the floor with a grunt and had to scrabble his way up the wooden half of the door to look at the panes again. This time he landed in front of the blue glass on the left. He whined gently.

Aidan thought at first that this was simply doggish clumsiness. Then he realised that he could still see Rolf's reflection, faint but clear, with its ears pricked, in the yellow glass. The beautiful hyacinth blue that Rolf was now staring into contained a different face.

"Clever!" Aidan said. Rolf's tail whirled so hard that he unbalanced himself and slid down to the floor again. Rolf was making serious scratches down the door, Aidan saw rather guiltily, as he bent down to look in the blue glass. The face in it, smoky and far away, seemed to be Shaun's. Unless it was Groil's. It could have been either of them.

Odd, Aidan thought, and crouched along to look into the red pane, lower right. The shape in this one, like someone silhouetted against a fierce sunset, had a battered hat on. Aidan knew the shape of that hat so well by now that he sprang up and opened the door, like Andrew always did, before Mr Stock could barge it open.

And, sure enough, Mr Stock loomed in the doorway, carrying a box.

Rolf gave a deep bark of pleasure and galloped outside past Mr Stock, where he raised his leg against the water butt and then trotted busily about, sniffing and occasionally raising his leg again to squirt on clumps of weeds.

Mr Stock came in and dumped his box beside Aidan's cereal bowl. It contained a heap of foot-long broad beans with lumps all the way along them, like snakes that had swallowed several nests of mice. Groil's going to be happy tonight! Aidan thought. He did not care for broad beans and he very much hoped Andrew didn't like them either.

"Where's the professor?" Mr Stock asked. "His car's not here."

"Gone to London," Aidan said. "He left a note."

"It's to be hoped he knows what he's doing then," Mr Stock said, and departed.

Aidan closed the door carefully behind him and then stood on tiptoe to peer into the top three panes. The orange glass, top left, had waves in it that made it hard to see that there just could be a face in it too. But a face was there, like someone dissolving in fruit juice. Aidan could pick out the hairstyle, the slightly bulging eyes and the thin, sucked-in cheeks. It really did look like Mrs Stock. He opened the door again, in case Mrs Stock was outside now, but the only person who came in was Rolf, all sprightly from his run round the garden.

"So it doesn't work to summon people," Aidan said. "How *does* it work then?" He turned his attention to the green pane, top right.

There was no mistake here. It was Stashe. She smiled merrily at Aidan out of a fog of spring green, almost as if she was about to speak, make a joke, tell Aidan he had to help her with the papers today, or else. There was a line of green bubbles across her, like spring sunshine.

"And she doesn't come today," Aidan remembered. "So it's not summoning."

He went on to the purple pane, in the middle. He expected, if he saw anyone, to see Andrew there. The purple pane had struck him all along as the important one. Instead he looked into a space full of lilac twilight, not a peaceful space. There was a storm, or a high wind, in there, tossing trees against rushing clouds and occasional small zigzags of lightning. Among the glittering and shifting purples and greys, Aidan thought he could pick out a face. But he could not see it clearly enough to say whose it was.

While he was trying to see it more clearly, Aidan was almost knocked backwards by Mrs Stock coming in, followed by Shaun. He put his glasses back on quickly and the windowpanes were empty again, nothing but glowing colours and accidental streaks, lumps and bubbles.

In the time it took Aidan to hook his glasses behind his ears, Mrs Stock had read Andrew's note, snorted out, "Men!", sent Shaun off to work and looked disgustedly at the broad beans. "What does that man expect me to do with *these*?" she said. "They'll be like wood wrapped in leather. Can't he *ever* bear to pick veg when they're tender?" She picked up the empty cereal packet and shook it. Then it was Aidan's turn. "Look at this! You and that great greedy dog have eaten the lot between you! Go and get some more, this instant. And get some dog food while you're at it. The shop sells that too."

Before Aidan had collected his wits enough to turn from magical thoughts to everyday ones, he and Rolf were outside with a large pink shopping bag.

"Well, it'll make a walk for you," Aidan told Rolf. The two of them set off up the village.

The shop, labelled simply THE SHOP, PROPRIETOR R. STOCK was beyond the church and next door to TRIXIE HAIR STYLIST. Rosie Stock, who kept the shop, looked at Aidan with gossipy interest. She plainly knew just who he was. "Is that dog yours?" she said. "Make him sit outside. He's not hygienic. I thought he was a stray really. I've seen him around for years. I've only got chocolate cereal left today, or would you like the set of little packets? And does the dog eat the dry food or the meat in tins?"

Aidan chose both kinds of both. As Rosie packed them all into the pink bag for him, it dawned on him that he had no money to pay for them. Rosie Stock seemed the firm kind of lady who would never let a person promise to pay later. Aidan doubted if she would agree to let *Andrew* pay later. There was only one thing to do in that case. A bit nervously, he fetched out the old battered wallet, took his glasses off and opened it.

For a moment, it seemed to Aidan that someone in the distance said, "*Ah!*" But this was mixed up with the fizz of magic from the wallet and Aidan's own delight when he looked inside it and found a twenty pound note. There was so much change left when he had paid for the cereals and the dog food that Aidan bought Rolf a gluey-looking pretend bone and a chocolate coconut bar for himself. He still jingled with coins when he came out of the shop.

Using the wallet had made him miserable. It brought back the time Gran had given it to him – with the sarcastic look she always had when she talked of Aidan's father – and the way Gran had not looked at all well that day. Gran must have known she was going to die, but Aidan hadn't even properly noticed she was unwell. And Gran must have had some kind of strong protection around him that Aidan had never noticed either, because the moment she died, the Stalkers had crowded into the yard.

Aidan didn't want to think of these things. To take his mind off them, he walked on up the village with Rolf, until he came to the football ground, hoping that someone was playing football there.

They were. All his new friends were there. They were having to play on a shorter pitch than before because the near end of the field now had two large dusty vans in it, labelled in curly letters, *Rowan's Travelling Fair*. "They always come for the Fête," Gloria Appleby explained. "There'll be more of them coming next week. Glad to see you again. We lost yesterday."

Everyone was glad to see Aidan. Some of them said, "Where were you yesterday?" And others said, just like Rosie Stock in the shop, "Is that dog *yours*? I thought he was a stray."

Rolf shortly became a problem. Aidan sat Rolf down near the goal, beside the pink bag, and told him to look after it. But the moment the game got going, Rolf dashed off to join in. Aidan laughed at first. The sight of Rolf, ears flying, tail whirling, trying to tackle Gloria or, barking excitedly, dribbling the ball with his nose and front feet, was truly silly. And it got sillier when Rolf dribbled the ball to the end of the field and got stuck in the hedge.

No one else was pleased. "He's spoiling the game!" they objected.

Aidan hauled Rolf and the football out of the hedge and made him sit by the pink bag again. "*Sit* there," he said, "or I'll turn you out to be a stray again!"

This sobered Rolf for a while. He sat obediently beside the pink bag. But soon, whenever the ball came near, Aidan could see Rolf half rise to his feet with his ears pricked, yearning to join in. Aidan expected him to turn into his boy form in his excitement, but that never happened. Perhaps Rolf knew that this would cause even more trouble. Just to be on the safe side, Aidan tapped him on the nose and warned him to be good. Rolf sat and whined.

When Aidan next looked, Rolf was not there. There was only the pink bag.

"Where did he go?" Aidan asked the others. "Did anyone see?"

Before anyone could reply, the answer came in huge yelps and snarls from behind the Travelling Fair vans. Aidan dashed over there to find Rolf in the most vigorous fight with the Fair's guard dog. Both dogs seemed to be enjoying it wonderfully, but the woman who rushed out of one of the vans was not pleased at all. Aidan helped her haul the dogs apart, after which she handed him a piece of rope.

"Tie it up," she said, and stalked back into her van.

So Aidan dragged Rolf over to the gate and tied him to a gatepost. Rolf was laughing, dog fashion, with his tongue hanging out, and quite unrepentant. "Yes, I know you were winning," Aidan said to him, "but that's because you're not really a dog. You were being unfair. You're cleverer that it is. Now *behave*!" He gave Rolf the gluey fake bone to keep him quiet.

Rolf ate the bone in two minutes, but he gave no more trouble. There was peaceful football until Jimmy Stock looked at his watch and said he had to be getting home for lunch. Everyone else looked at watches then and said the same. Aidan untied Rolf and gave Gloria the rope to give back to the woman, and they all left, some up the road to the new houses and some the same way that Aidan was going. Rolf trotted demurely in the middle of the cheerful group like a dog that had never misbehaved in its life.

As he and Rolf turned into the lane leading to Melstone House, Aidan had a horrible thought. Suppose, because Andrew was away, that Mrs Stock did not think she had to get lunch, not even cauliflower cheese? Aidan was so hungry by then that he could have eaten those broad beans raw. Well – almost. He went round the house to the back door to give Mrs Stock her pink bag back and then, perhaps, to look pleading the way Rolf did.

Rolf dashed ahead, round the corner. Aidan heard him give a roaring sort of bark there, full of surprise. Aidan ran after him, lugging the bag. Groil was there, looming shyly round the corner beyond the water butt. Rolf was bouncing around Groil, giving yelps of greeting and standing up to paw at Groil's knees. Groil made Rolf look tiny. "Oh, hello!" Aidan said. "I thought you only came out at night."

"Not these days," Groil said, fending Rolf off with his enormous right hand. "I got zips now. And friends." His bush of hair was full of dust and cobwebs. He scratched a storm of it out with his left hand as he said, "I came to say we finished the glass in the roof, me and Shaun. Want to come and look? It's got faces in it now. Power's up. You could speak to the High Lord now if you want."

"What do you mea—" Aidan began.

A look of huge dismay came over Groil's big face. He put a large finger across his lips and fell to his knees, looking imploringly at Aidan to keep quiet. Then – it was a little like watching Rolf change – Groil shrank into something smaller and darker and harder. In less than a second you might have thought Groil was a boulder at the corner of the house.

Aidan was looking at the boulder, thinking, So *that's* why I can never find him in the daytime! when a loud, rather shrill voice cried out behind him, "Aha! *Found* you! *Got* you!"

Aidan whirled round. Rolf spun away from sniffing at the boulder. His hackles came up like a bush round his shoulders and like a hedge down his back. He bared his fangs and snarled.

The fat little man, standing beside Aidan with one hand out to grab his arm, backed away a step. "Keep that brute under control!" he said. He was wearing a black coat and striped trousers, as if he was going to a wedding.

Aidan stared. "I can't," he said. "He doesn't like you. Who are you? Are you going to a wedding?"

"*Wedding*!" exclaimed the little man. "What a stupid

idea!" His round face flushed. Aidan thought, Here is somebody else who looks like someone I know! Round and red and clean-shaven though the little man's face was, it was still remarkably like Tarquin O'Connor's.

"Then what are you doing here?" Aidan asked, not very politely. Gran would have been shocked and said something about manners maketh man. But Aidan knew the man had been about to grab him, and it was clear that both Groil and Rolf considered him to be an enemy.

The little man drew himself up to his full, fat height. "I am loyal butler to the King," he said proudly and added, even more proudly, "I am the Puck, no less. I come here to deliver a letter to the magician Hope from my master, when here I see *you*." He waved an expensive-looking envelope in one hand. He reached out for Aidan with the other hand. "You used the wallet. There is no doubt who you be. I shall take you prisoner forthwith."

Aidan backed away. Just like Andrew, he thought, I don't *believe* this!

But Rolf evidently did believe it. He was advancing on the little man step by slow step, growling deeply. Aidan would not have credited that Rolf could look so sinister. "I – I don't believe you," he said. "Go away, or I'll set my dog on you!"

Rolf didn't wait to be told. He went from crawling to a leap, snarling hideously.

The little man – Was he *really* the Puck? Aidan wondered – dodged nimbly aside and got his back against the water butt. Rolf went thundering by, scrabbled to a stop and turned to attack the little man again. The Puck held up both plump hands and sang out, "Change! All change!" and Rolf was suddenly a soft-skinned small boy, kneeling on the grass and looking most unhappy.

"Ow!" he said. "That hurt."

"I meant it to," said the Puck. "You traitor! You are by rights one of us who do not use iron. Why are you defending a human?"

"Because you wish him harm, of course!" Rolf said angrily.

"Not I," said the Puck. "I am going to take him softly and kindly to the King my master, and the King my master will put him softly and kindly to death." He gave Aidan a sly little grin. "Kindly," he said. He held both hands up again and sang, in a soft, buzzing chant:

"Come to me in hornet guise,
Come and carry off my prize."

A dark cloud of big flying things came streaming over the roof of the house and descended on Aidan. He took his glasses off and tried to back away from them, but they were all round him, circling him, up and down and round, buzzing louder and deeper and stronger than bees. Meanwhile, the Puck was chanting again:

"*Seven times round,*
Seven times round,
Bind the child that I have found,
Seven times round,
The child is bound."

Aidan tried to keep his eyes on just one of the creatures, to count how many times it circled him, but he soon realised he could be hypnotised that way. It was like trying to follow one snowflake in a blizzard. Without his glasses, he was not sure if they were exactly hornets, but he could see they had big bent, striped bodies and stings sticking out at the ends. Their wings made a snarling blur. Aidan remembered reading somewhere that you could die if enough hornets stung you. He was terrified. He looked across at poor near-naked Rolf, crouching on the grass, but the creatures did not seem to be interested in Rolf. That was one good thing at least.

"Help!" he shouted. Mrs Stock must be in the kitchen. Surely she would hear.

"*Seven times round*," chanted the Puck. "*Seven times round.*" And he added in a more normal voice, "Then walk where my hornets take you and you will not be hurt. Walk towards the front of this house."

"*No!*" Aidan screamed. "*Help!*" Was Mrs Stock *deaf*?

Help came from another direction instead. Uneven feet ran, one foot light, one heavy. "What the green festering devil is going *on*?" demanded a voice. It could have been the Puck's voice, except that it had an Irish accent. Tarquin came round the corner of the house and exclaimed at the sight of Aidan half crouching in a funnel of whirling dark creatures. He swore. "Call those things off!" he said, pointing his crutch at the Puck. "Call them off now!"

The Puck looked extremely dismayed to see Tarquin, but he shook his head. "Not I. This is in my master's service," he said, and went on with his chant. "*Seven times round, Seven times round...*"

Tarquin suggested several very filthy things the Puck could do with his master and rushed at the little chanting man with his crutch pointed like a lance. "*Stop* it!" he yelled.

"I take no orders from a man with *one leg*!" the Puck

screamed out, as Tarquin's crutch hit him in his bulging grey waistcoat.

Tarquin's missing leg promptly gave way. Tarquin landed in a crouch on his real knee. But he heaved with the crutch as he went down and the Puck went up and over backwards into the water butt. SPLASH!

Rolf cheered and seized the chance to become a dog again. And, Aidan saw out of the corner of his eye as he ran out from among the dwindling, vanishing hornet creatures, Groil also seized his chance. Aidan glimpsed him uncurling and whisking himself out of sight round the corner of the house.

Aidan knelt down beside Tarquin. "Thanks," he said. "What can I do for your leg?"

"The Lord alone knows, except it isn't there any more," Tarquin said wretchedly.

Here the kitchen door opened and Mrs Stock came out with her what's-going-on face. Shaun followed her, busily gnawing on half a French loaf filled with steak and lettuce. Aidan's stomach rumbled at the sight. Then they all had to shield their faces as the Puck came soaring back out of the water butt in a brown surge of rainwater.

"I'll be even with you yet!" he screamed at Tarquin, spitting out water and pond life.

"Evens is all you'll ever be with me," Tarquin said to

him. "I'm your human counterpart, so I am. Add in Shaun here and you're outnumbered. Go away. *Stay* away."

"What in the *world*…?" said Mrs Stock, watching the Puck come hovering down to the ground in his dripping morning dress. "Shaun, get that creature out of here before my nerves get the better of me, for Heaven's sake!"

"I'm going, I'm going!" the Puck said, glowering at her. "You needn't invoke That Place. And," he added to Aidan, "I shall find you again, soon enough. Whenever you use that wallet." He bent and popped the soaking envelope he was holding into the pink bag. Then he was gone. There was nothing of him left but a small shower of water falling among the thistles and the grass.

"We must ask the professor for some way to keep these creatures off you," Tarquin said to Aidan.

"Professor's not here," said Mrs Stock. "Gone to London. World of his own. Were you wanting him for anything particular?"

"Nothing, only hoping for a bit of physio, as you might say," Tarquin said. He was still kneeling on his good leg, propped on his crutch. He pointed miserably to the missing one, where his trouser leg draped across the grass.

"Help him up, Shaun," Mrs Stock commanded. She picked up the pink bag – which had got rather wet in the encounter – and looked inside it. "Wet letter for the professor," she said. "Damp cereal. At least you got proper food for that ungrateful dog." Rolf gave her a reproachful look and shook himself. Water sprayed across Mrs Stock's apron. "None of that, or I shan't open you a single tin," Mrs Stock said. "Aidan, your filled French will be ready in ten minutes. *Be* here." She marched back indoors with the bag. Rolf followed her, with his nose practically inside the bag.

Shaun, with his French bread waving in one hand, heaved Tarquin up with his other hand, and Aidan helped steady him. Tarquin's shoe fell off his missing foot as he came upright. "See?" Tarquin said despairingly. "Gone again."

There was a perfectly good sock on the missing foot. Aidan looked at it, glad of the distraction. He was still vibrating all over from the hornet creatures, and from knowing that someone here in Melstone wanted him dead now. He was like the strings of Andrew's piano, he thought, if you struck one of the deep keys hard and then went away.

"Your sock's still on," he said to Tarquin. He bent and felt the air above the sock. His fingers met a sharp shin and a bony knee and strong muscles at the back of them. "Your leg's still there. The Puck just made you *think* it wasn't." He put the shoe back on over the sock to prove it to Tarquin.

"Is that so?" The colour began to come back to Tarquin's bearded, elfin face. Very cautiously, he stood on both feet. He flexed the missing leg, then stamped. "You're right!" he said. "It *hasn't* gone!"

Shaun nodded, satisfied that Tarquin was now all right, and turned to Aidan. "Groil wants you to look in the shed. He got the window clean."

Groil came sidling back round the corner of the house, big again, with his head nearly level with the bedroom window beside him. He grinned down at Aidan. "That was a good parsnip last night," he said. "Sweet. Big. Come and look in the shed."

Here was another distraction. Aidan grinned back. "There's about a thousand broad beans for tonight," he said.

"Oh, good," said Groil.

Tarquin tipped his head back to look up at Groil. His mouth came open. "Who—?" he said to Shaun.

Shaun had just taken a massive mouthful of bread and steak. "Glmph," he said, with lettuce hanging down his chin.

"This is Groil," Aidan said. "He's one of those who don't use iron. My gran told me there's a lot of them all over the place if you look. Coming?"

Tarquin nodded wonderingly and limped after Shaun as

Shaun followed Groil and Aidan round the house to the yard. There Groil stopped beside the lawnmower and bowed Aidan towards the shed door with one huge hand outstretched. It was so courtly that it made Aidan laugh as he slipped inside the shed.

The place was quite different already. It glowed with strangely coloured light from the glistening clean glass in the roof. Aidan could see where Shaun had been at work on two of the walls, cleaning and polishing the carved wood. The oddly shaped birds and little animals stood out all over the back wall, shiny and almost golden. The polish revealed that there were carved people in there too, mixed with trails of leaves and flowers.

Aidan breathed in the honey smell of the beeswax. "It's lovely!" he called out. He took his glasses off and looked up at the coloured glass in the roof. You could hardly see where the panes had been cracked now, or if you could see a crack, it looked like part of the patterns in the glass. Those patterns certainly seemed to be faces, but the window was too high for Aidan to see them properly with his naked eyes. All he could see was that they seemed to be moving. Or was it that his head was moving because he was craning upwards?

Something strange happened then.

The shed went away from Aidan and, with it, the

footsteps of the others and Tarquin's voice – Tarquin was chattering as usual. But Aidan could still hear birds singing somewhere in the garden or in the orchard. He could hear trees rustling too, and smell damp leaves mixing with the scent of honey from the walls. Out of this, a voice spoke to him. It did not seem to use words, but it reminded him of Gran's voice all the same, even though it seemed to be the voice of a man.

What is it you need, young sprig of kindling?

Aidan answered the voice in his mind, not by speaking. I want to be *safe*. People keep coming after me.

The voice seemed to consider. Then it said, *Steps have been taken, by you and by others, but to be sure of safety you need to get rid of that wallet in your pocket.*

Why? Aidan asked, startled.

Because they can trace you by it, sprigling. Money from nowhere is always trouble.

This sounded so like one of Gran's sayings that Aidan believed it instantly. He said in his mind, I'll get rid of it then. Thanks.

But isn't there anything more you need? Have you no ambitions?

Well, Aidan thought, he would quite like to be a football star, like Jimmy Stock was obviously going to be. But what his *real* ambition was he knew suddenly... I want to be *wise*, like Gran and Andrew, and have my own field-of-care and write books about all the amazing things I find out and, and fix things magically that can't be fixed any other way and, and do lots of other things that need magic and, and—

The voice interrupted him. Aidan could hear the smile in it. *Good. That is a very proper aim. The perfect one for you. You shall have my help in this.*

The birdsong and the leaf smell receded into the background and Aidan found himself back in the shed again, with all three of the others. Shaun, with his mouth full, was waving his French loaf at a piece of the wall and Groil was bending down to inspect it. Aidan blinked and wondered however Groil had squeezed inside here. On the other side of him, Tarquin had both hands curled up around his eyes, as if his hands were binoculars, and was looking up through them at the window in the roof.

"I can't see all the faces clearly," Tarquin was saying, "but there's Wally and Rosie, and I think there's Ronnie Stock too, so I do. On a rough guess I'd say half the village was up there."

A hatted silhouette darkened the door. "Shaun," said Mr Stock, "what do you mean, leaving my mower out in the yard? Get it in at once. It's going to rain."

"Yes, Mr Stock. Sorry, Mr Stock." Shaun fled out into the yard, still munching.

Aidan looked round for Groil. Groil had crouched down in one corner and made himself hard and heavy. He was obviously not wanting Mr Stock to see him. He looked for all the world, Aidan thought, like one of those old bags of cement that Shaun had buried in the asparagus bed. Aidan went over to Groil, wrestling the wallet out of his pocket as he went.

"Can you guard this for me for a while?" he asked him.

Groil put out a surprisingly small dense hand and took the wallet. "Where would I keep it?" he asked anxiously.

"Your pocket. Zip it into one of your pockets," Aidan said.

Groil grinned, like a crack in a sack. "Ah," he said. "Yes. I got zips."

Aidan remembered then how hungry he was. Mrs Stock had said ten minutes and *be* there. He pushed past Mr Stock and ran.

"What went down?" Mr Stock said to Tarquin as soon as Aidan had gone. "I felt something. Do you need any help?"

"Not now. I dealt with it myself," Tarquin said. "But I warn you, Stockie, Aidan's going to need us all on maximum alert from now on, so he is."

As Shaun began to trundle the mower towards them, Mr Stock scratched worriedly under the back of his hat.

"All right. But it's the professor I seem to be homed in on really."

"Revamp yourself to home on both of them then," Tarquin said. "I think it's urgent."

Shaun and the mower arrived then. Beyond Shaun, rain began to pelt down. Tarquin made a face and raced away to his car, carrying his crutch like a rifle and quite forgetting he had only one leg.

Chapter Twelve

It rained all that afternoon and evening. Aidan moodily went with Rolf into the dark, chilly living room, wishing yet again that Andrew could bring himself to own a television, and wondering what to do with himself instead. He scrounged around the room, looking for something – anything! – interesting. In this way he found the two packages from Stashe that Mrs Stock had hidden quite cunningly in a pile of music on the piano.

One was for Andrew. Stashe had written on it: "Andrew. No parchment yet but I found this. And please read the letters and notes I put in your study. I think they're important. S."

The other, to Aidan's pleasure, was for him, and it was big. Stashe's note on this one said, "*Aidan. These were all in the bottom of that box. You should have waited. Enjoy. S.*"

When Aidan unwrapped this packet, he found a stack of old comics, each labelled in round black schoolboy writing, *Property of Andrew Brandon Hope*. **Do not throw away**.

"Hey, cool!" Aidan said. He settled himself, Rolf, all the cushions and the comics on the best sofa, turned on the reading lamp and prepared to enjoy himself.

Andrew came in hours later, tired, exasperated and damp from standing on stations waiting for trains. His first act was to go to the kitchen to make himself a proper cup of coffee. The memory of Mrs Arkwright's coffee still lingered, and it was painful. As he was putting the kettle on, he noticed the wet letter in the middle of the kitchen table addressed to him in curly, majestic writing. Here was something to take away the taste of London, he thought.

The letter was too wet to read as it was. Andrew sat down with his coffee, thought a little while and then used a variation of the way he had fetched his car out of the ditch. Resting his fingertips on the damp envelope, he thought Einstein again, and time, and time past, back to the moment when the letter was first written, when it was dry and crisp. He suggested to the letter that it return to the way it was then.

The letter obligingly did so. In a second or so, it was a large expensive envelope, new and dry, dry enough for Andrew to slit it open with the end of his coffee spoon.

Andrew drew the letter out from it. In the same curly, majestic writing, it said:

> *Mr Hope,*
> *It has come to my attention that you are now bribing and coercing my folk to join your side. Desist from this. Failure to desist will lay you open to reprisals when my plans for Melstone have matured.*
> *Yrs,*
> *O. Brown*

All Andrew's pleasure in his successful piece of magic vanished in a surge of fury. How *dare* Mr Brown command him like this! The, the *nerve* of the man! He swigged coffee and raged. As he poured himself a second mugful, he had cooled down enough to wonder just who Mr Brown thought he had been bribing. Groil and Rolf, he supposed the man meant. He certainly couldn't mean Security. "Absolutely *absurd*!" Andrew said aloud. Groil was still a child and his grandfather had been feeding Groil for years. Fat lot of care Mr Brown had taken of Groil, who had had no food and no clothes until Melstone House provided him with them. And the same went for Rolf, who was little more than a puppy anyway. "Absurd!" Andrew said again.

He threw the letter aside and went to look for Aidan.

Aidan looked up with a grin from among his heap of comics. Rolf sprang up from across Aidan's legs, tail whirling, and fawned on Andrew. Andrew rubbed Rolf's silky ears and felt slightly better. Aidan watched a moment, then said, "Was it a bad day?"

"Yes," said Andrew. "What's that you're reading?"

Aidan answered by turning the comic round to the signature and holding it up. Andrew bent over and was amazed to read his own signature. He had clean forgotten his comics collection. He had forgotten how he had stored the comics here in Melstone House because his parents objected to him reading such things. His grandfather hadn't objected. Andrew remembered his grandfather reading the comics too and enjoying them as much as Andrew did.

Except when it came to the supernatural parts, Andrew recalled. There his grandfather had got all annoyed and explained to Andrew where they were wrong, and how. "Were-dogs, weres of any kind, *don't* need a full moon to change," Andrew remembered old Jocelyn saying. "That part's just folklore, son. They naturally change at will." After this, Andrew remembered Jocelyn instructing him in the correct, real way of this magic, then that; telling him so many things that the present-day Andrew felt as if he were receiving an information dump. He felt quite dazed by the amount he now remembered. He laughed incredulously. He had made himself forget it all, first because his mother told him it was all nonsense and then, as a hard working student, because he had decided that magic was not an adult thing to know. And old Jocelyn had, after all, instructed his grandson very carefully in everything he would need to know when he took over his grandfather's field-of-care. What a fool I've been! Andrew thought.

Aidan watched attentively as the dazed, incredulous smile grew on Andrew's face. When Andrew finally laughed, Aidan relaxed. Now he could break the bad news. "There was a bit of trouble here today," he said, "but Tarquin's leg really *is* still there. I checked." He went on to describe his encounter with the Puck, although he did not mention the strange voice in the shed. That felt private. "So I gave the wallet to Groil to guard," he finished.

"Good," said Andrew. "I'd been meaning to warn you not to use that wallet. They can find you by it. So after that little scrimmage, it may not surprise you to learn that they've got the Arkwrights' house staked out in London. I had an encounter there too. But the Arkwrights seem to have made themselves believe that they sent you away for frightening the other children."

"Great!" said Aidan. "I meant them to."

Andrew decided that this was not the time to point out

to Aidan that doing this was bad magic. Aidan had been shaken enough to find someone in Melstone actually wanted him dead. "So it was *you*!" he said. "That's a relief. They had me wondering which of us was mad. But the kids knew the truth. It wasn't until the Chinese boy chased after me—"

"Henry Lee," Aidan put in. "He's brainy. Stashe left you a parcel. Over there, on the piano."

Andrew realised he was glad that Aidan had interrupted him. It would do no good to tell Aidan who his father was – although it did, now Andrew thought about it, account for Aidan's astonishing gift for magic. He went over to the piano. On the way, he paused to gesture at the fire that Mrs Stock had laid ready in the hearth. Pull out a wisp of Earth's fiery centre, his grandfather had taught him and Andrew now remembered, and flick it among the kindling. The fire blazed up, popping and crackling. "That's better," Andrew said, picking up Stashe's small parcel.

"Can you teach me to do that?" Aidan asked as Rolf trotted eagerly to the hearthrug and threw himself gratefully down in front of the fire.

"Probably," Andrew said absently. He opened the packet and was flooded with yet more memories. A small silver pendant fell out, trickling a silver chain behind it. It looked like a very ornamental cross, but when you examined it, it was more like a tree, or a man, or an ankh. It was, Andrew knew, very potent. His grandfather had made him wear it whenever, as old Jocelyn used to put it, there was "a spot of bother with him down at the Manor".

And there was a spot of bother now. Andrew held the pendant out to Aidan. "Wear this," he said. "It'll keep you safe."

Aidan inspected it disdainfully. "I don't *do* bling," he said. He had been rather scornful to find that nearly all his football friends wore gold crosses or silver charms round their necks. "Gran said charms are mostly superstition," he explained.

"Superstition," Andrew said, "is something you believe. *They* believe in this, so it works against them. Take it. Put it on."

Aidan remembered his conversation with the strange voice. *Steps have been taken*, it had said, *by you and by others*. He saw that he might be being silly. "OK," he said and grudgingly put the pendant round his neck. As soon as he had the chain over his head, he found himself sighing with a feeling of deep peace. The urgent, tense feeling he had had ever since the Puck had appeared was suddenly gone. "It works!" he said.

"Yes." Andrew relaxed too. He treated himself to a thimbleful of whisky and sat with his feet stretched out to the fire and Rolf stretched out by his feet. It felt very comfortable to have a snoring dog on the hearth – even if the dog was not quite a dog.

Mrs Stock had been generous that day and left them a fine, juicy pie. And the rain stopped while they were eating it. After supper, they were able to lug the box of giant beans round to the woodshed.

Groil was waiting for them, rather damp, leaning his elbows on the roof. He beamed when he saw the box and lifted it up on to the woodshed himself. "What are you wearing?" he asked Aidan uneasily as he dragged out two fistfuls of the beans. "It makes me feel sore."

Aidan thought of himself and Tarquin's leg. "It's a charm to make my enemies *believe* that it hurts them," he said. "It can't hurt *you* because you're a friend."

"Ah." Groil took a mighty bite of beans, pods and all. He munched a bit and thought. "You're right," he said, after one of his drainlike swallowings. "It's all a trick. Do you still want me to keep your wallet?"

"If you wouldn't mind," Aidan said. "It's safe with you."

"Fine," Groil said. "This could be fun."

"What did he mean by that?" Andrew asked as they went back to the house.

"No idea," Aidan said, pushing the back door open.

This reminded him. The glass. "I forgot," he said. "I meant to tell you there are faces in the coloured glass. I'll show you tomorrow when it's light."

But Andrew fetched the big torch from his study then and there, and made Aidan stand outside and shine the light through the glass. Aidan stood there patiently, listening to Groil's steady munching from around the corner, while indoors Andrew stared and marvelled. Here was one more thing he had forgotten his grandfather telling him. He had only remembered that this stained glass was somehow precious. "It shows you my counterparts," old Jocelyn had said. "But we've only got two so far." Indeed, in his grandfather's day, Andrew had only been able to pick out two faces: Mrs Stock in orange, left-hand top, and Mr Stock in red, right-hand bottom, and Andrew had never been sure if he was really seeing them or not. Now he could, very definitely, see six people, all of whom must have counterparts among Mr Brown's folk. Andrew could see Tarquin clearest of all, in the purple pane. Tarquin's elfin face stared out at him from what seemed to be the thrashing branches of a tree, with some kind of storm raging behind it. But Rolf was almost as clear, in the yellow glass at the bottom. Rolf must count as a person then. So who did he correspond to? Security's dog? And what about Shaun, in the blue pane – or was that Groil?

Andrew spent the longest time gazing at the misty image of Stashe, in the green glass, until Aidan complained that his arms were aching. Andrew ignored him. Really that girl was a delight. So beautiful. Like a spring day...

"My arms are *killing* me!" Aidan shouted. "This torch is *heavy*!"

Andrew sighed. There was still a day to go before Stashe came to the house again. "Oh, all right. Switch it off and come in then," he said, wondering how he was going to live through tomorrow.

The next day was clear and bright, as if the rain had never been. Andrew solved the problem of how to live through it by saying to Aidan over breakfast, "Get your boots and jacket as soon as you've finished. We're going to walk the boundary from where the rain stopped us last time. Does Rolf want to come?"

Rolf did. Energised by two packets of cereal, he bounded eagerly ahead until they reached the dip in the road. Then, nose down, he went off unerringly along the line of the boundary that they had somehow missed when they ended up in the wood.

"That's a relief," Andrew said. "No need to zigzag."

Aidan nodded a little morosely. He had hoped to play football today. And he was not at all sure that the silver charm was going to protect him if any creatures appeared.

In addition, he could hear the church bell across the fields, summoning people to Sunday worship, which made Aidan feel guilty. Gran had been very strict about going to church. He was afraid that Gran would have called Andrew godless.

Andrew became very godless indeed at the point where the boundary swerved away from the road to his old university and their way was blocked by an impenetrable tangle of barbed wire. Rolf turned back, whining. Andrew stood and swore. Aidan was astonished at how many swear words Andrew seemed to know. "It's Brown again," Andrew said. "I know it!"

It did seem to be Mr Brown's doing. According to the map, which Andrew spread out angrily over one knee, the grounds of Melstone Manor made a great bulge at this end of the village, surrounded by a wall. They could see the wall through the coils of barbed wire, but they could not get to it, although it was fairly obvious that the line of the boundary ran along outside the wall, following the bulge.

"Trying to take over more land!" Andrew said furiously. "Let him just wait until my lawyer gets back from holiday!"

"Is this bit yours too?" Aidan asked.

"No. It's the *principle* I object to!" Andrew said between his clenched teeth.

Aidan was puzzled. "Isn't Mr Brown one of those who don't use iron?" he asked.

"Yes," snapped Andrew.

"Then," said Aidan, "what is this barbed wire made of?"

Andrew stared at him. "That is quite a point," he said after a while. "Perhaps it's all an illusion. Let's try and push through."

They tried it. All that happened was that Andrew tore his jacket and Rolf whined unhappily all the time they were trying. Whether the barbed wire was an illusion or, as Aidan suggested, simply made of zinc or something, it was quite as impenetrable as it looked.

"Let's go home by the road," Andrew said disgustedly. "I need to think about this, before he surrounds the whole of Melstone in barbed wire."

They trudged back along the tarmac and arrived back at Melstone House hungry, hot and cross. Rolf was the only one who was even remotely happy. After lunch he led Aidan joyously up the village to the football field, where Aidan had a very satisfactory afternoon and Rolf vanished to chase rabbits in the fields beyond. Andrew spent the time soothing himself by playing the piano and telling himself that he was thinking what to do about the encroachments of Mr Brown. In fact he had not the remotest idea what to do.

He decided to ask Stashe when she arrived tomorrow.

That Monday Stashe breezed in wearing another green dress, this one with beads around its high waist. She seemed to Andrew like the antidote to all his troubles. "Have you read those letters yet?" she asked him cheerfully.

"No, I had to go to London," Andrew said. "And – er – other things."

Aidan looked carefully at Andrew's face and slipped away with the pendant winking round his neck, first to chase about the fields with Rolf and then to the football field. Andrew barely noticed him go.

"Have you any idea what I can do about Mr Brown?" he asked Stashe. "First he grabs half my wood, and then he seems to be putting barbed wire all along the boundary of my field-of-care."

Stashe thought about it. "I don't know," she said. "I don't know how you deal with those people. They're so strange. But I intend to finish that second box today, and the third, if I have the time. I think we *must* find that parchment. Dad told me about the trouble on Saturday and how he thought he'd lost his leg again. He thinks that a look at that contract, or whatever it is, might help sort things out. And *do* find time to read those letters. They'll surprise you."

She breezed away to the box room, moments before Mrs Stock arrived.

"Lovely weather," Mrs Stock announced, handing Andrew today's paper. "If it stays this way, it'll be just right for the Fête on Saturday. I've sent Shaun to go on with that shed, is that all right? Had a good trip to London, did you? Mind you, I *still* can't be happy about that sideshow Trixie's thought up. I think it's indecent really. Why can't she come on the old clothes stall with me, like last year?"

She was interrupted by Mr Stock with a truly massive box, which he bunted against the back door to attract Andrew's attention. Andrew leaped up at once to open the door. He knew now that the stained glass was even more precious than he had thought. Mr Stock was not particularly angry with anyone that day, but he had been sorting out the vegetables that were not up to the exacting standards of the Fête and he had nothing else to do with them. As he carried the box past Andrew, Andrew glimpsed a jumble of outsize marrows, colossal potatoes and a vine of tomatoes like pulpy cricket balls. He left Mrs Stock to deal with them and fled to his study.

Stashe had put several piles of letters beside his computer, carefully labelled. *Finance*, Andrew read, on the first pile. "I never knew he was a Lloyd's Name." And on the next, *Letters from fellow occultists, mostly technical.* The third pile read, *Fifty years of letters from Aidan's gran!*

Andrew carried them all to the living room and settled down to read.

Mrs Stock, who had decided to move the piano again today, whatever Andrew said, was thoroughly thwarted to find him there. She revenged herself on Andrew by throwing the French windows wide open and saying, on her way out, "I thought you were too old to be reading comics!" She then removed herself to Andrew's study, muttering, "Well, at least I can get to dust that computall today!" She proceeded to wreak chaos and mayhem in there by piling all the papers into neat, random heaps, pushing pamphlets into an old box she found there and stacking every book she could discover into a cupboard where Andrew would never find them. Finally she dusted the computer with a heavy hand. The machine was switched off, but it nevertheless gave out protesting whirrs and beeps.

"Nothing to do with me," Mrs Stock declared. "I never touched it. Stupid thing. World of his own!"

In the living room Andrew was interested to find that the first letter from Aidan's gran to his grandfather was indeed written fifty years ago. It said:

Dear Jocelyn Brandon –
May I take a liberty? – we are such a

divided family – my parents quarrelled with
your parents – and then they quarrelled
with me for becoming a singer – but this
seems no reason why you and I should not
be friends – I have just acquired a
field-of-care here in London and it would
be a great boon to me if I could consult you
from time to time – I am told you are the
best occultist in the country – If you don't
wish to acknowledge me I shall understand
– but I hope this will not be the case.
　　Yours hopefully,
　　　　Adela Cain (née Brandon)

Andrew laughed aloud. Though some of it was at Adela's idea of punctuation, most of it was with astonished pleasure. Quite by accident, he had not lied to the Arkwrights, or not as much as he'd thought. Adela Cain really was a distant cousin, and so of course was Aidan. It meant that Aidan had a perfect right to come and live here, just as Andrew had a perfect right to go and ask the Arkwrights about him. Oh, good! he thought, turning to the next letter.

Obviously, old Jocelyn – who must have been in his fifties then and not that very old – had sent Adela a cordial reply. Her next ten letters, scattered over some years, were all friendly requests for advice, or thanks to Jocelyn for his help. In the next letter after this, Adela was giving Jocelyn advice in turn. *If your beastly Mr Brown*, this one went, *is really one of those who don't use iron, make careful note of what he actually* says *– they'll trick you if they can – those people – but they're quite careless too – they leave loopholes and so you can often trick them back.*

Two letters further on, there was a sad little note.

> *My dear Jocelyn –*
> *Thank you for your kind letter on the death*
> *of my beloved Harry Cain – I miss him*
> *terribly – but I shall pull myself together – I*
> *have my little daughter Melanie to care for –*
>   *Yrs*
>   *Adela*

Strange, Andrew thought uncomfortably. This feels like prying into someone's feelings.

He read more letters. *...and how do you stand on voodoo? – I wouldn't interfere myself – but some of their gods are actually walking my streets now...* and *...I don't know what is in her love potions – I only know one poor girl has killed herself...* And then suddenly *...Some personal* *advice now – as I know you too have a daughter you don't get on with – how do I deal with Melanie? – she is fifteen now and she seems to have nothing but sulky contempt for me...*

Andrew was jolted out of what seemed to be a story that had nothing to do with himself. Adela was talking about his own mother. By the date on this letter, this was long after his mother had stopped having any dealings with Jocelyn. Andrew never knew what their final quarrel had been about. He had been above such things then, a hard working and ambitious graduate student, studying furiously for his doctorate... And, yes! This must have been about the same time as he had had that sudden blinding sight of the true nature of history, the revelation that had led to his decision to write the book he was trying to write now... Anyway, on with these letters.

Melanie came into the letters a lot after this. She came home drunk. She came home high on drugs and was lucky that Adela prevented her being arrested for drug dealing. She insulted her mother all the time, in any way she could. Adela begged for advice in almost every letter. Andrew would have called Melanie a thoroughly bad lot – except that most of Melanie's insults were remarkably like the things his own mother used to say about Jocelyn. *Superstitious old fogey!* was entirely familar, and so was *Ha ha! My parent believes in fairies, stupid old fool!*

Perhaps Adela was simply mishandling Melanie, being too strict with her, just as Andrew had always suspected Jocelyn had mishandled his own mother and caused her to decide to be the opposite in every way she could. Rebels, both of them.

Then came a letter of thirteen years ago, dated at the time when Andrew himself had been in France studying, and rather out of touch with his grandfather.

> *Dear Jocelyn –*
> <u>*Thank you*</u> *– I'll bring Melanie down to you myself – but I won't stay – You have no chance of sorting her out if I'm with her – I pray you can – arrive 2.15 in Melton -*
> *Gratefully*
> *Adela*

So Melanie had actually come *here*! Andrew thought. I wonder if that helped. *Wait* a moment. Thirteen years ago?

Sure enough, the next letter said, Y*es, Melanie is pregnant, I'm afraid – she insists it's none of my business – but from some of the things she says I suspect the father to be that odious Mr Brown of yours – no – no – not your fault – how can you stop a girl walking in your wood – I know* *how sneaky he is – and I know Melanie...*

Feeling more than ever as if he was prying, Andrew leafed on through the letters – or even more as if he was guiltily turning to the end of a detective story to find out who the murderer was, which was something he always felt ashamed of doing. Melanie ran away from Adela, disappeared completely for a couple of years, and then returned home dying of cancer... *and the child – she's called him Aidan because she says only the right people get that name right – and Aidan has fleas and head lice – Jocelyn – I'm not sure I can cope!...*

Andrew had just read this cry of despair, when Stashe knocked at the door and sang out, "May I come in, Andrew?"

"Yes, of course," Andrew said, laying the letters down.

"*Thank* you," she said, not from the door but from the open French windows. "We have to be invited in, you know."

She was not Stashe.

Chapter Thirteen

She was not Stashe, although she was remarkably like her. She was wearing a long, fluttering dress the same green as the dress Stashe was wearing that day. Her hair was a brighter gold than Stashe's and it fell in long curls around her shoulders. Her eyes were huge and green and slightly slanted, more luminous than Stashe's, and when she smiled at Andrew, he felt dizzy for a moment, as he did sometimes when Stashe smiled. She was beautiful. She was not Stashe, but she was so like her that Andrew knew at once that she must be Stashe's counterpart among the folk who did not use iron. He whipped his glasses off and took another look as she came undulating towards him. She was wearing a hefty layer of glamour, like thick make-up all over, but she was still beautiful and still very like Stashe.

What does she think she needs that glamour for? Andrew thought irritably. "And who might you be?" he asked her.

She came and leaned against the piano in a pose that showed off her curves. Andrew was reminded of nothing so much as a singing star from the fifties. A glamour-girl, he thought. Cheesy.

The room filled with her perfume, thick and heady, like may blossom with a touch of mango. Her voice, when she spoke, was now artfully husky, with a chuckle in it. "I'm Queen Titania, of couse," she said. "Darling." She blew him a kiss from her lovely pink lips.

Andrew winced. "Then go away," he said. "I'm busy."

She pouted the lovely lips. "Darling, you can't send me away without knowing why I'm here!"

"I do know," said Andrew. "You want Aidan." And, he thought, it would be just like their luck if Aidan were to come cheerfully charging in here along with Rolf. He crossed the fingers of the hand that was still holding Adela Cain's letters and prayed that Aidan would stay a long, long way from this room.

"Of course I want him," she said. "Do you blame me? That boy is about the one true hold I can have over my husband. I wouldn't *harm* Adrian. I'd just take him away, quite kindly and hide him somewhere where Oberon will never find him. Oberon will kill him if he finds him, you know."

She came drifting towards Andrew, staring at him from those big greenish eyes. He could feel the glamour coming over him in waves. Don't panic! he thought. His girl students had often tried this sort of thing. Andrew knew he had had a reputation for being a very hard-hearted tutor. They had come to him with their essays unwritten, in spectacularly few clothes, and they had wept at him, and writhed at him, and ogled him, and coaxed him, and he had managed to remain quite unmoved by it all. He was supposed to be *good* at this sort of thing.

He found himself backing off into a corner of the sofa. "Why would your husband kill Aidan?" he said, rather desperately.

"Because Oberon won't be King here any more once his son knows who he is," Titania said dreamily. "They say that the old King vanishes away then. Oberon naturally wants to go on existing. So you see why I need Adrian, don't you, darling? Oberon will do anything I ask, once I have the boy."

She came closer. The muggy, floral scents coming off her made Andrew push himself even further into the corner of the sofa, feeling as if he was suffocating in a may tree. Or maybe a heavily perfumed bathroom. He tried to distract her. "And I suppose," he said, "that Mabel Brown, or whatever her name is, wants the same thing that you do?"

This did seem to distract Titania a little. "Oh, Mab!" she said, pouting. "Mab just wants Oberon to take her back as his wife again. She's so crude! And she's let herself get so *fat*! One really wonders what Oberon ever saw in her."

"And what does Mab aim to do with Aidan?" Andrew asked, trying to distract Titania for all he was worth. Why didn't Mrs Stock come in here to move the piano? Why couldn't Mr Stock appear at the French windows with another box of veg? Why couldn't *somebody* come?

Titania shrugged beautiful shoulders and came on again as she shrugged. "Oh, pooh! Who knows what stupid Mab would do! Kill the child probably, as soon as she's got what she wants. But I am Oberon's most recent wife. It's my *right* to take Adrian, don't you see?"

"No, I don't see," Andrew said.

By now Titania was close enough to put one hand on the arm of the sofa and the other on the back of it. She bent over Andrew, trapping him in his corner. Thick waves of her perfume rolled languidly over him. He found it hard to breathe. Damn it! Her scent was giving him asthma! Andrew had not had an asthma attack since he was a boy. He had forgotten how unpleasant they were.

"Oh, come on, Andrew Hope," Titania breathed. "Give me Adrian. You won't regret it."

Andrew stared down her cleavage and up at her pink, pouting lips, and at the glowing golden curl dangling near his nose. He might know just what she was doing and he might know why. He might know this was a time-honoured approach, but the trouble with this old fashioned method was that it worked. In spite of the knowledge, in spite of the asthma, Andrew could feel himself drifting under Titania's spell. Slowly, slowly, he knew he was going under. He was going to give her Aidan, even if it was only to get rid of her.

"Er – I don't think so," he managed to say.

"There!" Titania said, smiling brilliantly. "You're going to give me Adrian any moment now. Aren't you?" She bent further down to kiss him...

And Stashe came bursting in, waving a folded parchment with a big black seal on it. "Andrew! I found it! Look!" She stopped and stared at Titania bent over Andrew. "Who are you? What's going on?"

Titania looked round poisonously. For a moment her face was not beautiful at all. "Go away, woman," she said to Stashe.

"No, don't," said Andrew. He had never been so glad to see anyone in his life. Stashe was clean and modern and straightforward. Beside her, Titania looked elderly and unwholesome and tawdry. "This," he said, "is Queen Titania. She wants Aidan."

"She can't have him," said Stashe. "She can just get out."

"Oh, no," Titania said sweetly. "He invited me in, darling, and here I stay."

"I thought her voice was yours," Andrew explained.

"I meant you to think so," Titania purred. "I shall only go when you give me Adrian."

"Not if *I* have anything to do with it!" Stashe said. "You're getting out of here *now!*" She threw the parchment aside and ran at Titania.

Titania, quite unprepared, put her hands up weakly against Stashe. Stashe batted the hands aside, grabbed Titania by one shoulder and a handful of golden hair, and shook her. And shook her. "How *dare* you sneak in here!" Stashe said between her teeth, shaking. "How *dare* you try to seduce Andrew!" Shake, shake. Little fairy jewels began to pop off Titania and roll on the carpet.

"Unhand me!" Titania squealed, red in the face and most unqueenlike. "I *order* you to let me go this instant!"

"Don't you *dare* try to give me orders!" Stashe snarled, equally red in the face. She let go of Titania's hair in order to hit her round the head. Titania screamed and began to try to defend herself.

Andrew seized the opportunity to jump up out of the corner of the sofa, but once up, he was not at all sure what to do. Stashe and Titania were whirling and staggering around the room, each of them with her hands in the other's hair, Titania flailing and Stashe bashing. All Andrew could do was to keep dodging. Titania kept trying to bespell Stashe. Andrew felt each try as a heavy, scented gust. But as soon as she felt a gust of enchantment, Stashe hit Titania again and forced her to stop. Magic and small beads rattled round the room, from Stashe's high waistline as well as from Titania's dress. Andrew felt he ought to be saying, "Ladies, ladies!" and making them stop, but they had become two screaming, battling furies and were taking no notice of him at all. He dodged, desperately, crunching small beads underfoot and gasping in the puffs of scented magic, until it was clear that Stashe was winning. She was stronger than Titania and knew more about fighting. She got an armlock on the Fairy Queen and ran her to the French windows. There Stashe literally threw Titania out. Andrew saw Titania sail through the air and land with a thump on the grass.

"Get out and *stay* out!" Stashe shouted. "Don't you dare cross this threshold again!" As Titania crawled to her feet, Stashe stamped twice on the doorsill. "You cheap trollop!" she added as Titania started to limp away. She stamped a third time. "There." Stashe turned towards Andrew, dusting her hands together.

"I think she's probably quite an *expensive* trollop," Andrew said, trying not to laugh.

Stashe was not in the mood for jokes. A frown grew on her flushed face and she pushed her hair back aggressively.

Andrew laughed and hugged her to him. "Thank you," he said. "What a splendid girl you are! Will you marry me?"

"Yes, please," said Stashe, and she hugged him back.

They stared at one another, entranced.

Naturally, Mrs Stock chose that moment to come in, saying, "I have to tidy in here *some* time toda— Oh!" The look on her face was a mixture of shock, anger and fear of losing her job. She asked acidly, "Is this wedding bells I see, or just fooling about?"

Andrew said hastily, "Yes, Mrs Stock. Wedding bells. Be the first to congratulate us, please. And of course we hope that you'll continue to work for us just as usual."

"Huh!" retorted Mrs Stock. "Fat lot of use *she*'ll be at housework!"

"That's right," Stashe agreed happily. "I leave all that to my dad."

"And perhaps you could wait to tidy in here until this afternoon," Andrew added. "Stashe and I will be going into

Melton then to buy a ring and see about a licence."

"All right then," Mrs Stock said ungraciously, and went away.

"Oh dear," Andrew said.

"She'll come round," said Stashe. "Don't worry."

A while later, Andrew said, "Did you read those letters from Adela Cain?" Stashe nodded against his shoulder. "Then you'll know that Aidan *is* actually a distant cousin—"

"Fourth cousin," Stashe said, having worked that out days ago. She gave a shriek and jumped away from Andrew. "Oh, good heavens! I came in here to tell you I'd found that parchment! Where the hell *is* it?"

They searched. At first they could not find it anywhere. They found large numbers of beads, some of which were certainly precious stones. Stashe scooped them up and dumped them in a vase for safety. "We'd better take these to the Melton jewellers this afternoon," she was saying, when Andrew found the parchment under a chair.

It was in a sorry state, as crumpled as a used paper handkerchief. At some stage in the fight either Stashe or Titania had stamped her stiletto heel in the middle of the black seal and cracked it right across. It fell off as Andrew tried to smooth the parchment out and became black crumbs strewed across the carpet.

"Never mind," said Stashe. "What does it say?"

They leaned eagerly over the parchment. It was dated 1809. The first part was written in the black, flourishing letters that Andrew remembered from the letter from Mr Brown. It said:

> *I, Oberon King, being minded to take up a safe abode in this magical enclave of Melstone House, do order and enjoin Josiah Brandon, owner and keeper of said enclave, to extend his field-of-care to cover me and mine for all time while this Our seal stands unbroken. Said Josiah Brandon hereby agrees to keep my incursion secret from the world and from my wives. Also he agrees to prohibit or destroy any Counterparts of my folk who may arise by virtue of Our magics leaking into his field-of-care. I also enjoin him most strictly to cover the enchanted glass in the roof of his Chapel and to leave said Chapel derelict on pain of my extreme displeasure.*
>
> *Signed on this day of Midsummer 1809*
>
> *Oberon Rex*

The couple of lines below were in more ordinary writing, thick and black and angry-looking.

*I, Josiah Brandon, Magician and owner of
Melstone House and its field-of-care, agree to
all the above, unless and until the black seal of
Oberon is broken.
Signed,
                Josiah Brandon Esq.*

Interestingly, in the round, pale place where the seal had
been, the same writing had added:

*This was signed under duress. You, my
descendant, may now be free of it. J.B.*

This part had a fresh, almost recent look to it. When
Andrew ran a finger over it, he could tell that it had been
designed by Josiah to be invisible until the moment the seal
cracked. No doubt Mr Brown had been leaning over him,
waiting to affix the seal as soon as Josiah had signed the
agreement.

"Phew!" Andrew said. "Just as well the seal got broken!
I seem to have disobeyed his orders in all directions. What
do you think he'll do?"

"Let's see if we can find out," Stashe said, dragging
today's paper out from under a mixture of Adela Cain's

letters and Andrew's old comics.

They bent over the racing pages. The winner of the first race at Pontefract had been Queen's Mate. This struck Stashe and Andrew as so funny that they hardly noticed that the second horse home had been Reprisal, followed by Country Fair. They were still laughing at how exactly right Queen's Mate was when Tarquin put his head round the door.

"Stashe," he said anxiously, "what have you *done*? Are you all right?"

Stashe told him, ending with, "Then Andrew asked me to marry him and I said yes."

Tarquin was delighted. "I couldn't have hoped for better!" he said, more than once, and he waved his crutch in the air and hugged his daughter mightily. When he had calmed down a little he said, "Well, let's have a look at this contract then."

"Not so much a contract," Andrew said. "More a set of orders."

Tarquin read the crumpled parchment several times. "So it is," he said. "I wonder what he did to the poor man to make him sign it. Took his wife or his children hostage maybe. That seems to be their way. Is Aidan safe?"

"I hope so," said Andrew. "I gave him a fairly powerful talisman and he promised to wear it. But what I still want to know, Tarquin, is why it was so important to – ah – Mr Brown not to have counterparts in the village."

Tarquin pulled at his beard, considering. "I think," he said, "that if we have enough of them, it tips the balance of power to us humans – or at least makes both sides more equal. The coloured glass in that shed of yours does seem to show that things are tipping our way now. Brown won't like that."

"And why is my shed so important?" Andrew asked.

Tarquin was amused. "That I think I do know. Your Shaun *and* his counterpart are both working on it, aren't they? That makes their working very strong, so it does. It's old, that place, from long before old Mr Brandon and this poor Josiah who signed that contract. And to my mind, from the carvings I saw in it, it must belong to – well – let's say to one of those powers that even those who don't use iron have to bow to. My guess is that your whole field-of-care belongs to that power really. So Brown says cover the glass and let the building fall into ruin and none of the Brandons have anyone to appeal to. Brown can do as he likes, so he can. Does that make sense?" Andrew nodded. Tarquin's face went bright with another new thought. "Did your grandfather never tell you how to summon that power?" he asked.

Andrew stared into Tarquin's earnestly twinkling eyes

and tried to send his mind back to Saturday night, when the sight of his own signature on the comic Aidan was reading had caused him to remember so much. It was not easy. His mind kept going to Stashe instead, lovely, bossy, clever Stashe whom he was going to marry. He took hold of her hand. Then it was easier. He could hold her and still let his mind work.

Memory came at last. You said a string of old words, Jocelyn had told him, in a language that was no longer spoken. Andrew could see his grandfather now, standing with his back to the fire in this very room, slowly repeating the strange syllables, one by one. It almost felt as if his grandfather was *there*, at that very moment, staring at him, willing Andrew to remember. Andrew had been Aidan's age at the time and he had known he would never remember those words. So he had written those words down, sound by strange sound on – on – on… What had he been writing on? Something he had had in his hand. Of course! On one of those very comics!

Andrew let go of Stashe's hand and dived to collect the comics that first Aidan, and then Stashe and Titania, had left scattered around the room.

Chapter Fourteen

idan was startled and depressed to learn that Andrew and Stashe were getting married soon. It did not help that he had seen it coming.

It was Mrs Stock who sourly broke the news to him, when Aidan and Rolf came galloping in for lunch. Mrs Stock didn't exactly *say*, "They won't want *you* around now," but Aidan knew she meant it. He tried very hard to be as nice as Shaun was about it. Shaun beamed. He took Andrew's hand and shook it, up and down, up and down, with his hairstyle glittering. "Good," he said. "*Very* good, Professor."

Aidan had very little chance to say more than "Congratulations!" before Andrew and Stashe were off to Melton, Stashe clutching a rattling vase that she told Aidan was very valuable. Aidan blinked a bit. It struck him as a very ordinary and ugly vase, but he supposed Stashe knew what she was talking about.

Aidan mooched about with Rolf for the rest of that afternoon, anxiously wondering what would become of him now. He couldn't go back to the Arkwrights. He had arranged for them not to want him. Thinking about it, Aidan rather wished he could have thought of some other way to stop them sending people after him, but he had done it, and that was that now. Meanwhile he tried to avoid Mrs Stock, who was in her sharpest mood, and kept out of the way of Mr Stock. Mr Stock looked like the cat that had had the cream. Stashe was his niece and he was extremely proud of her. Mr Stock knew he had started it all by visiting Tarquin that day. He even whistled as he sorted out another huge box of vegetable discards.

And there was no football to take Aidan's mind off things. The football field was filling with tents and dusty lorries loaded with fairground machines. Where Aidan and his friends had played football, people were walking solemnly about, putting in markers for the roped off enclosures where the various competitions were going to be. At any other time, Aidan would have been highly interested and excited about Saturday's Fête, but not now. The field was just one more place to avoid.

To add to Aidan's gloom, Groil did not appear that

night. Andrew, helped by Stashe and Aidan, piled the woodshed roof with vegetable discards, but they were still there the next morning.

Ronnie Stock needed Stashe urgently that day. Andrew had a good mind to tell the man that he needed Stashe even more urgently, but at least he could send her off to the stables with a bright new emerald ring twinkling on her elegant ring finger. Titania's jewels had turned out to be worth quite a lot. With Stashe not there, Andrew felt almost as gloomy as Aidan. He firmly turned his mind to other urgent things. He could get on with his book, but his computer had gone wrong again, probably when Titania arrived. Anyway, this was not urgent, not nearly as urgent as Aidan, who was seriously in need of explanations. Andrew and Stashe had had a long talk about Aidan. Stashe was insistent that Andrew told Aidan exactly what the position was. "I know how I'd feel if everyone kept me in the dark," she said. So Andrew decided to talk to Aidan while they went on walking the boundary. This was urgent too. It proved the field-of-care was Andrew's and not Mr Brown's.

"Get your boots on and bring Rolf," he told Aidan. "We're walking the boundary again today."

Aidan listlessly agreed. He wanted to hit Rolf for being so glad to do it.

They walked down the village and started from the Stables – where else, with Stashe so near? – from the place by the gates of the Grange where the boundary wheeled off beyond the other side of the village. It was good walking weather, not too hot, not too cold, with just a hint of rain in the air. Andrew and Rolf appreciated it. Aidan didn't. Aidan was more unhappy still that the first bit meant they were definitely trespassing. The boundary curved through the gardens of the Grange, right across the corner of a rose bed and over a lawn, before plunging among a copse of ornamental trees. Aidan was not happy about this, not even slightly, until they came to a stile beyond the trees, where they had to lift Rolf over into the fields and heathland on the other side. There Rolf uttered an excited "Yip!" and set off with his nose down on the line of the boundary.

Then the only problem was keeping up with Rolf. Luckily, Rolf realised and kept coming back for them. As they toiled after Rolf's distant golden figure, Andrew began a careful explanation to Aidan.

"What?" Aidan said. "You mean I am your cousin?"

"Certainly," Andrew assured him. "Distant, but it means I have a perfect right to have you to live with us. More than the Arkwrights anyway. Stashe is going to look into what we have to do to make it official – whether we need to adopt you or get made your legal guardians. I probably need to be married before I can adopt you. Is that all right? Do you mind?"

Did he *mind*! Aidan felt his face stretching into a smile that beamed wider than any of Shaun's. "*Thanks!*" he managed to say. It was as if a heavy weight had been levered off his back and from inside his head. There was such a lightness to him that he began to walk faster and faster, still beaming. Perhaps, he thought, he might persuade Andrew that a telly in the box room wouldn't really be in his way. With a beanbag to sit on maybe. And he thought he could get round Stashe to let him have a mobile phone, if he went at it carefully. Oh, joy!

They were now walking up a long hill, among gorse bushes. Aidan was going so fast that Andrew struggled to keep up. He was more than a little out of breath as he gave the next part of the explanation. And six months ago, Andrew thought, I wouldn't have believed a word of what I'm saying now! Telling a boy that his father was Oberon and that his father wanted to kill him. Am I giving him too much of a shock?

Aidan was still too happy to feel much of a shock. The Puck had told him some of it after all. And Gran had always been very clear that Aidan's father was a very bad thing indeed. Aidan had always believed that. Instead, he worried about something Andrew had never expected. "Does that mean," he asked, "that I'm half *something else*?"

"They're not as different as everyone likes to think," Andrew panted, thinking of Stashe battling with Titania. What was the difference between two angry women? Except one of them was Stashe of course. "Think of yourself," he puffed, "as having the best of two worlds. A lot of people would give their eye teeth for a heredity like yours."

"Mm," Aidan said, taking this in. As long as it didn't show...

Up ahead of them, Rolf stopped and sat down. Warned by this, Aidan and Andrew stopped too. Andrew stood getting his breath back, wondering what Rolf had heard or smelt.

There seemed to be a jogger out on the faint path that marked the boundary. He came looming up over the brow of the hill, taller and taller, rushing towards them in great strides and huge leaps, most unlike the usual kind of jogger. He saw them and swerved away and went bounding down into the meadows below the hill, where they saw him dodging past bushes and splashing through patches of marsh. Over the brow of the hill after him came pouring a smoky stream of *somethings*. Whatever they were, they checked at the exact spot where the mighty jogger had left the path and then went pouring down into the meadows after him.

Andrew and Aidan both whipped off their glasses. Although the smoky stream was still hard to see, the long, galloping shapes of what might be dogs were part of it, and the upright, running figures of – maybe – men. The jogger they were after was much plainer.

"It's Groil!" Aidan said. "They're chasing him because he's got my wallet."

There was nothing either of them could do. Groil and his pursuers were going far too fast. Andrew led the way slowly upwards to where Rolf was sitting. Neither he nor Aidan could stop themselves from staring down into the meadows most of the time. Groil was jinking, turning, racing round bushes, and the smoky stream of the pursuit faithfully followed his exact path, even when he ran round in a circle. They watched Groil lead them into a figure-of-eight, leave them crossing their own path, mindlessly, and then set off uphill again in great energetic leaps. At that point the pack seemed to lose Groil. At any rate, just as Andrew and Aidan reached Rolf, Groil was nowhere to be seen, but the horde of pursuers was streaming uphill towards them.

Rolf, Andrew and Aidan all froze as the smoky pack came up against the line of the boundary just ahead. It seemed as if they could not cross it and Groil could. For a moment, they billowed round and round aimlessly. Then something in their midst cried out. A horn sounded. And the whole cloudy crowd of them came streaming downhill towards Andrew, Aidan and Rolf.

Andrew hastily pulled Aidan, and Aidan pulled Rolf, out into the hillside beyond the boundary. There they stood and watched the chase pour soundlessly past, mean dogs, big catlike creatures, Security in his woolly hat, manlike beings with stags' heads, staglike creatures with men's faces, and a crowd of tall, skinny people in golden helmets, who all looked rather like Mr Stock.

"They seem to have lost him," Andrew said. "And us," he added thankfully, as the chasers rushed away downhill and out of sight. He had had a feeling, for a moment, that the hunt had started to home in on Aidan, until Aidan had crossed the boundary.

They walked carefully back to the line of the boundary and climbed on up the grassland. Aidan was feeling guilty, wishing he had not asked Groil to keep that wallet for him. But then they passed a large gorse bush and Groil stood up out of it, laughing.

"This is fun," he said. "I go small and hard and they lose me."

"Are you sure you don't mind?" Aidan asked anxiously.

Groil shook his great shaggy head. "Not had so much fun for years," he said. "Hi, Rolf. You being tame these days?" He put a massive hand down on Rolf's back.

A look of extreme alarm came over Rolf's face. All four of his legs buckled. Before his legs could quite give way, Rolf was forced to change into boy shape, lying face down on the turf. "Stupid!" he said over his shoulder.

Groil grinned. "That always happens when I lean on him," he said. "Funny that."

"I'll bite your leg," Rolf said.

Groil laughed, waved to Aidan and Andrew, and went bounding away down into the meadows again.

"Oaf!" said Rolf. It turned into a bark as he went back to dog shape.

"They must have known one another for ages," Aidan said to Andrew. "I think they tease each other all the time."

They went on. Beyond the top of the hill, the boundary took a wide curve. To balance the bulge where the Manor was, Andrew thought. It was so much wider than the oval shape Andrew had been predicting, that they only walked half of it that day and had to come back to the village by a cart track level with the lane that led to Melstone House.

They got back to the house to find that Mrs Stock had made cauliflower cheese again. She was not going to forgive Andrew for marrying Stashe in a hurry. Mr Stock had also been in again, with bundles and bundles of weeded-out carrots. Andrew thought those could possibly have been a reward. But there were far too many to eat, so they put them up on the roof for Groil, on top of yesterday's heap. Aidan anxiously hoped that Groil would manage to get back to eat them soon.

He must have done. The vegetables were gone the next morning, carrots and all. That's a relief! Groil must have worked up quite an appetite! Aidan thought, while he waited impatiently to set off walking the boundary again. Stashe was back that day and Andrew did not seem able to leave her side.

They got going in the end. They were halfway down the drive, with Rolf charging ahead, when Stashe came racing after them. "Wait! Wait! You must come and see this. Both of you!" They turned back, to Rolf's annoyance. He sat down in the drive and yawned disgustedly.

Stashe had begun unpacking the third box. The first layer had been more of Andrew's comics collection, mixed in with numbers of old Jocelyn's irritable notes to himself. Andrew picked one up at random and read, *O. Brown trying to take over my wood again. What does he make all that barbed wire out of?* Ah, he thought. So he's done this before, has he? There had been no sign of the barbed wire when Andrew first came into his inheritance. He would very much have liked to know what his grandfather had done to get rid of it.

The rest of the box contained nothing but fat, dusty cardboard folders. Andrew took the one that Stashe handed to him and opened it dubiously. It was full of accounts from an investment firm. Form after form announced that Jocelyn now had so many thousands of pounds invested and that these had earned him so much more money that Andrew's mind reeled.

"They're *all* like that," Stashe said. "There's a small fortune here, Andrew. Did you know about them?"

"No," Andrew said. "I only knew about what he had in the bank."

"Then I could *smack* Mrs Stock for bundling them all in this box!" Stashe said. "And you take a look at *this* one, Aidan." She passed Aidan a much thinner folder.

Aidan, who had been standing by, rather bored, stared at the front of it. It was labelled in Jocelyn's writing: *Blind Trust for Aidan Cain. The least I can do after my failure with Melanie.* Inside, official forms stated that, ten years ago, Jocelyn Brandon had set aside some thousands of pounds, to grow into more thousands of pounds, until Aidan was eighteen. Then the money was Aidan's.

"Wow!" said Aidan. He had to whisk his glasses off, because his eyes flooded with tears. He found himself longing, hopelessly, that he could have known Andrew's old grandfather. He must have been quite something, to do this for a baby he had never met.

"Good man, wasn't he?" Stashe said. "Mind you, he could be a right old curmudgeon too! He used to growl at me and call me 'Tarquin's silly little bitch'. I put my tongue out at him once or twice. Anyway, Andrew, I'll get on transferring these to your name, shall I? Don't worry. I know just what to do. I did it for Ronnie Stock when his mother died." Stashe took hold of one end of the box and began to tow it towards Andrew's study. She stopped. "Is your computer still working?"

"It went down when Titania appeared," Andrew said, sighing.

"Then I know how to put it right," Stashe said and went on towing the box. They heard her in the distance muttering, "Honestly, I could smack Mrs Stock!" as she went.

Andrew and Aidan set off for the second time. Andrew had decided they would join the boundary where it crossed the Melton road, this time, and walk back to the cart track they had taken yesterday. So they went up the village, past the church and the football field. There was now a gate across the entry to the field and a big notice on the gate saying that Mr Ronald Stock would open the Fête at 2.30 on Saturday.

"It gets going before that," Andrew told Aidan. "As I remember, there is usually a procession with the band and people in fancy dress. The entries to the competitions have to be in by midday. Mr Stock will be wheeling in his vegetables most of the morning. He practically empties the garden for this."

Aidan stood on tiptoe and saw more tents beyond the hedge and a glimpse of a roundabout being put up. He was suddenly quite excited about this Fête. He had never been to one before. It looked as if it was going to be fun.

Otherwise their walk was uneventful that day. They found the place on the Melton road and a stile that led to the same faint path that they had followed yesterday. When they were in any doubt about where the boundary was, Rolf found it for them. There was no sign of Groil anywhere. Andrew suggested that Groil was probably sleeping off the vast meal he had eaten last night. Aidan hoped so. He hoped Groil was keeping thoroughly small and hard and well hidden.

As they walked home down the cart track, Andrew sighed and said, "Well, there's only one thing more for tomorrow and that's getting round the Manor grounds somehow. I vote we try to get round outside Mr Brown's barbed wire. It must be possible. He can't have covered the whole countryside in it. Can you help us do that, Rolf?"

Rolf looked up and nodded. He was thinking of supper.

"Won't that make your field-of-care bigger?" Aidan asked.

"Possibly," Andrew said. "But I'm not going to let Brown get the better of us. Hurry up, Aidan. I want to get back before Stashe has to leave."

Stashe had waited for them, saying she had made a good start on the folders and would do more tomorrow. Shaun had waited too. He wanted Andrew to come and look inside the shed and see what it looked like now he had finished it. He waved both hands and looked so pleading that Andrew went there at once, without taking his walking boots off.

Once inside, he stood and marvelled. The place glowed. In the multicoloured light from the window, the carved walls were a luminous honey colour, where small creatures peeped out from among a riot of tendrils, leaves and flowers, and man-shaped people seemed to dance in a line that wound in and out and through the other carvings, up and down across each wall. Shaun had made efforts to clean the floor too. Andrew had assumed it was concrete, but it was actually honey-coloured tiles, cracked and old but still beautiful. It all made the mower, sitting in the middle of the floor, look completely out of place. I must find somewhere else to keep the thing, Andrew thought while he was telling Shaun what a marvellous job he had done.

Shaun beamed and then looked anxious. "What do you want me to do now, Professor?" he said.

Trying not to leave mud from his boots on the tiles, Andrew took Shaun outside. He pointed to the thistles, nettles and small struggling blackberry plants that were crowding round the base of the walls. The walls themselves outside were brick, covered in old whitewash. "You can clear all these weeds away," he told Shaun, "and then give the walls a coat of white paint. This place is a chapel, as you told me once, and it ought to look as good outside as it is inside."

Shaun looked relieved. Andrew could see Shaun had been afraid that his usefulness was now over and Andrew would dismiss him. "I'll do that tomorrow, Professor," Shaun said. "I've almost finished my robot. For the Fête," he explained, when Andrew looked blank.

"Good. Great," Andrew said, and found himself adding, "and after that, there are hundreds of jobs for you inside the house."

Shaun's hands were waving happily as he went away.

He was rather late the following morning. "Up half the night finishing the robot," he explained when he arrived with Mrs Stock, who was also late.

"I'll give you robots!" she said. "I was up at five,

pinning prices on my old clothes. And I wish you wouldn't encourage Trixie, Shaun. That sideshow of hers makes me feel ill."

Andrew did not attend to much of this. He was talking to Stashe and waiting for Aidan to get his second-best boots on. Aidan was slow. His legs ached and there was almost a blister on his left foot. He was wondering if all this walking was good for him. But Rolf and Andrew were determined to finish the last lap of the boundary, so Aidan sighed and went with them.

He cheered up when they came level with the football field. There was bunting up now. If he peered over the new gate, he could see a platform at the other end being covered with flags and a red carpet.

"I'm really looking forward to this Fête," he told Andrew. "I've never been to one before."

Andrew was startled. He had not considered that the Fête was anything to do with him or with Aidan. He remembered being bored out of his mind when his grandfather had taken him to to admire Mr Stock's Prize Vegetables, year after year. "You may not enjoy it," he said.

"Oh, I know I will," Aidan said. "Will I need any money?"

Andrew sighed. "There's an entrance fee," he said, "and

all the stalls and rides cost money. All right. I'll take you to it."

Aidan's joy at this carried him round most of a tedious morning, while he and Andrew and Rolf walked carefully along outside Mr Brown's massive coils of barbed wire. There was so much of it that they were forced almost over to the road in places, and in other places found themselves stumbling among nettles and clawed by brambles that were almost as bad as the wire. The weather was hot and grey, which seemed ideal conditions for midges, mosquitoes and horseflies. When they sat down for lunch halfway, they were bitten all over, even Rolf. For the rest of the way, Rolf had to keep sitting down to give himself big, thumping scratchings.

Aidan was not enjoying himself at all by then. The almost-blister from yesterday had developed into a full-grown one, large, squashy and painful. He could feel another growing on his other foot. But at last, long last, the walk was almost over. They were walking on the road by then, because Mr Brown's defences had filled the space between that and the marshy place, and it was a great relief to Aidan when they arrived at the dip in the road and he knew they had finished.

It was even more of a relief to see Wally Stock driving his cows out into the field beside the road. Wally waved to

Andrew and came over. He wanted to talk, as usual. Aidan sat thankfully in the grass beside the scratching Rolf, while Wally told Andrew what a terrible price the Fête Committee was having to pay for the hire of the bouncy castle and how unreliable some of the Fair people were.

"And what's Mr Brown up to in that wood?" Wally asked eventually. This seemed to be what he had really come over to say. "I thought it was *your* wood."

"It is," Andrew said.

"Well, you better look into it," Wally said. "It's all barbed wire in there now. Man with a dog turned me out of it when I went in to get a sheep that had got herself caught on the wire."

"*What*?!" Andrew was, for a moment, almost too angry to speak. What was the *point*, he thought, of trudging right round the boundary, when Mr Brown quietly expanded to take over from inside? "Come on, Aidan," he said curtly. He waved to Wally and set off in long, angry strides towards the wood, with Rolf bounding ahead and Aidan limping behind.

They came to the sheep field. Rolf had almost reached the wood by the time Aidan had clattered the gate shut behind him. Andrew, halfway across the field, could see that the wood was full of pale coils of wire between the trees. He swore.

A grey, snarling dog shot out from among the trees and raced towards Andrew. It was coming straight for him and he knew it meant to attack. He stood still, wishing he had a stick. But his walking boots were quite stout. He supposed he could kick it.

Chapter Fifteen

efore Andrew could think what to do, or even move, Rolf came hurtling round the edge of the wood and threw himself on the grey dog. The air filled with snarls, growls and hoarse yelping – all the clamour of a serious dog fight. The golden body and the grey one rolled in a tangle on the grass.

Aidan forgot his blister and ran. "*No*, Rolf!" he shouted. He remembered only too well what thick muscles that grey dog had and the drool on its yellow fangs. It didn't seem fair that Rolf should die defending Andrew. But he had only run about ten yards when the fighting yellow body beside the wood dissolved into a blur and then into a small boy, clinging to the back of the grey dog, holding it by one ear and punching its head mightily.

The grey dog howled with pain and heaved the boy

away with a twist of its huge shoulders. Then it too became misty. It rolled over and it was Security, in his ragged coat with his knitted cap on crooked, diving to to strangle Rolf with his big knotty hands. But by this time Rolf was a dog again, snapping at Security's hands. Security snatched his hands away and scrambled to kick Rolf in the head. Rolf dodged the flailing boot and became a boy again. And Security was a dog then, snarling and going for Rolf's bare legs.

Aidan pelted onwards, frankly fascinated by the way were-dogs fought. They were man, boy, yellow dog, grey dog, boy, man again, almost quicker than Aidan could think. Andrew was circling warily in on them, watching for a chance to kick the grey dog in the head. But the changes were too fast for him to find his target. The snarling, hoarse shouting and screams were horrible.

"Go it, Rolf!" Aidan panted. "*Get* him!"

The fight was over as he said it. Security rose up into a man again, with one big boot drawn back to kick Rolf as soon as Rolf's yellow blur became a dog. But the yellow blur dissolved into a boy instead. As a boy, Rolf ran at Security head down and butted him violently in the stomach. Security went "Bwah!" as all the breath left his body, then toppled over on to his back. Andrew saw his chance and, quite unscrupulously, raced in and kicked

Security in his knitted hat. Several times. It helped that he did not think of Security as human any more.

"Get out!" he roared. "Get out at once!"

Security rolled over into a cowed, dazed dog. Andrew threatened to kick him again, but Security did not wait. He put his whiplike tail between his bulging back legs and bolted away into the wood. Rolf sank down on to his stomach, panting out a pink triumphant tongue. His plumed tail flapped on the grass. Didn't I do well?! every inch of him said.

Aidan dashed up and hugged him. "You were brilliant!" he said. "You used your brain." Rolf licked Aidan's face contentedly.

"I'm afraid it's not over yet," Andrew said.

Aidan looked up and saw twenty more grey-hatted figures standing at regular intervals along the edge of the wood. They were all identical and they all reminded Aidan – just faintly – of Shaun. As he looked, they began to advance out into the field.

Andrew was furious. This was *his* wood, *his* property, *his* field-of-care. How *dare* they set a pack of were-dogs on him in his own place! He had just walked round every inch of it, making it his own, hadn't he?

His own. It dawned on Andrew that he was now able to draw on all the power in his field-of-care, even

Mr Brown's, since he had just walked round the Manor too. He drew in a deep breath and, with it, the whole strength of Melstone. It made him feel huger than Groil. He spread out both arms and then flung them forward in a great scooping push. The power of it roared in his ears.

"Get out of here!" he shouted over the noise of the power. "*Get out of here NOW!*"

And he rolled the lot away backwards through the wood, all the grey-hatted figures and the coils of barbed wire, tumbling over and over. Beyond, he could feel most of the barbed wire melting away around the Manor walls. But not all of it. It stopped at one sparse coil and the Securities stopped when they were behind the ruined wall. He did not seem to be able to send them any further than that, although the trees thrashed about in the storm of magic. Leaves flew off them as if it were autumn and birds came up in a screaming cloud. But that was all. Mr Brown had clearly done something that fixed his boundaries at the walls. Andrew made sure that they could not come any further again by stamping three times, like Stashe when she threw Titania out.

"And *stay* there!" he said as the storm died down a little. Aidan said, "Wow!"

There were shouts in the distance. To Andrew's

surprise, Mr Stock was rushing across the sheep field, carrying a spade.

"Need any help?" he asked as he approached.

"No thanks. I think I've fixed it for the moment," Andrew said. He was feeling strange. Nothing he had done in his life had been like this.

Mr Stock surveyed the heaving trees. He nodded. "Trying to take over again, wasn't he?" he said. "Old Mr Brandon warned me he might. They need a lesson, to my mind. I'll think of something after the Fête. Let's make what you did stick for now." He went to the edge of the wood and drove the spade into the earth, so that it stood upright. "Iron," he said. "That should hold them for a day or so."

They went back to Melstone House. There, Andrew sat rather limply in a chair in the kitchen, while Stashe attended to Aidan's blisters.

"Honestly, Aidan," she said, "you should have mentioned these before. They deserve to be in the *Guinness Book of Records*. I've never seen any so big."

Aidan agreed with her. He was feeling very smug and cared for, with Stashe's shining fair head bent over him, smelling of clean hair mixed with wafts of disinfectant, and Stashe's face turning up to him and smiling every so often. Rolf groaned enviously. He was lying where he was most in the way, stiff all over from the fight, waiting for Aidan to notice him.

Mrs Stock sniffed as she got ready to go home. She still had not forgiven Andrew. "You'll be lucky to get to the Fête, any of you," she said as she opened the back door. "Cauliflower cheese in the oven, Professor. If there *is* a Fête to go to," she added, looking up at the sky. "It feels like thunder out here. At least if they do have to cancel the Fête we'll be spared Trixie's dreadful sideshow. Look on the bright side." She shut the back door behind her with a snap.

"I can't *wait* to see what Trixie's doing," Aidan said. "I hope it doesn't rain."

"It does feel like thunder," Stashe agreed.

It did feel that way, although the sky was clear. Andrew knew it was the storm of magic he had raised. It had sunk to a sort of uneasiness at the back of things by then, and there it stayed all evening. It was still there late that night, after Tarquin had fetched Stashe home and Aidan had gone to bed, when Andrew let Rolf out for Rolf to hobble about on the lawn squirting half-heartedly at thistles. I wish my grandfather had told me how you stopped such a thing, Andrew thought, watching Rolf limp upstairs to share Aidan's bed. But I don't think he ever did. Andrew locked the front door and went into the kitchen to make sure the back door was locked too.

Moonlight was blazing in slantwise through the coloured glass, casting misty squares of colour on the floor, faint purple, pale, pale green and red that was hardly more than a smear. Andrew looked at the glass itself and found himself jumping, with surprise that was almost fear. The faces there were so clear and so easy to recognise. Pulled by the strength of the magic coming in with the moonlight, Andrew went up to the glass and stared through the panes.

The magic blasted in at him, icy but not cold.

He could feel it now, coming in from vast distances, and he knew it was age-old, as old as gravity, older than earth. As a boy, he had always wondered why his grandfather called magic "the fifth power" and then grumbled at the stupidity of scientists for not recognising it. He could almost feel his grandfather, here in the kitchen behind him, urging and imploring him to understand. And Andrew did understand. In a shuddering leap, rather like the strange moment when he had understood all about History, he knew that magic was one of the great forces of the universe, that had come into being right at the beginning, along with gravity and the force that held atoms together, as strong, or stronger, than any force there. Stronger, definitely. At need, magic could dissolve atoms and reassemble them, as it did when Rolf changed from dog to child. It was a great power, to be used with great care.

Now that he understood, Andrew could feel magic pouring in, homing in on Melstone from light years away. It was being *collected* here. Someone, long ago, had set up the two sets of enchanted glass, the one here in the kitchen and the one in the roof of the shed, to act like the two poles of an enormous horseshoe magnet, pulling magic into the field-of-care. The Brandons' main task was to protect this glass. They were supposed to use it for the good of the earth. But as soon as he knew this, Andrew could feel that at least half the magic was being drawn off into the Manor, where Mr Brown lived, feeding on the field-of-care like a slug on a lettuce.

Andrew smiled then and thought of Mr Stock. Mr Stock was paranoid about slugs.

He went on staring at the glass for a long time, drenched in moonlit magic, wondering what to do about Mr Brown, wondering about the various uses of the colours that the glass split the magic into. He had inklings about that, but he knew it would take months or maybe years of study to use the colours accurately. No, to get rid of Mr Brown he would have to use the purple pane, the powerful glass that brought in all the others. How to do it without harming Aidan was the problem...

"Fête today," Aidan said to Rolf as he looked into the fridge that Saturday morning. Rolf groaned with his chin on his paws. "All that shape-changing was bad for him," Aidan explained to Andrew. "He's bruised all over. Can I give this cauliflower cheese to Groil?"

"If you like," Andrew said, yawning. The magic-filled night had left him feeling bloated and slow.

Aidan whistled as he took the cauliflower cheese to the larder and put the bowl of it into the box he had carefully labelled "GROILFOOD". He was coming to dislike cauliflower cheese almost as much as Andrew did. "And I know what," he said, coming out of the larder, "I can go down to the shop and get you a paper."

"Only if you're wearing the silver charm," Andrew said, sleepily making coffee. "Tell Rosie to put the paper on my account."

"Wearing it," Aidan said, jingling the charm on its chain. He had become fond of the way it lay warm against his collarbone. He swallowed a bowl of cereal and said, "Coming, Rolf?" Rolf groaned again, mightily. No. Aidan set off cheerfully on his own to see what was going on in the village.

Aidan was not disappointed. Much was going on. Mr Stock rumbled across Aidan's path trundling a wheelbarrow in which reposed the mighty zeppelin marrow, a green and yellow monster of a marrow carefully packed around with turf to prevent it from bruising. At the end of the lane, Aidan met Mrs Stock pushing an old pram piled high with old clothes for her traditional stall.

"Doing this early," she explained to Aidan. "I have to get back and make my cake for the Best Sponge competition. Tell the professor that Shaun's on his way. He's just finishing his Best Robot."

And so it went on, all the way to the shop. Aidan passed person after person with barrows or old pushchairs, or carrying mysterious tins or packages, each of them making for the competition tent in the football field. In the shop, Rosie Stock was cursing. Her Best Sponge had gone flat as a pancake, she said, and she was having to make do with Best Rock Cakes instead.

Aidan bought the paper and slipped off back to Melstone House. Shaun was just arriving. "My robot's the greatest!" he told Aidan, waving his arms and starfishing his fingers. "Does things you'd never believe. Make sure you see it." And he put a copy of the same paper on the kitchen table.

"Curses!" Aidan said. "Shall I take my paper back?"

"You don't need an excuse to snoop round the village surely?" Andrew said, opening Shaun's paper and looking for the racing results. "We can always use newspaper."

Aidan laughed and darted off again, to spend a happy morning watching the roundabout being powered up and coloured rolls of plastic being delivered and pumped into a bouncy castle. Shaun took himself off to the shed, saying wistfully over his shoulder that they always said he was too big for the bouncy castle. "But I bounce real careful, Professor. It's not fair!"

"Shame," Andrew agreed without listening. He was puzzling at the result from yesterday's first race at Goodwood. Rich Ronnie had won it, followed by Takeover Brown and Freeforall. "Now what is *that* supposed to mean?" he was saying to himself when Stashe breezed in, carrying a third copy of the same paper. Andrew laughed. So did Stashe.

"Three times is the charm," she said, giving Andrew a swift kiss. "Sorry. The paper was just my excuse to get out of the house. Dad's got ten Best Roses and six rose holders and he can't make up his mind which to enter. He's cooking rock cakes and sponges and trying to ice his Best Iced Cake while he dithers, and he's still got Best Bunch of Roses and Best Vase of Flowers to do. I tell you, it's bedlam in there!"

"I can see it is," Andrew said, still laughing. It was wonderful how Stashe and laughter seemed to go together. "But what do you make of this result?"

Stashe took up one of the extra papers and examined the

racing page. "What this means," she said, "is that you're not as good at this as I am. What were you trying to find out?"

"Whether it's safe for Aidan to go to the Fête," Andrew said. "After all, Brown's going to be there and Takeover Brown came second—"

"To Rich Ronnie and Ronnie Stock's going to open it," Stashe said. "That looks like the main event and it's got nothing to do with Aidan. Let's see what it says won the last race at Lingfield then." She read out, "Thunderstorm came first and Gigantic and Rain of Fire tied for second. Honestly, Andrew, all I can see there is bad weather. And seeing that this was the last race, we can hope that it holds off until later. Oh, let him go, Andrew. He'll go mad if you tell him he can't, and he'd probably sneak off there anyway."

Andrew sighed. He had hoped to be spared the boredom of the Fête.

He spent most of the morning watching the weather. In this he was not alone. Everyone in Melstone watched the sky and muttered that it felt like thunder. There were clouds, true, but high up, with hazy silver edges. The air felt hot and thick. But no rain came. By two o'clock, when the procession started, Andrew was resigned to the fact that the Fête would go ahead. He and Stashe went with Aidan to the end of the lane to watch the procession go by.

People carrying banners came first. Naturally there was a Best Banner competition. Aidan was a little pitying here. He had seen much better ones a couple of years back, when Gran took him to Notting Hill to watch the Carnival there. But he did concede that the billowing red dragon with MELSTONE on its side, which took four men to carry it, was probably quite good. Andrew preferred the stark black and white one that unfolded to show FÊTE in white letters on the black parts. "Huh!" Stashe said and laughed with delight at the motorbike disguised as an elephant, on which rode no-good boy Arnie Stock dressed as an Indian rajah. He was encased in a sort of cage with MELSTONE RULES on it in curly letters. The rest of Melstone agreed with Stashe. There were cheers and yells of, "Nice one, Arnie!" up and down the hedges from people walking in the road to watch.

The yells and whistles were almost drowned out by the band, who came next, marching quite smartly and playing the traditional Melstone Dance tune. It was a strange tune, jolly and sad at once. Stashe told Aidan that folklorists were always on about it. Aidan would have asked more, but he was distracted by seeing his football friend, Jimmy Stock, in a big and baggy uniform, playing the cornet in the band. Jimmy shot him a look as he marched past that said, "Don't you dare laugh!" and Aidan had to turn away or he would have started to giggle. He was quite glad when the band thumped onwards and was followed by the morris men, striding jingling after. They were to give a display of dancing once Ronnie Stock had opened the Fête.

The procession was surprisingly long. Beautifully groomed ponies came next, whose small, solemn riders looked thoroughly nervous at the thought of the competitions they were entered for. They were followed by equally tense people with dogs on leads who were entered for the Obedience and Obstacle Course. None of the dogs looked nervous or anything like obedient. They kept trying to fight each other.

Aidan thought of Rolf, left lying groaning on the living-room floor. He wondered if it would be cheating to enter Rolf for the competitions next year. Probably. He couldn't see Andrew letting him or Rolf get away with it. Pity. They were bound to win.

Meanwhile, the Children's Fancy Dress entrants were coming by, marching, shuffling and – in the case of the kid disguised as a tube of toothpaste – tottering past. There were enormous numbers of them. If he craned to look, Aidan could see them winding away into the distance, filling the road.

"What happens if a car or a lorry wants to come past?" he asked.

"Oh, they have police on duty to hold up the traffic," Stashe said. She craned out too. "I can just see a policewoman down the end there, I think."

At this, Andrew craned to look as well. There *was* a dim figure in the distance, who seemed to be holding up a few cars, but although he took his glasses off and put them on again, he simply could not tell whether it was a real policewoman or Mabel Brown pretending to be one. He checked that Aidan was still wearing his silver charm and, just to be on the safe side, he said, "I vote we all walk up and watch everyone arriving at the Fête."

They did this, sidling along the verge and being jostled by other people doing the same. They reached the football ground just as the band was turning in through the gate, while Wally Stock held it wide for them and the band's music clashed with the mechanical tune from the roundabout. There were two policemen on duty in the road there. One was holding up a line of cars with interested faces leaning out of them, and the other was directing more cars into the field opposite, which was labelled CAR PARK FOR MELSTONE FÊTE ONLY. Everything seemed to be orderly and unthreatening, Andrew thought, with relief.

They stood among the rest of the spectators and watched the procession all over again. There was quite a gap between the dog owners and the Fancy Dress children by now, almost certainly caused by the child dressed as a tube of toothpaste. They watched one of the Darth Vaders take her by her almost hidden hand and haul her through the gate. Then the rest of the children could go streaming through: gypsies, a skeleton, several more Darth Vaders, Supermen, Batmen, brides, footballers, fairies – lots of those – butterflies with big purple wings and crowds of aliens. Very realistic most of those aliens were, mostly green, with bobbing antennae on their foreheads…

Hang *on*! Andrew thought and looked at Aidan. Aidan was looking dubiously at those aliens, wondering if he had seen them before. "Would you like to go home now?" Andrew murmured to him.

As he spoke, the policewoman went past, shepherding the last of the aliens. She was definitely Mabel Brown. "I really think we should go away," Andrew said.

"*Please*, no!" Aidan said. "I want to see what prizes Mr Stock has won."

"And I've got to be here," Stashe said. "I promised Ronnie."

"In that case, we must be very careful to stay together," Andrew said, wondering how feeble this made him.

Wally Stock shut the main gate with a clang and opened the small gate beside it. Then he went behind a table with a cash box and books of tickets on it. "Selling tickets now!" he bawled. "Please form an orderly queue. Each ticket is a raffle ticket and entitles the bearer to enter for sumptuous prizes."

As cars began to go by in the road behind them, Aidan, Andrew and Stashe joined the other onlookers and shuffled forward through the small gate to buy their tickets. Out in the field everything seemed orderly and unthreatening again. The band was taking seats to one side of the platform. The roundabout was turning, but with no one on it. The bouncy castle was empty as yet. Someone was up on the platform testing the microphone in front of a row of chairs. Other people were arranging ponies, dogs and Fancy Dress children inside the different enclosures. The only odd thing was that there were very few aliens inside those ropes and no sign at all of Mabel Brown.

"It does feel like thunder," Stashe said, looking nervously at the sky.

The clouds were as they had been all morning, hazy and silver-edged, and the air was perhaps a little heavier, but there was no sign of rain. Stashe led Aidan and Andrew over to the tents and stalls against the hedge to the right. Opposite, the bouncy castle was suddenly filled with children and there was a long queue outside the ice-cream van. The Fête was definitely under way. This side, beyond the noise of the Fair, Mrs Stock was presiding over a stall covered with artistic heaps of colourful clothing.

"My forecast is for rain," Mrs Stock told them as they passed. She picked up a large golfing umbrella and waved it at them.

"I hope she's wrong," Stashe said.

They moved on beside a jewellery stall, a pottery stall, a stall selling eye-catching heaps of home-made fudge, and the stall Aidan slowed down beside, piled with more home-made cakes and pastries than he thought even Groil could eat in a week. But Andrew and Stashe kept going. Aidan sighed and followed them past the beer tent. This tent was mysteriously full of people who seemed to be well into their second pints. But it's only been open five minutes! Aidan thought. There was singing in there already.

Beyond the beer tent was a small structure massively filled with Trixie. Andrew and Stashe stopped as if they couldn't help themselves.

Trixie was sitting in a wide chair holding a notice which said GUESS MY WEIGHT!!! She was wearing an enormous, shapeless green garment that was probably meant to be Hawaiian – at any rate, she had a garland round her neck and paper flowers in her hair – and she had stuffed this green garment with pillows, enough to make her look twice her usual size. She was gross. She was enormous.

Shaun was standing on the grass outside, shouting, "Guess the lady's weight. Fifty pence a guess. Prize of £50 to the winner. Roll up, roll up! Hello, Professor. Don't my mum look a scream?"

Trixie was giggling and preening at the joke. "I reckon no one's going to guess right," she said. "Like to have a guess?"

"Certainly," Andrew said politely. He was thinking that Trixie looked more than ever like Mabel Brown in this get-up. "Are we guessing in kilos or pounds?"

"Oh, I'm doing both," Trixie said. She pointed cheerily to two bathroom scales on the grass beside her chair. "Come four o'clock, I weigh myself on both and Shaun shouts out the name of the nearest guess."

Andrew paid over money for the three of them and they all guessed. Andrew guessed in stones, Stashe in pounds and Aidan guessed one hundred kilos because he thought that was a lot. Trixie, laughing heartily, carefully wrote the guesses down in an exercise book and told them to remember to stick around for four o'clock.

They left Shaun shouting and Trixie laughing and made for the next tent where the competition entries were. That was where they all really wanted to be.

Chapter Sixteen

The dim, hot, grassy space inside the tent was lined with long tables carefully covered with spotless white cloths, as if someone was preparing for a banquet. The entries were dotted along them. Some were very sparse, like the Best Bunch of Wild Flowers. No one had entered for that except Mary Stock, aged nine. She had won First, Second and Third Prize for a remarkable collection of dandelions. By contrast, the Best Home-made Robots covered most of a long table. There were cardboard constructs, Meccano creatures, Lego Daleks, things made of dustbins and junk, things with wheels, things with legs, things that steamed rather ominously. Towering out of them was a tall, man-shaped silver robot, most impeccably and neatly made. It had flashing blue eyes and a mechanical voice that kept saying, "I am Robot Appleby, at your service, sir or madam." Then it raised one hand and bowed.

"Wow! Look at that!" Aidan said.

This robot had a gold card propped against it: *First Prize, Shaun Appleby.*

"Oh, good! Shaun will be pleased!" Aidan said.

They all three stared at Shaun's robot with smiles of family pride for a moment, before moving on past the Best Home-made Jams and Chutneys – where Andrew noticed that Mrs Stock had won Second Prize for the tomato chutney he had told her to make – and arriving at the Best Vase of Flowers.

There were a lot of vases and they were all impressive, but no one Andrew or Aidan knew had won. They noticed, sadly, that there was no Prize card propped against the vase labelled *T. O'Connor.*

"Mrs Blanchard-Stock *always* wins this one," Stashe said disgustedly. "She's one of the judges too. It's not fair. Let's hope Dad's won Best Single Rose at least."

But, alas, when they reached the array of rose holders, they found the golden First Prize card propped against a blowsy golden yellow rose labelled *Mr O. Brown.* Mrs Blanchard-Stock had won Second and Third Prize for a red rose and a white one, both quite ordinary. Tarquin's rose, a perfect creamy whorl with delicate pink edges, had won nothing at all.

"I've a good mind to change these cards over!" Stashe said angrily. "Do you think I dare?"

Aidan caught sight of Tarquin on the other side of the table. He looked across, meaning to tell Tarquin that his rose was by far the best, and realised that the face peering at him between the rose holders was not Tarquin's after all. It had no beard and it looked sly.

"Don't any of you try anything," the Puck said.

Aidan's hand flew to the talisman round his neck. It was still there. By the time his fingers touched it, the Puck was gone.

They came to the bakery section next, smelling deliciously of cake and new bread. The real Tarquin was there, propped on one crutch, grinning merrily, making the best of things. He said to them, "At least I won Best Sponge Cake. By way of compensation, so it is. *And* a Second for Rock Cakes too."

"I don't think Mr Brown eats cake," Andrew murmured.

Aidan said loyally, "I think *your* rose was *best*!"

"Yes, you've been cheated, Dad," said Stashe.

"Never mind. There's always next year," Tarquin said.

Tarquin went with them to the last table at the back of the tent, where the vegetables were. This was by far the largest set of entries of the lot. When Aidan touched the table, it creaked noticeably under its sheer weight of Prize Marrows, Largest Broad Beans, Bunches of Best Carrots, Best Boxes of Mixed Veg, Prize Onions and displays of carefully polished Roots – not to speak of the load of Prize Fruits up the other end. Melstone people seemed to have devoted the entire year to growing Prize Produce.

Halfway along stood Mr Stock. His arms were folded and the glower on his face was enough to curl a Prize Lettuce or fry a Best Onion. "Will you look at that! Just take a look at this!" he said to them.

He was standing beside the ecological zeppelin. Huge as it was, it had no card at all. Beside it was a whole row of other people's marrows, some stout and yellowish, some nearly as big as the zeppelin, some thinner and greener, and none of these had prizes either. Beyond them, a whole row of pale, narrow marrows labelled *Mr O. Brown* had been given all three prizes.

"You too, my friend," Tarquin said sadly.

"It's a scandal!" Mr Stock said. He led them along the table, pointing angrily at each group of vegetables they came to. "No prize for carrots," he said. "Nothing for onions, while as for cucumbers and tomatoes…! Not even my potatoes, and I swear they're biggest of all! That Mr Brown has got First Prize for almost everything here!"

Stashe tried to be tactful. "Perhaps," she said, "they're

not just going for *size* this year, Uncle Eli. They could be going for edible—" Mr Stock responded to this with such a glare that Stashe stopped, coughed and looked at her watch. "Andrew," she said, "we'd best be getting along. Ronnie Stock will be arriving at any moment and I said I'd be there…"

She began to drift away, pretending she had not seen the look on Mr Stock's face.

Andrew hesitated before following her. He was wondering if he should tell Mr Stock that, even with his glasses on, he could see that Mr Brown's entries had all been heavily enhanced by magic. But when he took his glasses off and looked at the polished potatoes that Mr Stock was pointing at, each one a pinkish-brown mini-boulder, he knew that Mr Stock himself was not guiltless of magical enhancement either. So he said soothingly, "I shouldn't wonder if Mr Brown isn't trying to take over all Melstone."

He stopped there, with his mouth open, knowing he had just spoken the absolute truth. This was exactly what Mr Brown was aiming to do: take over the entire field-of-care. When Mr Brown's letter had talked of his *plans for Melstone*, this is what it had meant. The First Prizes were simply an experiment on Mr Brown's part, to see if this could be done.

"Then *stop* him!" Mr Stock snarled, advancing his glare into Andrew's face.

"I'll try," Andrew said. Urgently wondering how, he followed Stashe and Tarquin out of the tent.

Aidan followed Andrew, hoping that this Fête would turn out to be more exciting soon. He had a feeling of something gathering, waiting, hanging ready to happen, and he could hardly wait for it to be there.

Rolf surged out from under the Best Rose table and barged into Aidan's legs, panting and whining.

"You're not supposed to be here!" Aidan said. "Go home."

Rolf glanced round, saw that nobody was looking, and dissolved into a small boy clinging to Aidan's left leg. "Come away!" he growled softly. "You're not safe. They're all here."

"I *know* they are," Aidan whispered. "But they can't find me when I'm wearing this charm." He jingled it at Rolf.

"Then I'll have to stay and guard you," Rolf growled.

"Oh, all right. If you must," Aidan said. He was fairly sure that Rolf did not want to miss whatever excitement was coming. "Be a dog then – a *good* dog – and walk to heel."

Rolf obediently dissolved back into a dog and followed

Aidan, tail waving sedately, as Aidan hurried after the others.

There were now important-looking people gathered on the platform beside the band. They were ladies in hats mostly, but there were one or two men in smart suits too. The vicar was there, in worn black, and so was Mr Brown, very tall and suave in a better suit than anyone else's, with a rose in his buttonhole. A crowd was gathering in front of the platform. People were coming out of the beer tent to watch.

"Ronnie's ever so chuffed at being asked to open the Fête," Stashe told Andrew. "He's planning a grand entry. I do hope he doesn't make too much of a fool of himself."

"He might. He never had much sense," Tarquin said. "Outside horses, that is."

The vicar stepped up to the microphone and tapped it to see if it was working. It caused a noise like an immense ear-popping all over the field. "Ladies and gentlemen," the vicar began and was then drowned out by barking. The dogs in the roped-off enclosure had spotted Rolf trotting past behind Aidan. They seemed to know at once that he was not really a dog and they hated him for it. They yapped, they growled, they bayed and they barked, and hauled the owners on the ends of their leads towards Rolf. Mr Brown's head turned sharply towards the noise and he seemed to be searching the place where Aidan was.

It was not pleasant. Aidan and Rolf scuttled hastily into the edge of the crowd, where they tried to stay quiet and hidden.

"Ladies and gentlemen," the vicar began again when the noise had died down, "it gives me great pleasure to introduce Mr Ronald Stock, whose Stables add such lustre to our village, and who has graciously agreed to open this humble Fête of ours."

Everyone was bewildered. Heads turned, looking for Ronnie.

The vicar pointed dramatically towards the distant gate. "Mr Ronald Stock," he announced. "Applause, please."

The band began to play the Melstone tune.

Everyone swung round as Ronnie Stock came cantering through the gate and across the field towards the platform. He was riding a white horse caparisoned like the steed of a knight of old. The horse did not look happy. It was draped round with blue and gold cloth and adorned with a blue and gold visor topped with a gold spike. Ronnie himself was in Elizabethan dress: a red and gold doublet and cloak, red tights and small puffy pants, also red and gold. On his head was a large feathered hat, like an outsize beret, which he swept off and waved to everyone as he cantered up.

Stashe turned her face away. "Oh dear," she said.

There was no doubt that this was a grand entry. Everyone clapped. The people by the beer tent whistled and hooted. Ronnie beamed as he reined in stylishly beside the platform, slapped the hat back on his head and gracefully dismounted. A young lady came briskly up to take charge of the horse.

"Hey!" said Stashe, starting forward. "I thought *I* was supposed to do that!"

"I'm glad you're not," Andrew said.

The moment Ronnie was off its back, the horse made a serious effort to rid itself of the blue and gold outfit. The young lady was carried high into the air and then had to dodge irritated lashing hooves.

"But that's *Titania*!" Stashe said angrily. "I hope poor Snowy *steps* on her!"

Tarquin and Andrew each took one of her arms to stop her rushing off. Tarquin said soothingly, "There, there, there." Andrew was speechless, watching Ronnie Stock gracefully swaggering up the steps of the platform. He had not seen Ronnie before this. He had always imagined him as short and wide, perhaps with a bluff red face. Not a bit of it. Ronnie was tall, thin and elegant-looking, with a narrow, aristocratic face. In fact...

Andrew found himself looking across at Mr Brown on the other side of the platform. Ronnie Stock could almost have been Mr Brown's twin. Mr Brown was staring at Ronnie in utter white outrage, because the unthinkable had happened and Oberon himself had a counterpart in Melstone.

Well, Andrew thought, this is your own fault for living here so long!

Mr Brown turned, slowly, and searched the crowd for Andrew. He found him and raised an elegant white finger. Andrew had to brace himself against a charge of electric magic. The world turned grey and dizzy for him and he had to hold himself up on Stashe and Tarquin.

Mr Brown then turned the finger towards Ronnie Stock. Ronnie had no defence against magic. He swayed for an instant and then went down on the platform with a hollow crash, like a tree falling.

There was consternation all over. Ladies in hats bent over Ronnie. People began pushing through the crowd, shouting, "Let me through, I'm a nurse!" or, "Make way! St John's Ambulance!" or, "I know First Aid!" while Mr Brown simply stood where he was, angry but otherwise unconcerned.

In the confusion, the horse got away from Titania.

Aidan felt somebody nudge him. The Puck stood beside him giggling. "Think you're safe, don't you?" he said to Aidan. He made a little wriggling gesture with one plump hand.

To Aidan's horror, the silver charm flew off his neck and landed some yards off in the grass.

Rolf dived for the charm, picked it up in his mouth and dropped it at once with a scream. Silver is poison for weres. Aidan dived for the charm too, scrambling after it on his knees in the grass. He had almost reached it when a gap somehow opened up in the crowd and he saw Mr Brown standing on the platform staring at him. It was a merciless and contemptuous stare. Aidan knelt where he was, staring back and feeling utterly worthless, small, foolish and stupid. He knew at once who Mr Brown was and he knew that Mr Brown had no value for him whatsoever.

"Well, too bad!" he said to Rolf. "As if I cared!" He looked round for the charm and found that it had disappeared.

Across the field, Titania stopped chasing the horse and pointed at Aidan. Over the other way, the policewoman looking after the Fancy Dress children was pointing at Aidan too and yelling. Strange beings rose up from all parts of the field and advanced on Aidan. He was suddenly alone with Rolf in a wide circle of grass, with Securities and tall, helmeted people coming at him from one direction, smaller folk with antennae rushing at him from another, and stranger creatures with cobweb wings flowing towards him from all around. It was worse than anything that had happened in London. The mad, nightmare part of it was that the band was still playing and clashing with the mechanical music from the roundabout. And it was all in bright daylight.

Andrew, still swaying and dizzy, saw Aidan kneeling in the distance and the creatures converging on him. "Got to help him!" he said. He thought he said it to Stashe, but only Tarquin was there. Stashe had said, "I *must* catch poor Snowy!" and gone dashing away.

Before Andrew managed to move, there was queer wailing and dim screaming that grew louder and louder. Groil came crashing through the hedge behind the platform, with his army of pursuers close behind him. It was obvious that Groil had had no idea that the Fête was going on here. He vaulted up on to the platform – which swayed and creaked under his weight – got mixed up in a line of bunting, and stared round in amazement as he struggled free of the little flags. Then, as his pursuers came streaming up on to the platform behind him, Groil hurdled Ronnie Stock and leaped to the ground, knocking two ladies in hats sideways and strewing bunting across the band as he went. He sped across the field in great strides and went to ground somewhere near the beer tent. His pursuers lost him. They went rushing this way and that, searching for Groil, getting in the way of the creatures advancing on Aidan and overturning the bakery stall. Some swarmed on to the bouncy castle and others invaded the roundabout, which stopped with a loud steamy squeal.

In seconds, the Fête had dissolved into confusion. In the roped enclosures, the dogs and most of the ponies went mad, while the Fancy Dress children huddled together screaming and Mabel Brown ran back and forth shouting orders that no one attended to. From the beer tent came yells, crashes and the sound of drinks being spilt. Mrs Stock, slipping and sliding on buns and chocolate cake, darted out from behind her clothes stall and went for Groil's pursuers with her umbrella. "Get *out* of it, you beastly things!" she shrieked, poking and bashing and swiping, and broke several sets of antennae.

Nearby, Shaun dragged one of the pillows out of his mother's vast dress and beat on any creature that dared to come near. Trixie followed him with another pillow. Feathers flew. Creatures winced and wailed and ran about.

Mr Stock came out of the competition tent carrying his zeppelin marrow on one shoulder and demanding to know what was going on. When he saw the hordes advancing on Aidan, he charged off that way, whirling the great vegetable. The Puck, who was rushing behind the horde, yelling at them to grab Aidan and kill Rolf, was Mr Stock's first victim. The marrow caught him THOCK! on the side of the head. It laid the Puck out cold on the grass, but the mighty vegetable remained intact, mottled and glossy.

Meanwhile other people came out of the competition tent and hurled Prize Potatoes into the confusion.

The whole crowd, including Mr Stock, was scattered by the galloping Snowy, hotly pursued by Stashe. Snowy was now in a panic. He could not seem to shake off the tattered cloth trailing off him and he kept finding strange beings among his legs. Everyone, human or immortal, kept having to dodge Snowy's violent back legs and his iron plunging front hooves. The advance on Aidan slowed and spread a little.

I must *do* something! Aidan thought. With the talisman gone, he was quite unprotected among scrambling clawed feet. He remembered Andrew telling him that the name Aidan meant "new fire" or something like that. It was all hazy with panic. But he thought, That's it! Fire!

On the platform, the vicar pulled himself together and, draped in torn bunting, took the microphone and tried to appeal for calm. "PEOPLE, PEOPLE!" his voice boomed out. "PLEASE PULL YOURSELVES TOGETHER!" As his voice boomed on and on and nobody listened to it, Aidan put both arms round Rolf and tried to surround both of them in impenetrable flames. The clawing arms and the vicar's booming distracted him. He panicked. I can't do it! he thought, and tried harder.

He was suddenly in the middle of a bonfire. A mistake! he thought as Rolf's coat sizzled and his own hair started to burn. "*Help!*" he screamed, surrounded in tall orange flames.

Tarquin and Mr Stock tried to push their way towards Aidan. "Though what we do when we get there, I don't know!" Tarquin said to Mr Stock.

"Lay about us," Mr Stock said grimly. "Beat it all down."

Andrew shook his head to clear at least some of the muzziness away and began to push the other way, towards the platform. He knew what he needed to do, if only he could think properly. He could see Mr Brown standing on the platform with his arms folded, quite unmoved by the confusion. In fact, he seemed faintly amused by it and not at all troubled by the way Aidan seemed likely to burn himself to death. Andrew pushed through the crowd in great strides and took his glasses off as he went. This transformed Mr Brown into a strange, wavery, tall being with a face that was not really a person's. Andrew looked away from him and tried to fix his dizzy mind instead on the window in his own back door. Green for Stashe, blue for Shaun, orange for Mrs Stock, yellow for Rolf, red for

Mr Stock. No, the pane he really needed was the purple one with the face in it that might have been Tarquin's. And he needed the other window in the shed too...

Groil must have seen the trouble Aidan was in. He surged into sight near the beer tent and marched towards Aidan's bonfire, towering above everyone else in the field. He burst in among the creatures crowding outside the flames and trampled on through. The first Aidan knew of it was Groil's feet sizzling as Groil seized Aidan and lifted him up into his arms. It was the strangest feeling. It took Aidan right back to the time when he was small enough for Gran to carry him about. But he did his best to put the fire out before Groil was badly burnt. He knew Groil's feet were like leather, but all the same...! And there was poor Rolf leaping and yelping.

Aidan felt Groil's chest buzz as Groil shouted, "Leave him *alone*! He's my *friend*!" He swung Aidan this way and that to avoid the Securities reaching for him and the clawing fingers of the cobwebby people.

How do I put the fire out? Aidan wondered frantically. Do it backwards, or what?

Andrew, at the same time, with his mind firmly fixed on the two windows, shoved past the edge of the crowd and marched up the steps to the platform. Mr Brown turned to watch him, consideringly, as Andrew stepped over the scarlet figure of Ronnie Stock – who was starting to roll about and groan a little – past the ladies in hats and up to the vicar. "Excuse me," he said politely and took the microphone out of the vicar's hand. "I need to speak," he explained as he fumbled in the back pocket of his jeans for the scrap of paper he had torn off the old comic Aidan had been reading. The trouble was he had to put his glasses on again to read it. As soon as he did, he saw Tarquin now standing at the bottom of the steps, staring up at him anxiously, and Mr Brown starting to edge towards him.

Hoping very much that this would work, Andrew ignored them both. He held the microphone up to his mouth and the scrap of paper to his eyes and read out the strange words he had written there long ago when he was Aidan's age.

The words did not boom like the vicar's voice. They came out of the loudspeakers like rolls of thunder and like long trumpet calls. Every other noise was drowned in them. All round the field people and creatures were forced to stand still with their hands over their ears. When Andrew had finished speaking, there was utter silence. Total stillness.

During that silent time Andrew felt the magic streaming inwards from eternity to focus on the two purple panes of glass, in the door and in the roof of the shed. It took effect.

The great oak tree behind Melstone House seemed to Andrew to stir and then lift its branches. Its crowded twigs filled with zigzags of lightning. Thunder rolled around it. Bearing the thunderstorm in its boughs, the huge tree advanced upon the field and the Fête. It seemed an age on the way. Andrew stood for what felt like an hour, feeling the thunder tree coming, with the storm swirling in its canopy and energy flashing through its roots. But it seemed to be there in instants too.

It advanced across the field, passing through Groil, Aidan and Rolf, leaving scorched grass behind it and a ring of creatures terrified and kneeling. It strode through the crowd and made straight for Tarquin. Tarquin's mouth opened in a scream of silent pain.

"Oh no," Andrew said. "He's not big enough. He's had a lot of pain already." His voice in the microphone added to the thunder already pealing round the field.

But the great oak had merely paused at Tarquin. It swept on through the crowd and on to the platform and became part of Andrew himself. NOW SPEAK, it said.

Andrew felt himself towering taller than Groil. He was a mighty trunk, huge twisted branches, twigs of lightning and a thousand leaves crackling with force. His mind thundered. He fought to find a voice people would understand. He fought to find his own brain. It was a frail human twist of a mind, but he found it and he clung on to it. He pointed a finger, or perhaps a branch at Mr Brown, now nearly beside him on the platform.

"*Errant king*," he thundered, "*you have fed in this field too long. Take your followers and your wives and the followers of your wives and return to your own country and live there in peace. Do not try to take this field for your own.*" He found Mabel Brown in the roped enclosure and Titania somewhere near the bouncy castle and swung his foliage to point at them too. "*Now go!*"

They went. They had no choice. With a strange hollow moaning, all the creatures swept up into the air in three smokelike swirls. Titania went with them, and Mabel Brown and, last of all, with a contemptuous shout of pure annoyance, went Mr Brown. Like dead leaves in a wind they went spiralling away, and away, crying out their sorrow and their protest as they went. Andrew thought he saw all three swirls of them plunge into the side of Mel Tump and disappear.

Now that's odd, he thought. I can't even *see* Mel Tump from here!

This made him realise that the great oak presence had left him. It had left him charged up and enlarged. He knew he would never be quite the same again.

To everyone else it seemed as if a tremendous

blue-purple flash of lightning struck down near Aidan and Rolf, followed almost instantly by a bellow of thunder. Then the rain came down, in heavy white rods, mixed with what seemed to be hail. Nearly everyone ran for shelter in the tents. Mrs Stock put up her big umbrella. The field emptied except for those in the enclosures or on the platform.

Then it stopped. Yellow sunlight blazed on wet grass and on wet, steaming ponies and bedraggled fancy dress. The hats on the platform dripped. Out on the field, Aidan shook his singed and soaking hair and tried to clean his glasses. He was kneeling in a ring of sooty-smelling burnt grass. There was no sign of Groil. Aidan was miserable about that. It stood to reason that when Andrew sent all the creatures away he would have to send Groil off too, and Aidan had lost a friend. But Rolf was still there, burnt brown down one side and trying to limp on all four paws. Rolf was, very cautiously, hobbling to sniff at a melted silvery lump nearby.

"Leave it, Rolf," Aidan said sadly. "It's only my charm. The lightning struck it, but I suppose I don't need it now."

On the platform, Andrew handed the microphone politely back to the vicar and bent to help Ronnie Stock to his feet. Apart from being soaking wet, Ronnie seemed none the worse. "That was a storm and a half!" he said to

Andrew. "Thanks. You're that Hope fellow from Melstone House, aren't you? Pleased to meet you."

As Ronnie stood up, he and Andrew both stumbled on things that crunched. The platform was covered with fallen acorns. Andrew bent again and gathered up a handful, but no one else seemed to notice. The vicar was irritably tapping at the microphone and getting no sound at all. It seemed to be broken.

Like my computer when it gets a charge of magic, Andrew thought, putting the acorns in his pocket.

"Never mind," Ronnie Stock said cheerfully. "I'm used to yelling at riders on my gallops." He strutted into the centre of the platform and shouted, "Ladies and gentlemen!" When enough people had emerged from tents, he shouted again, "Ladies and gentlemen, I *was* going to make a speech, but in view of the weather, I think I'll just declare this Fête well and truly open. Thank you."

The band, in a shaken way, emerged from the beer tent and started to play. Ronnie looked past them across the field, to where Snowy was now rolling on the ground, tangled in wet blue cloth. "Somebody rescue my horse!" he bellowed.

Stashe was trying to. The trouble was Snowy was not being in the least helpful. Stashe would never have got the horse on his feet if somebody had not come up and helped her heave. "Thanks, Dad," she panted, thinking it was Tarquin. But when she looked, it was somebody very like Tarquin, but without the beard. "Oh," she said. "Sorry. Thank you anyway."

"You're welcome," said the Puck and vanished beside the roundabout.

Andrew quietly jumped down from the side of the platform and made his way to Tarquin, who looked white as a sheet. "Come back to my house," Andrew said. "I'm leaving now. You look as if you could use a drink."

"I could use a cup of tea," Tarquin admitted. "I've the devil's own headache, so I have. What *was* that thing?"

"Best not to ask," Andrew said, as they both went over to Aidan. "Do you want to stay?" Andrew asked.

"No," said Aidan. "Groil's gone. But I think I'll have to stay. Rolf can't walk."

Luckily, Mr Stock came up just then, trundling his barrow, in which reposed the vegetable zeppelin. "I'll give the dog a ride," he said. "You hold this." He picked up the great marrow and seemed about to hand it to Andrew. Then it clearly struck him that Andrew was too importantly powerful now to carry produce about. He turned and dumped the mighty vegetable into Aidan's arms instead. It was very heavy and still quite undamaged.

Rolf scrambled into the wheelbarrow in the greatest relief, where he lay and licked his paws, and they all set off home. They passed Mrs Stock, shaking out her umbrella. "Trixie and Shaun between them burst both her pillows," she said to them. "And a good thing too! See you Monday, Professor."

They came to Stashe, fiercely ripping blue cloth off Snowy. "Leaving?" she said. "I'll be along when I've led Snowy back to the stables. I think he's pulled a muscle. Ronnie can just *walk* back, and serve him right! Honestly, what an ass he made of himself!" She stopped, with the blue spiked visor in her hands. "Do you think anyone else here knows what really happened?"

"I doubt it," Tarquin said. "I can't see anyone believing they saw a giant, let alone all the other creatures. My guess is they'll just remember that the Fête got interrupted by the father and mother of a thunderstorm. Or so I hope. I don't want to spend the next ten years explaining to people like Mrs Blanchard-Stock. Do you?"

Whatever people believed, the Fête was in full swing as they left. The roundabout was turning and the bouncy castle was full. Cracks rang out from the rifle range and singing from the beer tent. In the distance, the scarlet figure of Ronnie Stock was to be seen, solemnly choosing the tube of toothpaste as the winner of the Fancy Dress, before moving on to judge the dogs and the ponies.

And the sun shone.

Chapter Seventeen

Aidan continued to be miserable about Groil, although Andrew kept telling him that he was sure he had not sent Groil away with the rest. "I know I didn't include him," he said.

"Then why did he *go*?" Aidan protested. "I think he had to go because he was Shaun's counterpart."

Andrew tried to set Aidan's mind at rest by heaving the giant marrow up on to the woodshed roof that night. But it was still there, untouched, on Sunday morning. "Well," Andrew said, "the thing's practically indestructible. Maybe even Groil couldn't get his teeth into it."

Wally Stock called that morning to tell Aidan he had won a bottle of sherry. This did not console Aidan in the least.

Trixie called in the afternoon to tell Andrew that he had

guessed her weight correctly. Andrew thanked her and politely gave her back the £50 prize. He was very absent-minded that day, sitting on the mower under the stained glass in the roof of the shed, working out just exactly what each colour did. By the evening, he felt he almost had it.

During Sunday night, the giant marrow fell off the roof and burst.

Rolf, meanwhile, was making much of his burnt feet. He lay all Sunday in everyone's way on the kitchen floor, moaning gently. On the Monday, Mrs Stock got so annoyed with him that she made Shaun carry him out on to the lawn, where Rolf lay in the sun and continued to groan, until Aidan came out with a dish of dog food. Rolf sprang up eagerly and galloped towards it.

"You," Aidan told him, "are just a big fraud." An idea struck him. "Hey!" he said. "I wonder if Groil's had burnt feet too!"

Andrew sent Shaun up into the loft to see if he could mend the roof. After seeing that Best Robot, Andrew had boundless faith in Shaun's ability to mend anything. "Humph!" said Mrs Stock.

Andrew ignored her and opened the front door to Stashe and Tarquin, who had come to discuss the wedding. They had barely done more than fix the date, when they were interrupted by tremendous roars from Mr Stock, followed by Mrs Stock screaming, "Don't you go blaming our Shaun! He was only doing his best!"

"Now what?" said Andrew.

They all hurried outside. "By the way," Stashe said as they went. "Did you know that Melstone Manor's up for sale now? Ronnie Stock's thinking of buying it. He thinks the Grange isn't grand enough for him."

"Very fitting," Andrew said.

Out on the lawn, they found the mower standing there and Mr Stock now arguing with Aidan. "I tell you it won't start," Mr Stock was saying. "That lobby lout has been and spoilt my knack!" He pulled at the starting handle in his special way. Nothing happened. "*See?*" Mr Stock roared at Aidan. "Let me at that Shaun!"

"No, I'll do it," Aidan said. "Look." He pulled the handle and the mower throbbed sweetly into life. "See?"

"Stay with him, Aidan," Andrew said, "and start it again whenever it runs over a thistle."

Mr Stock glowered. He was so annoyed that, later that day, when the lawn had become brown and bristly, he marched into the kichen repeatedly to dump six boxes full of his Fête entries on the table. Mrs Stock complained loudly.

Later that day, Aidan scooped up the sad remains of the

marrow and helped Andrew load the woodshed roof with giant potatoes and vast tomatoes instead.

On Tuesday morning, while Andrew was getting breakfast, Aidan came dashing indoors with Rolf. "They've gone!" Aidan shouted. "Groil's been here! He must just have had sore feet after all."

"Good," Andrew said, catching the kitchen door before it slammed. "Great. Now is there any chance that I can get on and write my book today?"

"Oh yes," Aidan said happily. "Everything's all right now."

But it was not, or not exactly. In the middle of the morning the doorbell rang. As Mrs Stock was upstairs and Andrew's computer had once more inexplicably gone down, Andrew went out into the hall to answer it. "It's probably Tarquin," he said to Aidan, who was nosily going to answer the door too. "His leg will need firming up, I expect."

Andrew thought it *was* Tarquin for a second when he opened the door. But the little man standing there had two sturdy legs in floppy knee-length trousers and, though his leather jacket was very like Tarquin's, this person was much plumper and had no beard. He held a large envelope out towards Andrew. "A letter from my master," he said.

Aidan recognised the Puck and began to retreat at once.

Unfortunately, he backed straight into Mrs Stock, carrying an armload of plastic packets. "These were under your bed," she said. "Did I or did I not tell you to put them in the bin? You come upstairs with me at once and collect all your rubbish properly."

The Puck grinned.

"Yes, Aidan," Andrew said. "Go along and face the music. Does this letter need an answer?" he asked the Puck.

The Puck, still grinning, watched Aidan hurry away after Mrs Stock. Then he said demurely, "I am to wait for your reaction, sir."

"Indeed?" said Andrew, taking the big stiff envelope. It was addressed in the loopy, spiky writing that Andrew now felt he knew quite well to *A. Hope Esquire.* Rather self-conscious with the Puck standing there looking at him, he tore open the envelope and held the letter into the daylight to read it. It said:

> *Mr Hope,*
> *Your action in banishing me was rather hasty.*
> *I was about to tell you two things.*
> *First, your exposing of both sets of enchanted glass was rash. The two together are much more powerful than I think you might guess and could be very dangerous in*

inexperienced hands.

Second, as soon as I set eyes on the boy Aidan, I saw at once that he was no child of mine. He is palpably and entirely human and probably a close relative of your own.

The girl Melanie almost certainly threw herself at your grandfather, just as she threw herself at me. I gave her the wallet as a precaution, so that I might trace her if need be, but since your people and mine do not readily breed, I was unconcerned until both my wives discovered its existence.

If you doubt the truth of this second piece of information, you have only to find a picture of yourself at Aidan's age. The likeness is fairly striking. I saw you often as a boy.

You can now take charge of your new relative. I have no further interest in the boy.

Oberon Rex.

"Well, I'll be—!" Andrew muttered. He had no need to go hunting for photographs of himself at Aidan's age. One of the traditional fixtures in the living room, which Mrs Stock always put exactly in the middle of the mantelpiece, was a silver-framed photo of Andrew when he was twelve.

The likeness was certainly there, if you allowed for the fact that Andrew had had fair hair and Aidan's was brownish. In fact, Andrew rather thought that the reason that he had been so ready to have Aidan to live in Melstone House was that Aidan had a familiar, family sort of look about him "Well, I'll be—!" he said again.

"Is that your reaction, sir?" the Puck asked from the doorstep.

"Not exactly," Andrew said. "Tell your master that I am very grateful for both pieces of information."

The Puck looked decidedly disappointed. "Very well," he said and vanished from the porch.

Andrew reread the letter pensively. He wondered whether to tell Aidan. Stashe would have to help him decide.

Diana Wynne Jones

HOWL'S MOVING CASTLE

"How about making a bargain with me?" said the demon. "I'll break your spell if you agree to break this contract I'm under."

In the land of Ingary, where seven-league boots and cloaks of invisibility exist, pretty Sophie Hatter is cursed into the shape of an old woman. Determined to make the best of things, she travels to the one place where she might find help – the moving castle on the nearby hills.

But the castle belongs to the dreaded Wizard Howl whose appetite, they say, is satisfied only by the hearts of young girls…

HarperCollins *Children's Books*

Diana Wynne Jones

House of Many Ways

"You are rather lost, my dear. Turn round once, clockwise. Then, still turning, open the door with your left hand only. Go through and let the door shut behind you. Then take two long steps sideways to your left. This will bring you back beside the bathroom."

Charmain Baker is in over her head. Looking after Great Uncle William's tiny cottage should have been easy, but he is the Royal Wizard Norland whose house bends space and time. Its single door leads to any number of places: the bedrooms, the kitchen, the caves under the mountains – even the past!

In no time at all, Charmain becomes involved with a magical stray dog, a muddled apprentice wizard and a box of the King's most treasured documents, as well as irritating a clan of small blue creatures.

HarperCollins *Children's Books*

"There's one absolute rule," said Chrestomanci.
"No witchcraft of any kind is to be practised by
children without supervision. Is that understood?"

No witchcraft? Gwendolen Chant – a gifted witch
in the making – has other ideas and
is determined to get the better of the great
enchanter. Her brother Cat, who has no
magical gift, is powerless to stop her.

Winner of the Guardian Award.

HarperCollins *Children's Books*

Diana Wynne Jones

FIRE AND HEMLOCK

Polly has always loved the fire and hemlock photograph
which hangs above her bed, but now it sparks memories
that don't seem to exist any more. Memories of Thomas
Lynn, who became her greatest friend… Memories of the
stories they made up together – adventures in which Tom
is a great hero and Polly is his assistant… Memories that
these adventures had a nasty habit of coming true…

Why has Tom been erased from Polly's mind, and from
the rest of the world as well? And why is Polly so sure
that she must have done something dreadful?
Determined to uncover the truth, she casts her mind back
ten years to when it all started. At the funeral…

HarperCollins *Children's Books*